# SWEET WATER

## LANIE VLADIMIROV

CRANTHORPE
MILLNER
PUBLISHERS

First published by Cranthorpe Millner Publishers (2024)

ISBN 978-1-80378-241-6 (Paperback)

www.cranthorpemillner.com

Cranthorpe Millner Publishers

Printed and bound by CPI Group (UK) Ltd
Croydon, CR0 4YY

MIX
Paper | Supporting
responsible forestry
FSC® C013604

*For my family*

*I knew you the moment we met,*
*even though you were wrapped in different skin.*

# CHAPTER 1

## CHIARA

A single drop of rain slid down the grimy window as the bus driver beeped the horn. I clicked my tongue nervously, squinting through the foggy glass at the dark air filled with blazing red lights. Cars, trucks and buses were all lined up back-to-back.

My hometown seemed like a lifetime away.

Leaning my head against the window, I traced the path the raindrops made as they fell with my finger, ignoring the two girls giggling behind me. It was interesting how life could so drastically change in an instant. Like the snap of two fingers, I was at the mercy of the world.

I sank deeper into my seat as my window turned misty like the heavy clouds in the air.

*'Are you ready for this?' Mr Becksworth had asked me earlier that day.*

*I dumped my drawstring bag beside a crate of bananas. His grocery store was small, but I had always liked that about it.*

*'Is that a serious question?' I picked up a bunch, twisting my mouth to the side. 'One or two?'*

'One banana?' he scoffed, his round belly jiggling with laughter. 'I would tell you to take two since it's a long way to Paris an' all that – but you wouldn't listen to me, would you?'

I nudged his arm and smiled. 'You know I don't get that hungry.'

He heaved up a box of tinned tomatoes as his face blossomed bright red.

'Chiara, have you thought 'bout what you're gonna do once you're in Paris?' he panted.

I looked away with a sigh, glancing out the shop window. We'd had this conversation a thousand times and I always gave him the same response: get a job and figure it out. Once I got there, what to do was never going to be the issue; the issue was getting out of England. Out of this small, small town filled with memories I didn't want to have. He stretched his back beside me with a groan, his shoes scuffed with years of wear.

'An' Sophie? Did you say g'bye to her?'

I nodded, hoping he didn't notice me swallowing the knot in my throat. The stories in the fields, the singing in the playground at break time and the conspiring over the escape plan itself. Ever since I began to believe I could, she'd wanted to help me do it. We poured all our hopes and dreams into each other, sharing secrets we'd never tell a single other soul. A pang hit my chest as I thought of her and how I'd probably never see her again. She tried to convince me to stay for the rest of the school year; there were only a few months left. I cursed that my eighteenth birthday had been so late in the year; I would've left much sooner if I could.

Mr Becksworth watched me when I looked up. But his brown eyes were softer than I had ever seen them.

'You're all grown up now, Chiara,' he said quietly, almost as if to himself. He looked as if he wanted to reach out, but *something must have stopped him because he pushed his mouth together and nodded firmly at his feet.*

*I threw myself at him. He chuckled in surprise, but when he hugged me back, it was warm and safe.*

*'I'm gonna miss you,' I said, squeezing him as hard as possible. Perhaps it was something about how the only good people in my life would be stripped away. Maybe it was the realisation that my life would never be the same again. Maybe it was fear. But when he let go of me and I saw the tears glazing his eyes, something in me broke.*

*'I'm sorry,' I burst out as several tears dislodged themselves from my eyes and started to freefall.*

*He patted my shoulder gruffly with his bear-sized hands. 'Nothing to be sorry 'bout. It's tough, that's all.'*

*I nodded, attempting to suck it back in. Leaving, I realised, would be harder than I had ever imagined.*

A baby wailed somewhere in the front of the bus, lurching me back to the present. I ran a hand through my uncombed curls, then pulled my legs onto the seat. The large stone buildings of London were already looming overhead in the grey air, the streets below them scattered with solemn-looking people. I pressed my face so close to the glass that condensation wet my nose. We passed a colossal building with round stone columns that sunk into its steps. My hometown was a million times smaller than this monster of a city, even though it had a certain beauty.

The mother was cooing her baby by now and her soothing whispers did something to soothe my mind. Mr Becksworth hadn't understood why I had to leave so soon. Running away looked immature and unplanned, something only a fool would do. But I wanted a new life more than anything.

A female robotic voice chimed, telling us it was time to leave. I folded over and shoved open my drawstring bag, pushing my hand deep inside it.

'Money, where's my money?' I muttered, feeling around the clothes, passport, second bus ticket and my paints at the bottom until I felt my fake leather wallet. I pulled it out and carefully placed it in my beige coat pocket, just in case.

I pulled at my fingers as I waited for the people in front of me to get off the bus, craning my neck to get a better look outside. There wasn't much to see but it was something. Something different. Fresh pink blossoms lined the street and I inhaled the damp air as I stepped off the bus. It was a cold reality, but it was getting warmer as I walked toward the tube station. I looked up at the sky, noticing how the pieces of light splayed out from a parting in the clouds, like a north star.

After running down the steps to the underground, I found myself squashed between two old women on the tube. It started with a screech that made my hands shoot to my ears and I promptly lowered them so I didn't look like an idiot. With my drawstring bag tucked between my legs, I looked around the closed faces of the other passengers before staring decidedly at their shoes.

'Samantha, do you remember when Gerald cheated on me with that pansy?' I half-glanced at the wrinkled woman sitting to my right. 'Thirty-four years and I can still smell her blasted tulip perfume.'

I stared at my dirty trainers, tracing the curve of the laces. The woman to my left cackled as she rocked forward in her seat, slapping her walking stick against the floor. 'Don't you worry; she had nothing on you, dear,' she said, leaning across me to pat the other's knee.

I squirmed.

She leaned back as if noticing me for the first time, pursing her lips as her shrewd eyes took me in with one swoop. I looked away. Something sour pinched at my stomach.

'And you know what?' the one on the right started again, 'I was cheating on him too!'

The two of them roared with laughter, turning several heads. No longer able to stand it, I pried open my drawstring bag and retrieved my flip-phone. Most people now had a smartphone but I didn't have that kind of money and I didn't need one anyway. The women continued babbling and I ignored them, caressing the small black thing with my thumb.

*"Course, you don't have to call me when you get there, you know,' Mr Becksworth told me once. He looked down at the thick, calloused palms of his hands. "Course, you don't have to ever talk to me again, if you don't want to.' I smiled, putting my small hand in his.*

*'I'm sure I will,' I affirmed brightly. He glanced up, brown meeting green. 'And if I don't, I will never forget you.'*

I flipped open the phone, shaky fingers pausing on the first number. But the train started to slow and another robotic voice informed us we'd arrived at Victoria Station. I sighed, shutting the phone and throwing it back into the bag with finality.

*Maybe some other time*, I told myself.

As I scanned the street I emerged on, something caught my

eye. A raven, dark as night, perched atop the telephone wires. She was beautiful, with sleek feathers that glistened in the dusk. I watched as she leapt into the air and flew. An ache that was deep and hollow rang throughout me as I stood rooted to the spot. People scurried to and fro around me, the ceaseless traffic and noise blurring into a haze.

*Snap out of it.*

I blinked at the empty telephone wire, then turned to look at the shops lining the street. My stomach grumbled. I still had the banana but I knew it wouldn't satiate me like something fatty and unhealthy would.

As I started walking towards a familiar fast food joint, I thought about the likelihood of seeing a raven in the streets of London and wondered if it had even been a raven at all.

'Hi, can I take your order?' yelled the lady behind the counter. The room was packed, stuffy and hot.

'Um,' I stalled as I looked at the menu behind her head. She tapped her fingers on the counter. 'Can I have the chicken burger?' I asked, even though I didn't really want it. She nodded curtly, looking at me from under her hat before entering the order into a machine.

'Next!' she called.

I sidestepped towards the other end of the line where people waited for their orders. Some had their hands in their pockets and others were pulling their kids back from running off. A heavier woman glanced back at me, jerking her finger towards the line.

'It's gonna be a while,' she helpfully informed me, the whites of her eyes glistening in the fluorescent lights.

I smiled. 'If I go to the bathroom, can you hold my spot?'

'Sure, hun.'

I walked into the women's room in the back of the restaurant, finding it empty. Dumping my bag on the ground, I ran the water from the tap without looking at my reflection and splashed it over my face. It was so cold it stung. The noise from outside was muffled behind the thick door, the smell of cheap disinfectant and baby oil lingering in the stale air. I laid an icy hand over my eyes and suppressed the urge to moan. Eating was the last thing I wanted to do right now, yet my stomach clearly had other plans since it was growling at me like a wild animal.

*There's only one more bus to take*, I reminded myself.

I sighed and ran my hands through my hair, forgetting they were still wet. I looked at my reflection and cursed. The girl was tired, with dark half-moons under her light green eyes, her skin pale. I looked away.

My phone rang, causing me to shoot down towards my bag so fast I almost bumped my chin on the sink.

'Come on, come on,' I muttered, rummaging through my things as the ringing continued.

Something shifted in the air then, a dark and silent presence in my periphery, but I was only vaguely aware. A rough hand clamped over my mouth and an arm made of iron snaked around my waist. Terrified, I screamed uselessly as I was pulled backwards from the ringing phone. The grimy hand tightened on my mouth. I writhed and kicked my legs, hoping to loosen their grip on my waist, but it only seemed to piss them off. They grunted and in a split second spun in front of me, grabbing my neck with both hands and shoving me into the wall with a thud. The man looked at me, and I whimpered.

His gaze burned with hatred, his eyes so dark his irises looked as though they had been consumed by his pupils

There was no point in screaming; no one would have heard me. He used the hand on my mouth to yank my head to the side, his entire body pressed up against mine, stiff and cold. Unable to move, I cried out as something tore through my throat, the pain like fire in my veins. Tears ran down my cheeks, hot and stupid and useless, as his mouth bruised my skin, sucking at the wound he had made; draining me.

When he let go, I collapsed in a heap on the bathroom floor. Through bleary eyes, I could just about see him slip through the heavy door, before the world turned dark.

My entire body seized up as my eyes flew open.

*Fuck.*

I sucked in a breath, then another and another as I glanced feverishly around the room. The man with the black eyes was nowhere to be found.

*What the hell just happened?*

I squinted, my eyes slowly adjusting to the harsh, white light of the bathroom.

Every single muscle and bone in me felt heavy and paralysed. I felt it would be a thousand times easier to stay there and sink deeper into the floor than pick myself up from it. But I remembered the ringing phone and my dream of Paris.

*There is no way in hell that you came this far to back out now.*

I groaned and pressed my palm into the floor. It was sticky. The blood rushed to my head as I sat up and I touched my throat where the man's mouth had been.

My eyes widened and I pressed all my fingers against it in disbelief. The flesh was puckered as though there was a scar. I frowned and stood up to look at it in the mirror. It was deep red and a little tender, but looked as though it had been healing for weeks, not minutes. I pulled my hair to the front to hide it, then frowned. That man had not been human. I was sure of it. No human would tear out another's flesh and blood in that way, in a way so precise – as if he had been doing it all his life. No human had eyes that merciless. No human could feel hatred so deeply for a stranger.

I ran my hands through my knotted curls and tried to think. But all I could think about was the feel of his cold body on mine and the way I wanted to melt into the wall or, even better, to run.

I shuddered.

Ducking down, I rummaged through my bag to find my stupid phone. But the person who had called me hadn't been Mr Becksworth like I thought. I frowned and listened to the voicemail.

'Bonjour, Chiara,' said a woman's voice. 'This is Juliette from Paris Rental Services. Everything is ready for your arrival, but I have been asked to inform you that the apartment will only be available to rent for a maximum of one month. The original owner is returning to Paris soon, so she has asked us to take the apartment off the market. If you wish to discuss other options, please give us a call. I hope you enjoy your stay!'

'What?' I whispered.

I listened to the message again, even though I was well aware of its content. It was bad enough that I'd been attacked by some psycho in the bathroom, but it was even worse that I was getting evicted before I even had a chance to look at my flat. I stared at my shoes, worn and scuffed.

I should have seen it coming. When had anything been as

easy as I'd hoped? This was the one dream I'd had for so long, the only dream that was even a tiny bit possible.

I sighed and pulled the drawstring bag over my back before peeking behind the bathroom door. To my surprise, the room outside was dry and noisy, almost identical to how I left it. I checked the time. It had been less than an hour. I half-expected the same woman to be in the line, still holding my space. I took a meagre step forward and carefully looked over the face of each person I saw.

But the man with black eyes was gone.

# CHAPTER 2

Luminescent blue dots lined the dark floor of the night coach from London to Paris. I kept my head down as I walked past the blank faces of the other passengers. The thick windows reflected the blue light that enveloped the space as I walked all the way to the end of the bus. There was no one else there.

Good.

I licked my finger and rubbed my face again instinctively, even though I had already checked and knew I had no blood on it. My hand dropped like a weight by my side and I closed my eyes, sinking into the seat.

I felt I was wasting away, heavy and weightless all at once.

Taking out the floppy burger, I forced myself to take a bite. It was past 11:30 p.m. and I felt I could have died then and there. But I knew it would help the hollow gnawing in my stomach.

The bus had long since taken off by the time I had finished eating and I tucked my head into the seat as far as it would go. There was something about the lulling motion of the bus as it pulsed along the road and the whir of the engine under my seat. I would have never allowed myself to sleep on public transport before; that was a surefire way to get mugged or worse. But the gentle rocking made me drop my defences, even for a little while.

When I next awoke, the sky had broken into streaks of pale yellow and crimson, with dark blue sailing above like an eternal bliss. The muted light filtered into the bus, rousing the sleeping passengers until the air was filled with whispers and tinged with excitement.

I pressed my palms against the cool glass. Deep green trees lined the motorway, blossoming into pinks and yellows the further in we travelled.

*So, this is France.*

I leaned against the window and watched the road ahead, even though the bumps the bus passed over were enough to rattle my skull. It was unlike anything I could have ever imagined, the way the freedom glided within me like a bird. Even being here, trapped in this bus when I would a thousand times have rather run alongside it, was new, was beautiful.

'Do you remember where I put the passports?' murmured a woman up ahead.

It took me a few moments to realise they were sitting at the front of the bus, where I shouldn't have been able to hear them. I frowned and shut my eyes.

'Why don't you check your coat pocket?'

I rubbed the scar on my neck, finding my skin was raised and smooth. *They were probably just loud whispers*, I told myself. Something strange had happened last night, but the doubt clouded my memories until they were black and foggy. It was best to move on, act like it had never happened.

The bus turned into the terminal. I hoisted my bag off the floor where I had it sandwiched between my legs, clutching it close to me as I waited for people to get off.

The air was musty and cold in the car park, not at all how I had envisioned my arrival. Even so, the moment my foot hit the ground, I knew it was real. The hours I had whiled away fantasising tasted like a long-forgotten memory compared with this reality. I found myself sitting in the backseat of a taxi, half in a daze as I stared out the dusty window. Closer. It was still early morning but somehow that didn't stop the streets from being backed up as we entered the city. My eyes were glued to it. Rows and rows of creamy buildings rose to the sky and slender trees lined the cobblestones. It was lovely, yet it looked nothing like the photoshopped picture on the postcard I used to sleep with under my pillow.

After winding through countless tiny streets, the taxi screeched to a stop under the darkest sky in Paris. I exited the car in front of my building and stood, frozen. It was too similar to back home. Several storeys high, it was crafted from thin, textured concrete walls, blackened with age. The building had an eerie glow, something like bad intentions and bad news.

*Maybe it looks better on the inside.*

The main door to the building was open and I climbed the stairs until I reached the third floor. I entered the pin the agency had given me into the key-safe mounted on the wall, opening it and retrieving the keyring that tumbled out. Inserting the larger key into the lock, I had to jiggle the door a few times before it opened. A familiar sinking feeling of expected disappointment lodged itself in my stomach.

The moment I shut the door behind me was the same moment I collapsed. Slumped on the floor, I stared at the white-washed walls I had slaved away to pay for. Not that it mattered any longer. *One month*, I reminded myself. It was enough time to look for a new place to live. I took a deep breath, my body shaking as I let it out. A couple were arguing in the flat next-door. It reminded me of my old home. Too much.

I stood slowly, shuffling towards the bedroom.

It wasn't much: just four walls, a single bed and a chest of drawers. The couple sounded like they were hurling abusive French at each other. *Thin* four walls.

I pressed my palms over my ears and crammed my eyes shut. I thought about calling Mr Becksworth. What would I even tell him, that I was safe and everything went swimmingly?

The couple were still arguing. To distract myself, I rummaged through my belongings. I dumped out the heaviest things from my bag into the dresser's top drawer: my paints. They were gorgeous, in deep hues I'd spent a good deal of money on. The nice ones. I thrust in most of my clothes, passport and used bus tickets. I left the banana in the bag and then I took the bag and left the flat.

Meandering through the streets and alleys, I searched for a bench, eventually sitting down and peeling the banana open. A bike flew past as I took the first bite and licked my lips. The more I sat and watched Paris awaken, the more the initial shock and disappointment I'd felt faded. I leaned back in my seat. There was something magical about the air that morning, about how I had overcome my expectations so fully. Maybe it didn't matter so much that it wasn't exactly how I'd imagined; I was still here and that meant more than anything else.

Gradually, more and more people filled the streets: business men and women, small children grasping onto their mothers' hands and various breeds of dogs barking at one another nonsensically. I folded my empty banana peel into itself before tossing it into the nearest bin. All the shops were open now, with the sun glinting off the polished glass windows.

Customers queued at a bakery and I watched, somewhat envious, as a woman dressed in a sleek black dress sitting at a circular table on the street bit into a croissant. It looked warm, soft and buttery.

It made me feel at ease to be the observer and know I had nowhere I needed to be. I weaved in and out of the crowd, staring in awe at the large stone buildings, bridges and street signs. It was almost too much, being bombarded with new sights and smells from all angles. Smells. I almost stopped as I sniffed the air, a wave of something deep and rich overcoming me. It was intense, intoxicating... metallic. I stared around me in shock, trying to identify its source. A woman accidentally bumped into me, apologising profusely in French as she continued to jog away in her high heels.

It hit me suddenly.

Revulsion threatened to rise to the surface as my stomach contorted upon itself. I wrinkled my nose, nearly gagging as I forced my way through to the nearest building.

I smelt blood.

Everywhere.

I doubled over against the cool brick, clutching my stomach. No, no, this had to be wrong. Curiosity surged from my mind, but I forced it back into its box. *Absolutely not.* I didn't understand it at all. I didn't understand how my body wanted something so out of bounds. I ran my fingers over the scar on my neck, my breath catching in my throat.

*Maybe I really am one*, I thought.

Maybe that man hadn't been a man after all. It was always something people in my small town would joke about. The myths and stories were told like they were living, breathing truths, although they weren't. And everybody knew they weren't, apart from some crazy old ladies who swore they'd seen them in the flesh. "Monsters" they'd called them. It was enough to scare kids into obedience and give them nightmares for a week straight. But I, like most people, had never thought any of it was real.

I glanced up towards the swarm of people. Hundreds of heartbeats now pulsated through my eardrums, the vibrations of blood gushing through veins and arteries all hitting my system at once. I opened my mouth in shock, unable to stop staring at the crowd. What I was hearing was beyond human range. I felt sick to my core.

I knew now what I had doubted before; I was certainly not human, not any longer.

Glancing down at my hand, I twisted my palm, examining my skin. Was I truly a monster? I didn't look any different. I didn't feel any different.

My eyes darted back to the throng of people as if by a magnetic pull.

Before I could do anything stupid, I gritted my teeth, hurled my bag across my back and held my nose as I ploughed through the street. I turned the corner onto a smaller street, panting a little. A group of friends waltzed past me, oblivious to what I could do if I were to snap. The throat was the most obvious place to do it – exactly where the man with hate in his eyes had attacked me in the bathroom. But I just couldn't bring myself to do something like that, to be the same as him.

Panicking, I looked up at the sky, exasperated. More people turned onto the street, their blood rich and luxurious. A deep, insatiable thirst rang through me and I drew in a sharp inhale to compose myself. There was nothing to stop me from... I couldn't even finish the thought. I took another deep breath, pulling my coat tighter around me before turning onto a nearby street, then another, almost running until I found my way into some sort of playground.

I inhaled the deep, clean air, registering that I was finally, blissfully alone. I sighed, dropping my bag to the ground covered with overgrown weeds and long grass. I stumbled forward. The day was beautiful and the playground should have been filled with children playing games, hanging off the monkey bars and chanting on the roundabout. But there was no one. I looked closer, wrapping my fingers around the bars as the dry paint crumbled away silently. The rusty chains that held the swings screeched in the gentle breeze, the roundabout stubbornly sticking in the ground. There was something eerie about the place. The quiet. The only movement happening of its own accord, as if the rubber and beams were alive.

I lay splayed out, with my back pressed upon the earth. The grass encapsulated me in a warm embrace, flowing around me on all sides. I leaned into it, closing my eyes as my breath lulled me gently.

*Nothing will be the same again*, I thought, bitterness mixed with excitement lingering in me. I looked up at the sky, so wide and empty. A small laugh escaped my lips. I had been dreaming so hard of this for years. I closed my eyes again as a solitary tear squeezed out and slid down my cheek. Nothing could have prepared me for what had happened, what I had become. My stomach contorted once again, disgusted by the very thing it craved.

*'It's dangerous there, Chiara,'* Mr Becksworth had warned me darkly one night. *'It ain't safe for a little girl like yourself to*

*be walkin' those streets all alone. You'll get raped, murdered an'*
*kidnapped... not necessarily speaking in that order.'*

*I had laughed at him, gently placing my hand atop his. 'I*
*can handle myself,' I said, giving him my best smile.*

*He laughed slightly, rubbing his balding head with his free*
*hand. 'I know you can. I'm just worried, that's all.'*


I wrapped my arms around myself, sinking deeper into the
grass as I felt a different ache. *Maybe I should call him*, I
thought. And a part of me really wanted to. But I couldn't do
it. I looked at the sky again as more tears ran down my face.

I was alone in an abandoned park in the middle of Paris, no
longer human. He wouldn't want to talk to me.

I curled into a small ball. My insides felt like they were
tearing themselves apart and my mind was on fire.

*Blood, craving, vampire. Mr Becksworth, alone, unsafe.*

'Stop,' I moaned, hugging my knees closer to my chest. I
inhaled over and over again, dragging air into my burning
lungs. 'Shh, shh, it's okay,' I whispered to myself, rubbing my
arm and managing a shaky exhale as the flow of tears slowed.

I lay on my back, watching the sky for so long that the sun
began to burn my skin. I sat up, swallowing a lump of mucus.
Long branches hung down from the willow trees beyond the
playground, their tiny leaves swaying ever so slightly. I picked
up my bag, wandering through the grass until I stopped in
front of one of the trees. It was like a curtain, the way the leaves
fell so thickly. I pulled a wispy branch towards me, running my
fingers along the leaves.

*It's beautiful.*

I parted the branches, entering a cavernous space. The

thick trunk twisted, its branches sprouting out from the top and pouring down on all sides to kiss the earth. I sat down on the roots, leaning my back against the bark. Pieces of sunlight filtered in; glowing embers amongst the dark green coolness of the leaves.

And for a moment, nothing mattered.

I watched the leaves dance as a slight breeze picked up, tingling against my sun-kissed skin. I smiled, leaning my head back against the trunk and listening to the soft chirping of small birds hidden amongst the branches.

The next time I opened my eyes, the sky had dimmed to indigo. I stood stiffly, swinging my bag over my back, listening to the quiet. My fingers momentarily swept through my curls, wrought in tangles, dirt and grime. I sighed – there wasn't much I could do about those.

Tiny specks of luminescence flickered across the sky, the midnight blue depths that reached on forever and ever. For a moment, I stood there, looking up with my head thrown back.

I waded through the tangled knee-high grasses, listening to the crickets sing their tune like the birds did during the day. The moon was still hidden in its shadow, the night black apart from the stars. For a moment, I felt something had lifted from me.

Liberated me.

# CHAPTER 3

The streets were filled with couples, tourists, travellers and young children up past their bedtimes. It was as if the cobblestones and painted lines themselves were moving with the same vibrancy of life as their occupants. I stayed on the sidelines, trying not to get too close to anyone. The sky covering these streets seemed different, tainted. The orange glow from lamps and restaurants seeped up into it. If I squinted, I could only just make out several pinpricks of light. I sighed. My home was near the countryside and stars covered the sky in large sheaths of unbroken constellations.

*You wanted something different*, the bitter voice reminded me.

I walked further down the street, watching as children kicked stones at one another and elderly people sitting on communal benches smiled as they recalled their own youth. This part of the city was quieter, the buildings steeped in shadow. I pulled my drawstring bag closer, cradling it like a baby. I didn't want to go back to the flat; I felt like I needed to be outside to see more of Paris, even if it was late.

I stepped towards the dark alley, ignoring the bitter part of my mind, the part that was always afraid. If it had its way, I would still been stuck in that miserable flat in England.

*Music.*

As I came closer, I could hear it and pinpoint its source from deep within the heart of the mass of buildings ahead. The darkness played tricks with my eyes, tricks that formed the shape of a man that lurked. But there was something about that darkness that was calling me now. My legs carried me towards it, straight down the centre of the alleyway. Even though I was close enough to see that there was no man, I wrapped my arms around myself and squinted my eyes at the edges of the cobbled street in case someone was hiding there. Someone like the creature that attacked me.

A flashing neon sign disrupted the darkness, and I started walking towards it, then stopped abruptly. A man was guarding the entrance. Instinctively, I pushed myself up against the cool brick. He was tall, over six feet of bulging muscle, and wearing a navy-blue uniform. I leaned forward. Was that a baton hanging from his belt? This place screamed trouble. Hell, I could smell it oozing out of the walls. Even so, I had come to Paris for a fresh start, for something different. I was different. I wanted to do something that made me feel alive, like I owned myself again. If I could control my impulses, it would be fine, surely.

'*Tu es perdu?*'

I whipped my head around to find two girls staring at me, miniskirts clinging to their thighs. I could smell their blood, but by now the wave of longing had decreased into a small, controllable ripple.

I squinted at the one who spoke. 'I, uh, English?'

She looked relieved.

'Sorry, you never know.' Her voice was low and definitely British. 'You just seemed lost. Are you okay?'

I opened my mouth, glancing back at the bouncer. The other girl tugged on the first one's shirt.

'I'm...' I paused, searching for the right words. The girl probably regretted wasting her time on me. 'Sorry,' I said finally, smiling shyly. 'It's my first time in Paris.'

Her eyes softened knowingly as she subtly smacked her friend's hand away.

I glanced back at the bouncer. 'I wanted to go in there.'

The other girl coughed. 'You ain't exactly dressed for it.'

I stared at her, her dark skin glowing in the shadows, her braided hair wound in a high bun on her head.

'Karlie!' her friend snapped.

I blushed, looking down at my bulky beige coat and trainers. I probably looked homeless even when I wasn't standing beside them.

Karlie's hand waved in front of her. 'Oh shit – I didn't mean it like that.'

Turning towards the first one, I forced a smile. 'Thank you for your concern. I hope you both have a good time.' I pushed myself off the wall, making to get around Karlie and back to the dimly lit street.

'Wait!'

She caught my arm. My heart stopped for a beat, thinking she meant trouble.

'Look, I didn't mean it like that. For real. I'm sorry.'

I pulled my arm away slowly as I studied her.

Karlie smiled mischievously. 'What do you say about going in there?' she tilted her head towards the entrance before looping her arm through mine. 'You seem like you need to let loose!'

My breath caught in my throat as her warm pulse leapt

against my skin.

I focused on the bouncer again, surreptitiously taking a breath to steady myself as she pulled me towards the door.

'I don't have an ID on me,' I managed to say.

'Karlie, I don't know about this...'

'Sweet Jesus, Luna,' Karlie cried. 'When have I ever done something that I'll later regret?'

'Do you really want me to answer that?'

'Hmm, no.' Karlie turned to wink at me. 'Gabriel's a friend.'

It took me a moment to realise that Gabriel was the security guard. I raised my eyebrows at her with an awkward laugh.

There was something warm about the two of them, something healing and light that I couldn't put my finger on. But even with that, I was still as good as an abandoned puppy they took pity on and saved from the streets. Helpless and easy to manipulate.

'Relax,' Karlie told me as though she'd read my mind.

'Wait—'

'Hi, Gabriel.' Karlie detached herself from me and slunk up to the giant man.

His stony face cracked for a split second as he ran his eyes over Karlie, a shadow of a smile gracing his mouth.

'We had fun the other night, didn't we?' she murmured, walking her fingers up his chest.

His hand slipped casually around her waist.

'I had a thought...' she purred. 'You see my friend over there?'

His eyes shifted, but barely even lingered on my face before being drawn back to hers.

'She's come a long way tonight and forgot to bring her ID

in that little bag of hers.'

He chuckled. 'Oh, Karlie. You never were subtle. I'll let this one slide,' he said, taking his arm away from her waist and leaning it against the door frame. 'But next time, I won't be so lenient.'

His eyes shifted back to me again, sending chills down my spine.

*What am I doing?*

'Thanks, Gabriel!' Karlie called back with a flick of her hand as he stepped aside to let us through.

I kept my head down, shuffling in as quickly as possible before he changed his mind. The heavy metal door clanged shut behind us. The air inside was cool, musty and full of noise. The beat reverberated in my eardrums so loudly that I thought they would explode. I gritted my teeth as I followed Karlie down the steps, with Luna tailing behind me. With each step down we took, the air became hotter and hotter, as if we were descending into the depths of Hell itself.

The room was dark and cavernous, filled with people stuck together in one blurred mass; bodies pressed together so tightly they shared the same air. I followed the lights that swung over them with my eyes. Hot pink, turquoise and yellow. Someone took my arm and I let them, still watching the crowd. There was something about the throbbing mass. It screamed belonging.

'Here, let's take off that coat,' Karlie yelled above the music, pulling it off before I even knew what had happened.

I grabbed it back, clinging to the pocket with my wallet.

'It's safe here, don't worry.' Luna smiled at me reassuringly.

Something about her smile made me believe her, though I still took out my wallet and tucked it into my bra, just in case

'And your bag, too, if you don't want to lose it.' Karlie

opened her palm as the person behind the counter waited.

I bit my lip and stared at the bag in my hands. It was small and dark, and mine. I would've rather kept it with me as I danced, but I knew I couldn't dance properly then. I handed it over, my bag that contained some of my only possessions in the world, to a stranger, who handed it to another.

'What's your name?' Luna yelled as we walked toward the dance floor.

'Chiara.'

They smiled and nodded, and I wondered whether they had heard it. Karlie's cool hand was wrapped around the bare skin of my arm and her other hand was around Luna's as she pulled us deeper into the crowd. I tried to shrink into myself as much as possible to avoid touching anyone but that was pretty much impossible. I inhaled sharply as a girl collided with me, apologised and then went back to her friends giggling.

Blood.

It was tangy, metallic. And everywhere.

'Ooh, I love this song!' Karlie shouted before swaying her hips to the side with a pout.

I laughed despite the unease that had risen within me. She was carefree in a way that made me think she was rude at first, but maybe that was just her speaking her mind. I glanced at Luna. Maybe she was the one who was harder to read.

'Ah!' Karlie shrieked. 'Girl, you're supposed to dance!' She took my hands and moved my arms back and forth.

'Not when people are watching!'

'Let it go – ain't nobody watching.' Karlie wiggled her body as she raised her eyebrows, making Luna and I laugh.

The place didn't reek so badly of blood now that I was more used to it. I glanced at Luna as she started dancing again.

25

She was tall and of a heavier build, her thick black hair hanging mid-back. It swung as she did, her body moving almost as easily to the beat as Karlie's. She smiled, noticing me watching, then looked away.

I blushed, but the lights were too low for anyone to notice. Not that anyone was noticing me anyway. I was the only one in the crowd not dancing.

And probably the only one who wasn't human.

Running my hands through my hair, I blew out a sigh. Maybe that was a good thing, though. If I wasn't human, I wasn't who I was before. I stood a little taller as I scanned the people dancing in the shifting lights. Let it go, Karlie had said.

The song ended for a brief moment in which everyone seemed to come out of a trance. Karlie and Luna swirled back to me as if they had been caught in a vortex and had only just awoken themselves.

My face broke into a grin the second I heard the next song. 'Okay,' I looked between them. 'You got me.'

'Let's jump!' Karlie took my hands and we giggled into each other's faces as we bounced.

Somewhere between the gliding voice in the speakers and Luna and Karlie around me, I started to melt into the moment. Soon enough, we were all body-pumping against one another, laughing and shrieking as we swayed and fell into each other's arms like we were drunk.

'Watch this,' Luna called out as she did the robot.

'Step aside,' I smirked, waving my body down to the floor like a scuba diver from the '70s.

Karlie screwed up her nose. 'You look like a seaweed.'

'You wish you were a seaweed.'

'You're weird,' Karlie yelled at me with a smile.

Luna shoved her to the side with her hips. 'So are you, idiot!'

Karlie bumped her back. 'Mm. You know what I do wish for though?' She threw her arms into the air and swung her hips with each word, 'Shots, shots, shots!'

I raised my eyebrows. 'Um, I have to pee.'

They turned to look at me as if they had just remembered I was there.

Luna softened first. 'I'll show you where the bathroom is,' she yelled in my ear.

I turned to look at the crowd and for the first time, I looked past it. Over on the far side of the cavern was a better-lit area and a group of people gathered around what appeared to be a bar. Even from this angle, standing on my tiptoes, I could make out the shine of the bottles stacked high on the wall.

'I'll find it.' I gave Luna a quick smile.

'Ooh, can you get drinks while you're there?' Karlie stuck out her bottom lip. 'Pretty please?'

My smile froze on my face. I knew I couldn't afford it. Before I was forced to admit it out loud, I felt my arm being gently nudged and turned to find Luna placing a blue plastic card in my hand.

'Use this to pay, if you're sure you don't want me to come with you.'

I stared at her. This girl barely knew me, and already she was trusting me with her bank card?

She was watching me. I composed myself and gave her a smile as if this was normal. I didn't want her to think I'd run off with her card.

She nodded, turning to Karlie, who had started dancing again. 'Hey! Tequila?' Karlie gave a thumbs up, and Luna's eyes flashed back to me. 'Tequila.'

I crossed some sort of threshold between the dance floor and this new area, marked by a wooden floor and little white lights in the ceiling. The dance floor was claustrophobic and stuffy, but here there was at least a three-body gap between each person. My eyes skimmed across the area until they landed on the small door near the shadows.

When I walked in, several girls were touching up their lipstick in the mirror. Their voices jarred against the muffled silence. I gritted my teeth as I walked past them into the stall, knowing they could hear everything. As if I already didn't look underdressed.

I sat down on the toilet and put my head in my hands. My first day in Paris and already I was clubbing with two random girls who took pity on me.

England seemed so far away.

V

A throng of people stood gathered around the glossy slab of mahogany. I weaselled my way in until my fingers gripped the edge of it.

'Excuse me!' I cried, waving my arm at the bartender. He was young, leaning towards a woman over the thick counter as he polished the same glass over and over. She twirled a blonde strand of hair and looked at him like she wanted a piece.

'Don't waste your breath. It'll be a while.'

I frowned at the depressed-looking middle-aged man leaning against the counter next to me. 'There are too many people here, all wanting a drink.' He barely passed a glance my way as he downed the contents of his glass.

I pushed my way back into the space between the two crowds of people. *Maybe I'll wait here for a bit, in case it clears up.*

My hand briefly passed over the card in my back pocket to check it was still there, when something unknown and stronger than I was made me turn.

He was leaning against the brick wall less than two metres away, wearing a thin shirt that clung to his torso. He looked like he was trying not to smile as his eyes trailed down my body shamelessly.

My breath caught in my throat. Those eyes were the colour of midnight.

And now they were on mine.

For the briefest moment, my mind flashed back to the previous night, to the man – the creature – with black eyes.

I peered at the man cautiously. He didn't look all that threatening, but I couldn't trust anyone, not anymore.

He held my gaze effortlessly, the black glistening like he knew me. As though he saw what most people didn't. As though he wasn't afraid of what he saw.

I sucked in a breath and turned back around. Why was he making me nervous?

Ignoring him, I stood on my tiptoes and craned my head, finding that the bartender had apparently left blondie hanging and was now attending to a large party. Luna and Karlie probably wouldn't be too pleased if I returned without the drinks, but I didn't technically owe them anything. The only thing binding me to them was the blue plastic card in my pocket.

I turned to leave a second time, with a plan to go find the other two and call it a night. Even if the last thing I wanted to do was go back to my flat. Alone.

But when I tried to move, I found my legs didn't want to. I gritted my teeth, my heart pulsing wildly as I turned to glare at the dark-eyed stranger. What was I, a piece of meat? The fire in my chest made it easier to ignore what his eyes did to me.

I marched up to him and crossed my arms, hoping to burn a hole through his stupid angelic face.

'Stop staring at me.'

His skin was tanned, the kind of smooth that those girls from the bathroom would have loved to trail their fingers across. His eyes gleamed at my demand and the corner of his lips turned up as if I was a good joke. I opened my mouth to give him a piece of my mind when his hand grabbed my wrist, and before I'd even registered what was happening, he'd turned us both and pushed me up against the wall.

I stared at him, my heart hammering against my ribs. The place where his hand had touched my skin burned.

He leaned in so closely I could feel the warmth of his breath and smell the tinge of lemongrass and smoky wood emanating from his skin.

His lips grazed my ear. 'I know what you are.'

I shuddered.

So, he was like me then. I didn't know whether to be glad I wasn't the only such creature in Paris, or to run far away. I hated how he made me feel – like my limbs weren't solid, like my heart was in my throat. I hated that he knew it, too.

He started to pull away, but I caught his jaw. He could hear how fast he made my heart beat, but I could also hear his. And it was no better than mine.

'I know what you are too,' I whispered.

His eyes glistened with a question. When he didn't speak, I

let go of his jaw. He moved aside so I could leave, and I didn't look back.

I could still feel his eyes on me until I disappeared into the crowd.

'Girl, where were you?' Karlie yelled as soon as I returned. She swayed her hips in breathless circles. 'You've been gone a while.'

Luna looked down at my empty hands. 'What happened?'

I handed her card back and sucked in a breath. 'There were a lot of people.' I ran my hands through my hair. 'And there was this guy...'

Karlie stopped dancing.

'Who?' she squinted her eyes. The song pumping through the speakers ended for a split second – enough to make the room sound far too quiet.

'Just some random guy—'

'Ooh!' Karlie squealed, pointing at my cheeks heating up to Luna, who rolled her eyes with a smile. 'You mean someone sexy as hell.'

*Shit.*

Karlie winked at me before starting to dance to the next song.

I pressed my hands to my cheeks, trying to cool them. 'Does she ever get tired?' I asked Luna, gesturing to Karlie.

'Oh yeah. You should see her in the mornings.'

I laughed awkwardly, shifting on my feet.

'You don't look so good,' Luna said, frowning at me. 'Do you have anywhere to sleep?'

I gave her a strained smile. 'I do, but... you know what? It doesn't matter. Sorry.'

Her dark brows pulled together as she searched my eyes.

'Look, I'm gonna go,' I yelled, jerking my thumb towards the exit.

'Wait!' Karlie cried. The look in her eye was dead serious as she stood before me, the same height as I was. 'Are we gonna see you again?'

I opened my mouth, then closed it. 'I-I don't know.'

'You can come over to ours for the night, if you want,' Luna offered. Her baby blue eyes were soft as they looked at me, and I wondered what she thought she knew.

I shook my head, tucking my hair behind my ear. 'Why? I'm a stranger – you barely know me and I barely know you.'

Karlie flapped her hand. 'Potato tomato. Doesn't matter to me – does it matter to you, Lun-lun?'

'Nope.'

'How 'bout it, Chiara? '

I looked between the two of them, trying to come to a quick decision. They both did seem genuine and I could always leave in the morning and never look back. Plus, my flat felt like the last thing from safe.

I found them still waiting for my answer. My lips cracked into a shy smile.

Smooth granite steps paved the way up to their flat. The air was still and quiet. I ran my hand along the silver rails that lined the steps as we climbed to the second floor, the scuffs of our shoes echoing throughout the building. It even smelt middle class.

'I feel like a princess,' I murmured, glancing up through the gap in the stairs. I turned back to the other two and groaned. 'I said that out loud, didn't I?'

Karlie scrunched up her nose with a smile. 'If you like this, you'll like the inside even better.'

'Are your parents here?' I asked as Luna turned the key, shoving the door with half her body. The creak of it echoed.

'Luna's parents live up there,' Karlie whispered, pointing up the stairs before we stepped into the dark room. 'But mine are across town.'

'Do you live here then?' I held up my hands. 'Sorry, I don't mean to intrude—'

'Nah, it's cool.' She shrugged as Luna flicked on the light. 'Yeah, I do.'

The question on the tip of my tongue dissolved into the air as I looked around. The small entryway opened into a living area with a wall stripped back to brick on one end. A plush sofa was pushed up against it and I walked closer to have a better look, my socks sliding over the smooth wooden floorboards.

'Do those work?' I pointed to the string lights weaving against the brick.

Luna laughed. 'Of course, they work, silly!'

She bent behind the sofa and, a second later, a soft orange emitted from each tiny bulb. I almost laughed at how perfect it all was, twirling to examine the beanbags and pillows strewn across the fluffy rug.

'Is that a fireplace?'

'Piece of shit.' Karlie kicked her heels off and sashayed over.

'Your home is... so beautiful,' I whispered, gazing around.

Luna looked at me strangely and spoke as if she was surprised by her own response, 'Yeah, I guess it is.'

I coughed. 'Are there... do you have somewhere I can sleep?'

I stopped myself from pointing down the hall, scratching my head instead. The girls laughed like it was a ridiculous question, and dragged me along with them, showing me into the guest bedroom.

'I think I'm in heaven,' I murmured, dropping my bag to the floor.

A double bed was pushed against a similar brick wall, and the white duvet on top looked more like a cloud than anything else. I trailed my fingers across it, feeling guilty for having to sleep in it and, in doing so, defiling it with my sweat-stained body. But it felt like even more of an insult to use their shower.

I turned around to Karlie and Luna. Their eyes were soft as they looked at me, gentle and compassionate.

'Thank you.'

My words lingered in the air and lessened the space between us. Luna shook her head as if to say offering this room to a stranger for the night was the most normal thing in the world. Maybe it was, to her.

Karlie winked, and with a "see you tomorrow", they shut the door and were gone.

I sucked in a breath, turned off the lights and peeled off my layers, belly-flopping on the bed.

*What am I going to do?*

It was too late to call Sophie, my best friend. She would probably be curious about how our escape plan had panned out.

*A best friend from another life.*

I swallowed the lump in my throat. She had told me to move on when I got here, to forget about her and everyone else in my life. "Leave the past where it belongs, Chiara," she had said.

I'd nodded, taking her words to heart like I did with everything.

She didn't want to talk to me anymore.

I rolled over onto my back and gathered all of my hair so it spread out to the side. Luna and Karlie were unbelievably kind, but they were also strangers. Once morning hit, I knew I would be in the same predicament as before I met them. I shut my eyes. This room was suddenly far too big and I was far too small.

Noise from the street drifted through the thick glass window. I allowed the quiet sounds to lull me to sleep, pretending the tyres on the tarmac were gentle rain instead.

As I dared to let my eyelids droop, a pair of sparkling midnight eyes sank into my mind.

Eyes I'd rather forget.

# Chapter 4

*My tummy felt numb like it always did when I got this hungry.*

*I'd checked all the drawers and cabinets in our kitchen that I could reach, but all I could find that was edible was dry pasta and some crackers. I didn't know how to make pasta. Besides, I knew if I spilled hot water on my skin, it would hurt really badly.*

*My foster parents were out somewhere, but there was an extra key on the table. I took a deep breath, grabbed it with my small hand and gripped it tightly so it wouldn't fall. In my other hand, I took the coins that were left over in the organiser by the door where my parents kept their wallets. I knew it wasn't much but I hoped it would be enough for something. My foster mother needed to go shopping. There was only a single tomato and some ginger in the fridge; there wasn't even any milk left.*

*The shop was just down the road. I knew because I'd been there plenty of times. There were crates outside full of fruit and vegetables and more crates inside. The shelves were always full. I didn't know where the man inside got all the food from, but I knew that if you gave him some money, he would let you keep what you wanted. I was glad there weren't any people inside; I didn't like too many people. They were loud and made me scared when they talked to me. I was also glad when I saw the crate with bananas; I liked those. The sign said £1.40 for a bunch. I looked at the coins in my hand and then I picked up a bunch and removed a single banana.*

*'Here,' I said quietly, laying the banana and the coins on the counter.*

*Mr Becksworth – was that his name? – peered down at me. I shivered.*

*He didn't say anything as he walked around the counter and disappeared somewhere into the back of the store. I wondered if that was it and I should go home when I felt a light tap on my shoulder. The same tall, round man was standing there, holding a whole bunch of bananas.*

*'On the house,' he told me in his gruff voice. When all I did was blink up at him, he added, 'Means you can keep 'em for free.'*

Swallowing down any reservations, I dialled his number. It was morning now and he was always up from 6 a.m. to open for 7. Mr Becksworth was almost like a father to me, somebody who was more consistent and trustworthy than my foster parents ever were. Why had it been so hard for me to call him until now?

My phone started to ring and it didn't stop until it hit a voicemail. I paused while I listened to his cheery voice, feeling the same old comfy feeling I always got around him. It turned into something anxious when I heard the beep at the end. I promptly ended the call.

If he'd picked up, maybe things would have turned out differently. Maybe we would've had a conversation and it would've been like a second goodbye. But what was the point of that anyway? It would've hurt more than cutting it off cleanly.

Sighing, I rolled out of bed before walking to the bathroom.

*I wish I had the money for a place like this.*

I caught a glimpse of my reflection in the mirror, then regretted it instantly. My hair had somehow clumped in a poof at the back of my head and I looked like death had snatched me in the night. I looked longingly at the bathtub. I couldn't remember the last time I'd had a bath; it felt like such a luxury.

*Snap out of it. They said you could sleep here, not knock yourself out on the facilities.*

I popped my head into the hallway. There were blinds at one end, but they were doing barely anything to stop the light from bursting through them.

Silence.

Grabbing my bag, I started to tip-toe down the hall. The front door would probably wake them up, but by then it would be too late for either of them to do anything about my sudden exit. Not that they would care anyway.

*Crash.*

I cursed under my breath and stuck my head into the kitchen. My plan fell into pieces as I caught sight of Karlie sitting in the middle of the floor with pans sprawled everywhere. A laugh bubbled up within me as she looked up in sheer bewilderment.

'Shh!' Karlie said in a whisper. 'Luna's sleeping.'

I let my bag fall to the ground, still holding onto the string.

'Well, if she slept through that, she needs to be woken up anyway,' I grinned, weaving the string through my fingers.

Karlie's smile faded as her eyes trailed down to my hand. 'You were gonna leave without saying bye, weren't you?'

I opened my mouth, glancing around the kitchen wildly as if an excuse would appear. 'I-I thought you might've regretted letting me stay. I thought it would be easier to just leave.'

I rubbed my shoulder, wishing she had been asleep more than anything. Didn't Luna say she was an evening person?

Karlie frowned. 'You really think we'd regret it after we had so much fun last night?.' She shook her head and stood up, a more playful look in her dark eyes. 'I've got an idea.'

Karlie's mood was infectious and we giggled and shh-ed each other as we tiptoed down the hallway, each armed with a pan and a wooden spoon. Karlie snorted as I stepped on the floorboard that creaked. I shuffled into Luna's room after her.

'Three, two, one,' Karlie whispered, her eyes glistening in the dark.

'Wake up!' we shouted in unison, banging as loudly as we could on the pans.

Luna fell out of bed.

Karlie and I cackled with laughter, the kind that made you wheeze and gasp for air.

'Oh no,' Karlie cried, pointing to Luna on the floor.

Another laugh escaped me as we leaned across the bed. Luna took one look at us, then yelled like she was about to go into battle.

'Run!' Karlie grabbed my arm and we fled down the hall, heading straight for the bathroom.

I laughed as Karlie slammed the door and dragged me into the bathtub, where we sat breathless, slumped against the curved edge. Luna's sluggish steps pounded down the hallway like a drumbeat in the silence.

'Do you think she hates us?' I whispered, chewing on my nail.

'Oh, definitely,' Karlie responded. 'She'll beat the crap out of us.'

'But I'm so young!'

Luna stormed into the bathroom with skewed glasses and hair resembling a bird's nest.

'If looks could kill,' I whispered to Karlie, biting back a laugh.

'It's a pity they don't.'

I glanced at Karlie, who looked like she was barely holding it together. *Don't you dare,* I said with my eyes. Luna glared at us and time stood still for several long moments.

Finally, she cracked. 'I hate you guys,' she moaned, slumping out of the bathroom.

I grinned with relief as Karlie cupped her hands around her mouth and shouted, 'You mean you love us!'

Forty minutes and two cups of coffee later, we were sitting around their little wooden table in the kitchen, the glow of the morning filtering through the windowpane.

'So,' Luna started, wrapping her fingers around her half-empty mug, 'What are you really doing in Paris?'

I shrugged, not ready to share my whole life story. 'Just looking for a fresh start, I guess.'

Karlie eyed me with a smirk.

'So,' I swallowed, pursing my lips slightly, 'what are you two doing here?'

Luna smiled, pushing her round frames up her nose. 'I'll pretend as if you actually answered my question. Our parents work here. It's all about business, of course,' she rolled her eyes, casting a knowing look in Karlie's direction. Karlie looked uncomfortable. 'We go to this English-speaking school just outside the city.'

'How long have you guys known each other?' I asked.

'Since we were little.'

Luna glanced at Karlie. 'Yeah, like four or som—'

'Nah, like two!'

I laughed. 'That's pretty cool. And you guys even live together?'

Karlie leaned forward towards Luna, eyes glittering. 'Girl, do you remember that time we almost got expelled?'

I spat out my coffee.

Luna laughed and her entire body shook with it. 'Oh yeah.' Her eyes were off in the distance. 'That was probably the stupidest thing ever.'

'Do you guys go to a public school or—'

'Private.' Karlie rolled her eyes. 'They're all stuck up.'

I looked around their kitchen. 'And you're not?' The words slipped out before I could control my tongue. 'I—'

'Ha!' Karlie cried. She fixed her head wrap, smoothing it down with her slender fingers.

Luna's light eyes examined mine. 'Maybe a little. Definitely privileged, but I hope not stuck up!'

'I didn't mean it,' I said sheepishly, then bit back a laugh as I added, 'your flat just looks a lot different from mine.'

'Do you want me to drive you back, by the way?' Luna glanced at the clock on the wall. 'If you have to be anywhere—'

'Oh no, I-I'm not doing anything,' I said, tracing the lines in the wood with my finger. 'I didn't have much of a plan of what to do once I got here.' I looked between the two of them. 'I just turned eighteen. Technically, I should be in school. But

I need a job so I can have enough money to...' I trailed off, cupping my chin in my palm as my eyes wandered through their kitchen. It must be nice to not need to even think about money at all.

'Do you have any hobbies?' Luna asked, probably sensing a need to change the subject.

'Um... I can paint.'

Karlie lit up like a crystal ball. 'I need to show you something.'

She led the way, her hand pulling me towards her room.

Inside, a glow emanated from fairy lights draped over the walls, covered in art prints. There was a floor-length mirror at one end, next to a wardrobe made of wicker. I stood by the bed as she dug underneath it, humming a tune I didn't know. The melody was sweet and deep; it carried well in the quiet .

'Here's one!' she called, sliding out and handing me a medium-sized canvas.

I felt my breath hitch. Vibrant colours slashed across the surface – gold, crimson and burnt orange – like a sunset. I traced the lines with my finger. They made a woman's face.

'You like it?'

I glanced up, noticing Karlie's dark eyes glittering.

I nodded, looking at the painting again. 'It's amazing.'

It differed from how I painted; the lines looked so much harsher and more abstract. But it was Karlie and it worked.

Her hands wrapped around the canvas I was holding, pulling it back towards herself.

'You actually like it?' She examined her work closely, as if trying to see something that wasn't there.

I knelt down and peered under her bed. My mouth slackened. Large and small canvases were strewn around on the dark floor, probably gathering dust.

'Karlie, why the hell are you hiding all these paintings?' I stood up, crossing my arms.

She laid the painting of the woman on her sheet. 'What am I supposed to do with them?'

I stared at her. 'Karlie. You are literally an amazing painter. You should be selling them or at the very least putting them on your walls.'

I picked up the woman's face again. For me, something about art made it easy to not compare between pieces. I could appreciate the uniqueness and beauty in every painting, even in my own. It was one of the few things I had the strength to view in that light.

Karlie adjusted her headwrap again with a nervous smile. 'But some of these are really personal. Besides,' her dark eyes slid to mine, 'have you ever sold your paintings?' Before I could announce that I had, she exclaimed, 'Oh, and I wanna see them, bitch! You can't be coming in here all high and mighty. I wanna see what you've done too!'

I bit my lip. 'I left them in England.'

She stopped. 'Are you for real?'

I nodded. 'I couldn't take them with me. I-I told my best friend to take them, but I don't know if she did. My parents might have thrown them out.'

I'd been painting for years, and each canvas was like a different piece of me, took up a different space in my mind and soul. I had almost cried when I realised I couldn't take them; I'd put all my love into my paintings, and they looked like emotions poured into the moulds of images or symbols or colours.

Karlie looked at her fingers. 'Damn. I know you kinda

develop an emotional attachment to your paintings.'

I gave a sad little laugh. 'I really wish I'd brought at least one just so I could show you. Now that you've shown me inside your mind, it's only fair I show you mine.'

Karlie tilted her head to the side. 'I wanna be your friend,' she said, as if the thought had only just occurred to her. She turned so her frown faced the paintings on her bed. 'Whatever you end up doing, I hope we can see each other again.'

'Even just to paint together?' I smiled.

She smiled back.

# CHAPTER 5

We rolled up to my building, Luna in the driver's seat. Karlie let out a low whistle from the back. The sky had now been dabbed with clouds, one of which had stolen the sun.

'It's a good location.' I shrugged, taking the drawstring bag from between my legs.

'Chiara, I don't know about this.'

I paused with my hand on the door handle, noticing Luna take in the upturned rubbish bins, graffiti and the lingering air of trouble.

'It looks worse than it is.' I stopped myself from adding it could actually be much worse and that they were clearly used to much better.

'I've got an idea,' Karlie announced.

I tilted my head. She looked as if she was struggling to say what she was thinking.

'What?' Luna eyed her.

'Um, well, since we've got a spare room...' Karlie paused, her cheeks heating up in a way I hadn't seen them do before, as if she knew she had crossed some unspoken boundary.

I tightened my grip around my bag, though Luna looked as if she was actually considering it. I opened my mouth to object.

'I don't have a problem with that,' Luna said, turning to me. 'Only if you want to, of course.'

Her expression was deep and sweet, like slow-moving syrup. Something I couldn't handle.

I glanced back at Karlie to see if hers was any better.

Hope. Expectation.

It was worse.

Without explanation, I pulled the car handle and swung open the door, turning back a single time before I ran up the steps. My fingers were clumsy and shaking as I fiddled with the key, finally shoving it in the lock and slamming the door behind me before I allowed myself to see if they had driven away.

I didn't exhale until I got inside my flat.

'Fuck.'

I dropped the bag to the ground and ran my fingers through my curls. I couldn't live with them, could I? Why had Karlie been stupid enough to even propose such an idea? I met them *yesterday* and already she had the audacity to assume I was ready to commit to being trapped with two strangers who could kick me out at any moment with the snap of their freshly manicured fingers. Did I really appear that desperate, as if I would cling like a parasite to a merciful rich girl without a second thought?

Karlie and Luna thought they knew me, knew what I was like. I almost laughed. They had no idea. What if they got bored of me? What if I opened up to them and they realised they didn't like me after all? Would they still let me live there out of the kindness of their hearts? Unlikely.

I dragged in a shaky breath, pinching the bridge of my nose. No, I couldn't rely on someone like that. It was completely ridiculous. Irrational.

I slung my bag over my shoulder, kicked off my shoes and waltzed into my bedroom. I glared at the thin, scratchy duvet on the bed before stepping up to the chest of drawers. It was made of chipboard and each drawer caught in such a way that made it stiff to open. I dug my fingers into the groove on the top of the first drawer and pulled. My paints.

They gleamed in the silken light, the tubes half-empty and stained with their own colours. My fingers reached for a deep blue shade. But I knew I had no canvas.

Reluctantly, I pushed the drawer shut and tied my hair up, surveying the room with my hands on my hips.

*If I'm going to live here, I might as well make it livable.*

I swept the floor everywhere I could, vacuumed and then mopped. Usually when I cleaned I had music, but now there was none and so my thoughts had space to run in wild circles.

Besides the obvious fact that I would be seriously endangering my freedom by accepting their offer, something much larger was at stake. I ran my hand over the smooth scar on my neck. It was a secret I didn't know I'd be able to keep, not to mention one I couldn't willingly keep without risking their lives. What if I lost control? It hadn't happened yet, but that meant nothing. If anything, it was only a matter of time.

I shoved the pillowcases and duvet cover into one of the washing machines downstairs, along with the clothes I'd worn yesterday.

Then again, there was something about them. It was inexplicable, illogical. Something I couldn't use any written language to describe; it spoke to me only through feeling.

Though I hated myself for it, I knew I'd rather live with the two of them than alone. I didn't want to be alone, especially now that I wasn't human.

I let myself feel the glimmer of excitement that ran through me at Karlie's proposal. I knew what I really wanted was to accept it, more than anything.

Taking a shower, I arched my back uncomfortably so the weird angle of water would actually land on my head. I changed, throwing on a dress, before cracking open the window in my room. The air smelt like garbage. I shut it again.

Sitting at the square table shoved against the wall in the kitchen, I rested my chin in my hand. Moving in with them would also solve my problem of finding someplace else to live. I wouldn't have to worry about that anymore.

The minute hand ticked loudly on the clock and though I was hungry, I didn't do anything about it. There was no food in here and I couldn't be bothered to buy any now. My hand reached for my phone absentmindedly before I jerked my fingers back.

Luna and Karlie had given me their numbers that morning in case we wanted to meet up sometime. Something deep in me urged me to call and that I was worrying about nothing.

*But what if it isn't nothing?*

Taking a deep breath, I closed my eyes, letting it out slowly. After a few seconds, I picked up the phone again.

'I'm glad you changed your mind,' Luna said as I opened her car door.

I dumped my bag in the back, the one carrying all of my belongings, before sliding in.

'I knew it, I told you!' Karlie bounced in her seat. 'Ooh, this is gonna be so much fun!'

'Did you have to come too?'

Karlie scrunched up her nose at me, but seemed too happy to be offended.

Luna hit the accelerator and we started off, back to their flat.

'Does this mean you're coming to our school as well?' Karlie asked.

'Oh, wow.' I didn't even bother with the seat belt as I leaned my head against the window, watching that seemingly unmoving sky.

'Is that a yes or a no?'

'Karlie, I only just accepted moving in with you guys – give me a break!' I rolled my head to find Karlie's lodged between the gap in the seats, brown eyes soft and open.

I frowned at her, wondering why she was putting in all this effort for me. I could usually tell when someone was ingenuine; I felt it straight away. I saw through their fake smiles and their sugary voices, but Karlie was none of that. She was real, and I guessed she must have taken to me in the same way I took to her.

Luna's voice cut through the silence. 'There are only a few months left of school – we should see what their policy is. Look,' she sighed heavily before turning a corner. 'Chiara, I know it's your life, but I think you really should finish school. You can't be a dropout; that's ridiculous.'

I felt a deep blush bloom across my cheeks. 'Luna, I'd need financial aid to go there.'

'We can arrange that – it's no problem, really.'

'That's not—' I cut myself off, not wanting to explain how uncomfortable the idea made me feel. How could I live

49

with them and rely on them financially? Besides, I needed to work, to have enough money to support myself in case they did decide to leave me on the streets.

I dug my nails into my arms. It was hard to remind myself I couldn't trust these people, that no matter how close I felt to them they were still strangers, and I was probably nothing but momentary entertainment.

Luna glanced at me as she turned into the parking space. 'I'm sorry, you're probably feeling overwhelmed. We can talk about this later.'

I didn't answer, thinking about how much of a drain I was already being on them, wondering how much time I had left before they decided not to bother anymore. Barely anyone had shown me kindness, and it always came at a price.

I didn't see why this time it should be for free.

We spent the rest of the day lounging around the living room, eating salted-caramel popcorn and talking about everything from what our favourite animals were to whether or not aliens existed. I almost peed myself laughing several times before erupting into fits of giggles. I couldn't remember the last time I'd laughed like that, or even had a conversation like that.

Karlie was easy to talk to and around her Luna seemed to open up more. Luna appeared to be the more emotionally tuned-in one, having skilfully steered the conversation away from why I was really in Paris; why I had run. Sighing, I stretched out on the beanbag, letting my hand drop to the floor above my head. I didn't want to even think about any of that now, much less talk about it. My past seemed murky and broken compared to this moment, the warm sun rosy on my new friends' cheeks.

'I've got an idea,' Karlie exclaimed.

I sat up, feeling the rush of blood to my head. 'The last time you had one of those...'

'Shh!'

Karlie clicked something on her phone, pushing her fingers into the side to turn up the volume all the way. I groaned as an Ariana Grande song started playing.

She leapt on top of the sofa with a wild grin, before belting out the lyrics in a pitchy voice, swaying her hips and using her phone as a microphone.

'Bloody hell, you sound like a dying cat!' Luna shrieked, holding her hands over her ears.

I laughed, which became an intense coughing fit as Karlie shot me a dirty look.

'Get up here, bitch!'

I screamed as she grabbed my arm and yanked me up.

'Come on! Sing, Chiara!'

I side-eyed Karlie, smiled widely and then joined in with the next line, laughing to cover the embarrassment. I knew I was a terrible singer, but something about them made me comfortable enough not to care so much.

Karlie decided it was time to change pitch, causing Luna to shove her head into a pillow and moan.

'Oh no, you don't!' I yelled, jumping down to pull her up. 'If I'm singing, there's no way you're getting out of it.'

I pulled Luna up onto the sofa, telling Karlie to move her ass over. As the next song came on, Karlie side-bumped me so hard I fell into Luna, who almost fell off. We were all giggling as we clung onto each other, then began to sway to the beat.

We held each other closely, and my heart soared.

# CHAPTER 6

'Karlie, get the plates!' Luna called from the steaming kitchen around seven o'clock. The sky was turning a light pink and the buildings out the living room window were ablaze in the dying sun.

'Why can't Chiara do it?'

Luna stepped out of the kitchen wearing an apron, hands on hips.

'How old are you, five?'

'Four, actually.'

Luna rolled her eyes. 'Get off your lazy bum.'

I laughed as Karlie groaned, shot me a helpless look and then sashayed to the kitchen with extra sass just to annoy Luna.

I padded over to the kitchen as well, standing awkwardly in the doorway. 'Do you want me to help with anything?' I asked.

'No, don't worry about it. Honestly, I like cooking, and Karlie never helps me anyways.'

Karlie made a face at her and I laughed, before peering into the pan on the stove.

Suddenly, a waft of chicken hit me, causing my stomach to lurch so violently that I felt the bile rise all the way to my throat. Their heart beats sounded as loud as my own, thundering in my head.

I sucked in a breath, squeezing my eyes tight and trying to calm the nausea.

All this time I thought I'd been hungry for food, when really it was for something far worse. These cravings were starting to be a real inconvenience. What was I supposed to do, hunt an animal?

I stepped back from the pan and walked as calmly as I could to the table, where Karlie was setting down the plates. She handed me a fistful of cutlery, but as I began to lay them down, my hands started shaking.

'You okay?' she asked, smiling like it was a game, not understanding the control it was taking to calm the craving.

It felt like a thousand knives were pressing against my chest. I dropped the cutlery with a clatter.

'I need some air.'

Karlie looked from my hands to my face. 'But the meal is almost done?'

I had already started backing away, feeling panic rise within me. 'I'll be back soon. I just have to clear my head.'

The soft wind hit me as I emerged onto the street, engulfing me like a soothing embrace. I gulped the early evening air into my lungs.

Something about it was healing.

I closed my eyes, massaging my throbbing temples with my fingers as my heart rate fell

The nausea was still there, fuelled by the disgust I felt for myself. I needed blood. I knew all this would go away if only I let myself have some. But from where? From Karlie? From Luna?

The world tilted sideways as if I was on a ship at sea. I clung onto a lamppost.

No, I wouldn't do it. I couldn't. My head started to pound, knives running along my skull. I blinked, gasping in the dying light. The noise from multiple streets flooded my ears in a mad tyranny as my head continued to pound, so sharply that my vision blurred for a moment.

I was only vaguely aware of sinking to the floor. But I felt the sharp jolt that rang through my bones as my knees hit the concrete and the even sharper jolt that shuddered through my skull as it crashed into the lamppost.

Then, darkness.

It was light when I awoke next. I blinked slowly in the perfect silence, squinting against the sun's rays.

*Where am I?*

I frowned as I sat up, noticing the duvet. Grey. Not white, like Karlie and Luna's was.

I inhaled sharply, grabbing a fistful of it as I kicked myself against the backboard.

But I was alone.

I exhaled and sank into the pillows. It was the softest bed I had ever been in, even softer than the one at Karlie and Luna's. I knew I should be scared; who in their right mind would take an unconscious girl back to their own home unless they were planning on kidnapping and raping her?

I looked down at myself. It didn't feel like either of those things had happened to me.

Sunlight filtered in through the floor-to-ceiling window. I realised I must've never made it to dinner last night. It was morning all over again.

*What happened?* All I could remember were the sharp points of knives running across my skull and the darkness that had followed.

I rolled onto my side, finding a picture on the bedside table. Apart from that, the room was clear of personal items, making it impossible to even identify the gender of the stranger who had taken me in. The wooden frame surrounding the picture was rough; hand-carved. I traced my finger over the smooth grooves before resting my eyes on the couple in the photo. A woman laughed into a man's chest. It was a beach. Sunset. I wondered if it meant something to the stranger or if I was lying in that couple's guest bedroom right now.

*Why though?*

I laid the photo back exactly how I remembered it before throwing off the duvet. It smelt familiar. I drew in a breath to catch another waft of it, but it was almost impossible to identify.

Sticking my head out into the hallway, I strained my ears for any signs of life. But it was as if the house was completely deserted.

Perfect.

While I was slightly curious about whose house this was, I didn't particularly feel like talking to the owner. I tiptoed down the carpeted steps and scanned the ground floor wildly, before snapping my head back around to ensure no one was behind me.

My eyes fixated on the front door. Without thinking, I ran and was there in an instant, about to fling it open and—

An arm looped around my waist, dragging me back. I screamed, kicking and writhing with all my strength, but they were stronger. Panic flooded my veins as they picked me up and flung me over their shoulder, as if I were no more than a ragdoll.

'Let go of me!' I cried, pounding on their back.

'Would you cut that out?'

Something about his voice made me freeze. It was also familiar. Low, rough and smooth at the same time. He carefully set me down on the marble kitchen counter, then straightened up with a grunt.

'Was it really necessary to hit me that hard? I think you might've left a couple of bruises.'

I widened my eyes.

It was the guy from the club. He had the same tousled dark hair, high cheekbones and tanned skin, but his eyes... they were not the same. They had never been black at all; it must've been the lighting.

They were blue.

Midnight blue, deep sea blue, the kind of blue you could drown in.

'I'm flattered, doll, but you should know that it's rude to stare.' He gave me a wicked smirk and I felt the heat rush high into my cheeks.

*Doll?*

'You're weak,' he stated.

I forgot my embarrassment, the heat burning differently altogether. 'Excuse me? You—'

'I didn't mean it like that,' he sighed, rubbing his hand over his eyes.

I was about to ask what he did mean when he turned around, rummaging through a compartment in the double-sided glossy fridge behind him. I watched the way his hands moved. Smooth, precise. I thought of the carved frame upstairs and wondered if he was the one who'd made it.

When he turned around, those hands were holding a package filled with dark red liquid. It bulged.

'No.' I forced the word out, digging my fingers into the counter.

But it was all I could do to not leap forward. It was almost too much, the blood being there alongside him.

I swallowed, then asked the first question that came to mind, tearing my eyes away from the blood. 'Are you stalking me?'

One side of his soft lips pulled up, his eyes glistening. 'I think what you meant to ask is why I, being a kind stranger, took you back to my nice home when I could've left you on the street?'

I scoffed. '"Kind stranger"? If you really were so kind, then you'd let me leave. Now.'

He rolled his eyes. 'I don't think so.'

His grip around the bag softened as he held it out to me. I swallowed hard, running my hands through my hair. *I shouldn't*. But it was right there.

My stomach turned in a million different ways as I stared at the liquid and then at the suntanned skin of his hand. His palm was calloused.

'Today, doll.'

I snatched the bag from his stupid hand, clutching it to my stomach. 'Stop calling me that.'

His eyes were smirking again, but I knew my request wasn't going down. The blood in the bag was O-negative, most likely stolen from the nearest hospital. It was even more vile this close to my lips.

I blew out a sigh. 'I can't.'

He made a noise of frustration as he clenched his jaw. 'Listen to me.' The smirk was gone. He was suddenly close, too close. 'If you don't drink this, you will die.'

I stared at him. 'I-I didn't choose this. I don't want to be like this.' I looked down at my hands, twisting anxiously in my lap. 'It's disgusting.'

He drew in a breath. 'I'm sorry,' he whispered.

I met his eyes, mine filling with tears. For once, I didn't care if it made me look weak.

'You know, I think I understand what I am. But it still feels unreal.' I pulled back my hair, showing him the scar on my neck. 'A man attacked me in the bathroom. He... bit me and ever since, I've been different.'

He reached out as I talked and gently ran his thumb over my scar. 'Different how?' he asked.

I sat back slightly, leaving his fingers floating in the air between us and gave him a look, gesturing to the blood bag I was holding.

'You don't need me to explain it to you anyway,' I said, ignoring the way his lips twisted in a smile, 'when you clearly know more. I just wish it was all a nightmare.'

'It's not that bad, actually,' he shrugged. 'You'll get used to it.'

When I looked at him, I found he was already looking at me. His gaze was captivating. We stared at each other, time stretching. Then I blinked, remembering myself, and he bit his lip, dropping his gaze to the blood bag and gesturing to it.

'You, uh, need to drink that.'

'All of it?'

The smirk was back. 'All of it.'

I chewed on my lip. Every cell in my body was yearning for it. Even for just one drop. I turned the bag over in my hands as my craving battled with the disgust. Both had been equally strong at one point, but it seemed now that the craving had won, stumbling out from the realm of inconvenience into a necessity. My hands shook as I undid the toggle at the end and held the tube extending from the bag to my lips.

He was watching me.

'Turn around.'

To my surprise, he did as he was told.

The blood was thick and cool as it seeped into my throat. I almost moaned in relief. I felt it working instantly, nourishing me in a way nothing else could. I had only planned to take a couple of sips, but the more I had, the more I wanted, and soon I had to push on the bag to get the last drops out.

He'd turned back around by the time I looked up, and I wiped my mouth with the back of my hand.

'That good, huh?' he smirked.

'Shut up.'

He took the bag from me and threw it in the bin. 'You're a new turner; you'll need blood more often.'

I watched as he leaned back against the fridge, regarding me with something like intrigue.

I pushed myself off the counter. 'And where am I supposed to get the blood from, Einstein? Your fridge? Or do I have to sneak into a hospital and steal it too?' I had the urge to walk closer to him and out the door simultaneously. But I did neither, settling for crossing my arms instead. 'You know people could be dying due to a lack of blood supply because of you.' I glanced around the kitchen. 'Do you live in this big house all by yourself? That must get lonely.'

He laughed, shaking his head. 'Do you always talk this much?'

I felt a pang in my heart. I usually didn't talk much at all.

'Goodbye, thief.' I saluted him, giving him my best smile before walking out of the kitchen and stopping at the huge front door. The lock system looked complicated and I wondered if I needed a key to unlock it from the inside.

'Turn the handle at the top and pull.'

I scowled at him, found the handle and pulled a little too hard; the door swung open so fast I almost smacked myself with it. He was smirking, leaning against the kitchen door frame as if biding his time.

I shut the door on him before I could wonder why.

# CHAPTER 7

'Holy shit.'

This was clearly a wealthy area. The road was freshly paved with smooth dark tarmac and wide enough to fit three cars down it at once. The houses were several storeys high, with large glass windows and, from the looks of it, probably around ten bedrooms each. I walked forward and gasped as my bare foot touched the sun-baked ground.

'He took my shoes?' I cried, whipping around, daring him to be watching me from one of his windows. But if he was, I wasn't able to see.

*Who is this guy, some kind of millionaire?* I squinted at his beautiful house before starting off decidedly down the road. He probably stole the money too. Or the house.

Halfway down, I stopped dead in my tracks.

*Fuck.*

I had no idea where I was and I had no phone. There was a reason he'd had that knowing look in his eye: I needed him to get home.

'Fuck's sake,' I muttered to myself, starting off down the street again. 'Chiara Beaufort, you got yourself into this mess and you will get yourself out of it.'

I had walked far enough down the road that when I turned around, his house seemed much smaller and much less impressive. I huffed, staring up at the blue sky. It, too, seemed to be mocking me.

I gritted my teeth and started to walk back. What I didn't understand was why he had gone through all that effort. And, come to think of it, what were the chances of meeting the same guy twice in less than twenty-four hours? Out of all the people in Paris who happened to be driving down Karlie and Luna's street at the exact time I had passed out, it had to be him?

I clenched my fists as I spotted him standing outside his garage, wanting nothing more than to put a dent in that rich idiot's angelic face. He flashed me a grin almost as shiny as the vintage car he was standing next to.

'Took you long enough.'

I scowled at him, which made him smile even wider.

'Why did you bring me to your house?' I asked, folding my arms over my chest as he unlocked the car.

'You would've preferred it if I'd left you on the ground?'

'Yeah, actually.'

'I'll keep that in mind for next time' – the corner of his lip tilted up – 'doll.'

I gave him an unimpressed look, muttering that there would be no "next time", before reluctantly slumping into the passenger seat. He slid in coolly and shut the door with just the right amount of strength: gentle enough to not rock the car and hard enough to make it click closed.

It was silent.

I dug my hands into my arms to stop myself from shaking; leaping out of the seat; exploding. He hung his arm across the back of my seat to reverse. My heart was pounding in my ears. I dug my fingers in harder. I didn't dare look at him, even though there was something magnetic about him that made me want to.

I swallowed, wondering how many other pairs of female eyes were helplessly drawn to his, how many other girls he had seduced without even trying.

It hadn't been more than a few minutes of silence before I snuck a glance. His eyes were fixed firmly on the road ahead as he manoeuvred the steering wheel with ease. It almost bothered me how unbothered he was, as if my presence did not affect him whatsoever.

'Done staring?'

I jumped, blood rushing to my cheeks. *Stupid, stupid, stupid.*

I scoffed to hide my embarrassment. 'You wish I was staring.'

He rolled his eyes, but I still managed to catch a glimpse of satisfaction in them.

We hurtled past cars, sticking to the fast lane and probably going well over the speed limit. I raised an eyebrow, wanting to ask if he was in a rush to get me out of his car, but stopped myself, a pang of hurt pulling at my chest at the thought of what his answer might be.

*He's just a guy, Chiara, like any other. He literally kidnapped you for God's sake. Get over it.*

I drew in a breath and fixed my gaze solidly on the sky. With the light white clouds stuck across it, it looked almost like a painting. I suppressed a smile, thinking about asking Karlie if she wanted to paint something together when I got back.

Did he usually drive without music? Even with the hum of the tyres on the road, the silence still unsettled me. Just like him.

And he knew it.

'Can I ask you something?'

Blue Eyes seemed surprised, briefly glancing at me.

'Why do we have to drink blood?'

He squinted, lifting a hand to scratch the back of his neck. 'It's a long story.'

I eyed the motorway. 'We have a long time.'

He glanced at me again before sighing. His hand loosely guided the steering wheel, but it held all the precision and control it needed.

'Then I'll give you the full story.'

'What?' I frowned at him. 'The whole history of vampires?'

He laughed. 'Only if you want to hear it.'

I rolled my eyes. 'Go on then.'

'Where to begin...'

I waited in the stillness while he organised his thoughts.

'The first vampires can be dated back to one thousand years ago, in a small village in Iceland. A peasant girl and a prince lived there, and the two of them were in love.'

The word hung in the air. It sounded good coming from his mouth.

'The prince asked the king, his father, for permission to marry her. But the king was an evil man and sent out his guards to kill the peasant girl.' He glanced at me. 'According to the king, the prince could only marry a princess. So the couple turned to Hades, whom they'd heard could grant any wish.' He laughed, but it was bitter. 'And he granted them a wish alright: immortality. To be together for eternity. But like any wish, there was a price to pay. Hades turned them into sadistic beasts who could only survive by consuming the blood of others.'

He winked at me, causing tiny flutters to erupt in my stomach.

There was a long pause.

'Is that it?'

'What more did you want?' His eyes glistened, an amused smirk playing on his lips. 'The two of them lived happily ever after, end of story.'

But I wished it wasn't the end of the story. I wanted to hear more of his voice. It was unlike anything I had ever heard, deep and with the slightest hint of an accent I couldn't place.

'I have a question,' I announced. 'If you were to drink a human's blood, would they always turn into a vampire?'

'It depends; if our saliva mixes with their blood, then yes. But since it's tricky not to do that, I usually just use blood bags.'

I nodded, feeling a chill. *So, the consequences of me losing control wouldn't be limited to injury or death of a human, but something even worse. They'd end up like me.*

My eyes widened. 'Wait. Did you say immortality? Please tell me that isn't real.'

He looked at me. 'It isn't real.'

He turned away fast, eyes back on the road, but I didn't need to see them to know he was lying.

'Shit.' I ran my fingers through my hair over and over. 'So that's it then.' My voice was bitter, tinged with emotion. 'One day, I get attacked and all of a sudden I'm a blood-sucking monster from a fairy tale who lives forever.' I paused, staring dead ahead. 'Yeah, it's not really sinking in.'

'Any idea why?'

I turned to face him. 'I will punch you.'

He laughed – it was the purest sound I had ever heard.

'Oh, I'm so scared.'

I crossed my arms, turning back to face the front. 'You should be. I've got some serious muscles you don't wanna mess with.'

'Yeah, and that's why it was so easy for you to escape when I flung you over my shoulder.'

'Hey, I gotta get warmed up first. You could've at least given me a five-second warning.'

He was grinning. I hated it and loved it simultaneously.

'You have an accent,' I told him, 'are you from Iceland? Like the original vampires in the story?'

He laughed again. 'Not even close, doll.'

'For fucks sake, stop calling me that!'

'But it fits you perfectly.'

I stared at him, hating how he made my cheeks and everything else less obvious light up with fire. But before he could chastise me for checking him out again, I tore my eyes away. Right as we rolled up to the block of flats.

He nodded towards it. 'You live near here?'

'Mm.'

His eyes were on me, I could feel them, making my every movement as heavy as lead.

I stopped with the door half-open and turned in my seat.

'You never told me your name.'

I said it quietly because the way he looked at that moment had taken most of my breath away.

The sun was lighting up his face, illuminating his blue eyes with such intensity it was as if he were the source of light. His soft lips were pursed slightly as he squinted through his lashes at me.

'Kaelan.'

My heart leapt.

Before I could do something stupid, I turned and shut the door behind me.

He rolled down the window. 'And yours?'

I paused, biting my lip. 'Chiara.'

It sounded foreign in my ears, as if I was hearing it from his perspective. There was silence between us, his eyes dropping to my lips for a moment, causing them to tingle.

He blinked, then rolled up the window again. I watched the smoke his car left as it drove off, out of sight.

*What's the point anyway?* I thought, kicking a small stone into the gutter. *It's not like I'll ever see him again.*

I shifted from foot to foot, pressing on the intercom for flat 3.

'Hello?' Karlie shouted.

I stumbled backwards. Did she somehow know I needed a wake-up call with her damn screaming?

Once I recovered, I pressed the button, yelling, 'Hello, Karlie. This is Chiara, from Planet Earth.'

'Wait— Chiara?'

I rolled my eyes. 'Dude, don't shout. You're breaking my eardrums.'

A muffled noise burst from the other side. This time, it was Luna's voice that played through the speaker.

'Chiara! Are you okay? What happened? Wait one second, I'll let you up.'

As soon as I stepped inside, Luna flung her arms around me, and Karlie somehow dived under her to hug me at the same time. I giggled, resting my head on Luna's shoulders.

'What happened to you?' Luna asked after letting go. 'Karlie said you had gone out for some air, but then you never returned. We went down to the street and couldn't see you anywhere—'

Karlie nodded seriously. 'We were gonna call the police.'

I sucked in a breath, guilt playing in my chest. I didn't realise they would be so worried. My foster parents had never cared if I left without saying anything, but clearly the same rules didn't apply here. Not with them.

Karlie looked at me with wide, concerned eyes. 'Where did you go?'

I gave them a quick rundown of what had happened, leaving out the part where I was practically force-fed blood... and enjoyed it.

Luna looked alarmed. 'What were you thinking, getting into a car with him? Do you not understand how dangerous that was? I mean, he could have killed you Chiara! You should have asked a neighbour for their phone and called me so I could've picked you up. You said it was the same guy you met at the club? What the fuck is his problem, I'm amazed you're not locked in his basement!'

Since I couldn't explain that we were both vampires and he was just trying to make sure I didn't die, I kept my mouth shut.

'You're okay though, right?' Karlie asked quietly.

I nodded, causing Luna to sigh.

'We were just worried, that's all.' She ran her eyes over me quickly, as if checking for any damage. 'Chiara, he didn't—'

'No.' I shook my head abruptly, knowing exactly where her

mind was going. He didn't seem like the kind of person to do something like that, not that I knew him well enough to know what kind of person he really was.

Luna nodded, before guiding me into the living room with Karlie a few steps ahead of us. Something cold and dormant within me started to melt with Luna's touch. She seemed to care more than I thought she did.

I groaned as I collapsed on a beanbag, throwing my head back onto my shoulders. Karlie was laughing at me. I sank in deeper and smiled. There was something so warm about being back with them, something familiar. Comfortable. And it reminded me how different it had felt to be with him, even though he was also familiar.

'Woohoo! Earth to Chiara!'

I blinked, registering Karlie's hands waving violently in my face.

'Stop!' I cried, smacking her palm away.

She gave me a death stare. 'I asked you a question.'

I bit my lip.

'Pizza or macaroni?'

'Macaroni sounds good,' I said quickly, hoping to distract her from my flustered appearance.

Karlie clapped her hands, proclaimed I had good taste, and hopped off the sofa to inform Luna of my choice.

I began to play with the soft rug fibres, twirling them in my fingers the way he must twirl girls' hearts around his.

# CHAPTER 8

It was Monday, and Karlie and Luna would be coming back from school any minute. I sat on the living room floor and watched as the rain fell outside. I'd wanted to go job hunting today, but I decided turning up at a coffee shop looking like a wet rat and begging for a job when I didn't speak French wouldn't have been a smart idea.

I stared at the empty flat. One of the lights flickered in the silence. I wished they didn't have school today. Either that or I wished I could be in school with them. Anything but being alone with these thoughts; with these memories.

We had already given the school all my personal information and appealed for student financial aid, to which they had yet to respond. I already knew that all the students attending would be rich, stuck-up brats who would probably spit on me given a chance.

I looked back out the window and sighed.

*Karlie and Luna are different; maybe this will be too.*

Later that day, having both finished their homework, Karlie brought two canvases and a box of paints to the living room. Luna was curled up on the sofa, reading one of her steamy romance novels and blushing like the rising sun.

'Just get a boyfriend already,' Karlie said pointedly.

'Easier said than done,' I muttered.

Luna rolled her eyes, sighed loudly and glared at Karlie. 'Not everyone is as desperate as you, Karlie. I'd prefer to find someone who will love me, not some lusty fling that'll last two days before either of us gets bored.'

'Ooh, she wants that ring, baby!' Karlie cried.

'Damn, just let her read her book. Clearly, it's filling a void.'

'Chiara!' Luna's jaw dropped, but she couldn't stop the smile from reaching her eyes. 'I'll have you know I am an independent woman and I am whole and capable of living without a man, thank you very much.'

'Is that your morning mantra? What do you have against men anyway?'

Luna wrinkled her nose. 'I'm not against them. I just don't need one at this particular moment in time.'

'I won't ever need one,' Karlie announced, swaying her hips. 'All they're good for is helping me in other ways.' She winked.

'All right, I've had enough of this.' I grabbed a canvas and propped it on my lap. 'Let's change the subject.'

Karlie's smile was wide. 'I'm gonna paint you.'

'I think not.'

'You just wait and see, Chiara. You'll be hanging it on your wall in no time.'

'I seriously doubt that,' I narrowed my eyes at her, 'but go ahead.'

She stuck out her tongue before nestling into a beanbag opposite. I smiled, embarrassed, and did my best to ignore her as she started tracing my outline. I picked up the pencil on the floor and frowned at my blank canvas.

I'd had a book of ideas, filled with colours and images from my dreams, but something about them now seemed childish and mediocre. Neither of them had seen one of my paintings before and I wanted it to be good.

I skimmed through ideas in my head, but I felt a thick, heavy block preventing me from coming up with anything halfway decent.

'I don't know what to paint,' I said finally.

Luna put down her book. 'Why don't you paint the sky?'

I gave her a look. 'Have you seen the sky? It's fricking grey.'

'Well, bloody hell, I don't know,' she said, exasperated. 'Mm, how about a concept?' She lifted her book to show me. 'Like, love.'

Love.

I frowned at the blank canvas, my mind already working on the colours I would fill it with.

I tilted my head at Luna. 'I like it. Thank you.'

We worked until late, the sky turning a darker grey. Luna got bored of her steamy romance novel and decided to put on a steamy romance movie instead, so we could all watch while Karlie and I painted. After a while, Karlie was having trouble focusing on me instead of the movie and I took the opportunity to steal her painting from her lap.

'Give it back,' she whined.

I swatted her away and leaned back against the sofa to inspect it. She'd done the base layers with rough olive-toned outlines and wide eyes. The lips were full and the hair fell out of the frame.

'It's good,' I said, handing it back to her.

She gave me the side eye but seemed pleased by my reaction. I looked down at my own painting, half-finished and even more abstract than the concept of love itself.

'It's not my best.'

Karlie grinned and took my painting. I watched her and Luna's eyes skim over the dark reds and flowing lines, over the white crests that faded away into nothingness. They looked up at me at the same time: Luna's expression warm, Karlie's excited.

'I think you're right,' Karlie said, 'we should be selling these paintings.'

I regarded mine. 'Maybe I've lost my touch.'

'Uh, uh, uh.' Karlie wagged her finger. 'Don't you be doubting your talents now, Chiara. Can I call you Chi-chi?' she smiled widely. 'I'll call you Chi-chi. Everybody's gotta have a nickname.' She pointed at the canvas on my lap. 'Look at that! That's beautiful and artsy and... well I love it, so you should too.'

'I agree,' Luna said softly. 'You can definitely sell that once it's done.'

I smiled at her, then looked over my painting again. Maybe I was just being hard on myself.

'Ew, Luna, why were you reading this trashy romance fanfiction?' Karlie cried.

Luna glanced back at her and in the short amount of time it took me to comprehend that Karlie had stolen her laptop, she'd leapt out of her seat and slammed it shut, almost catching Karlie's fingers.

Luna held her laptop to her chest, her face ruby red.

'Because. I was in a politics lesson and I was bored.'

'To be fair, politics does sound pretty boring,' I said.

'It is, but I want to be a lawyer,' Luna explained, 'so it's useful if I take it. Speaking of, can you guys read my essay? I need other opinions.'

'Just so you know, that sounds really boring, but I'll do it anyway 'cause I love you,' Karlie announced, before sticking her head over the top of the laptop.

I laughed as Luna pushed her away and told her to sit beside us so we could all read it.

They made me feel as though I was a part of them, as though I belonged. My heart squeezed as I leaned my head on Luna's shoulder.

This kind of love was a different kind altogether.

The next day, I set out to find a job, starting with a bakery nearby. The manager was the one to give me an interview, but seeing as he didn't know much English, I sensed within the first minute that we wouldn't get very far.

With a small dent of disappointment in my heart, I left the bakery behind, walking until I found another job advertisement. Eventually I came across a hotel, seeking an English-speaking receptionist. I ventured inside, thinking this one seemed a bit more promising.

'Miss Buchanan.'

*Beaufort*. I held my tongue and kept my face neutral as the interviewer shuffled her notes. This was after a series of questions which were delivered in a monotone and with the air of someone who thought the whole thing was a waste of time before I even finished my answer. The desk was broad and she was small, with thin wire-framed glasses she kept perched on the end of her nose.

'Do you know how prestigious a job such as this is?'

I swallowed.

'I thought not. Even the way you are dressed, it's...' she waved her hand over my body, her mouth in a stiff pout, 'well, a bit shabby, to put it lightly.'

I felt like I had been struck.

The heat spread from my chest up my cheeks and I knew it was way past the point of redemption.

She raised a thin eyebrow, glancing at my CV on the table. 'Furthermore, given that you have no credentials and your work experience is rather limited, I'm going to cut straight to it and inform you that we will not be hiring you today.' She gave me a forced smile. 'Thank you!'

'What a bitch!' I said loudly once I was ooutside her office. Who the hell did she think she was? '"Limited work experience",' I muttered, walking past the reception. 'Unbelievable.'

'I wouldn't take it too personally if I were you.'

I turned to see who the posh British accent belonged to and found a tall blonde woman in a black suit and matching glossy heels. The kind of woman they wanted.

'Okay.'

'I've seen about seven other girls today like you who also got rejected.' Her perfectly lined eyes scanned me from head to toe. 'Ma'am, of course, has higher standards.'

I scoffed, tears pricking at my eyes.

'There is a garden centre the next street over if you fancy.' Her red lips stretched in a short smile that barely made any crack in her face. 'I'm sure you'd be more suited to a position in a vicinity like that.'

I widened my eyes to stop myself crying in front of her and gave her one of my best smiles. 'That's very kind. Thank you.'

It took everything I had in me to turn and walk away slowly, knowing full well that the blonde bitch was watching me as I did, probably with a smirk on her stupid face.

The moment I stepped outside, my walls collapsed. It took all my strength to keep walking, even though the pit in my stomach welled deeper and the hurt seared through me as tears spilled down my cheeks. Unstoppable.

Strangers gave me looks and several mothers pulled their kids away from me. I couldn't blame them; my face was probably streaked with mascara and all the bullshit transferred via osmosis from those two rude women.

"Higher standards". As though I was the scum of the earth, a naive little girl who thought she was good enough for a job like that, only to find out how so very wrong she was.

I felt like a fool.

In a blur of tears and heart pain, I somehow managed to catch a bus and walk the ten minutes back to the flat, where I promptly slammed the door behind me, sunk to the ground and burst into loud, ugly tears.

I cried until I was numb.

v

It was lunchtime when I picked myself off the hallway floor and headed to the bathroom. I knew I was too sensitive; practically everyone in my old life liked to remind me of that immutable truth about myself. Even Mr Becksworth had told me to "toughen up".

I laughed when I caught sight of my reflection. No wonder I wasn't good enough to be hired – even without the trails of black mascara, the puffy eyes and swollen lips, I would've never looked the part.

My reflection screamed neglected, attention-seeking and desperate. All the things I hated, all the things I didn't want to be. I locked the door and stripped off my nicest clothes, which apparently weren't nice enough, glancing forlornly at the bathtub. But it would be a shame to waste water.

I sucked in a deep breath as the hot water from the shower ran down my back and thighs. I watched it trickle down my arm in spirals, dripping off onto the ceramic. It somehow took part of my pain with it, washing it down the drain in torrents until I was clean.

Luna and Karlie knew something was wrong that evening. From the way I was quieter, the way I kept my distance. And for the first time since I was an outsider in their home, I felt like one all over again. I didn't belong in a place as beautiful as theirs, where I didn't have to pay rent, with home-cooked meals and two friendly, loving women who were everything when I was nothing. They loved and were loved, wealthy and smart, kind and talented.

I was nothing.

The thought of moving out crossed my mind – after all, what was I but a drain on their money and time? They probably regretted letting me live here, but I knew they were too nice to say anything about it.

The worst part of it was that I felt I had little choice. If I were to leave, I'd be in the same predicament I'd been in earlier, with no home and little money. It was easier to rely on them than forge my own way. I was like a parasite, clinging to their resources while hoping they wouldn't notice how fucking desperately I needed them.

I hated myself for it.

Try as they might to coax the truth out of me, I wouldn't tell them a single thing. I shook my head, even as the frustrated tears betrayed me. They shared a glance and, before I could protest, their arms were around me. How could I tell them that I didn't deserve it? That I didn't want their love; it wasn't mine to have.

But for all I wanted to push them away, I found I didn't have the strength. I was tired of crying alone. I wanted to be held.

After a while, I sniffed and found it in me to pull away slightly. 'I'm sorry. I'll go cry in my room.'

'Don't be stupid, Chiara.' Luna moved my hair to one side and guided my head into her shoulder.

I laughed a little as Karlie wrapped her arms around my waist from the side, leaning her head on my ribs.

'I don't understand either of you,' I said, my voice sounding thin in the warm room.

Neither of them said a word, but they hugged me harder to prove that even if I didn't understand, they did.

Several days passed and I managed to apply online to the garden centre the blonde bitch had so kindly pointed me towards. They'd get back to me soon, said the automated response.

The school also sent me an admissions test to do, comprised of mock questions from my 3 A-level subjects as well as basic maths and English. I was pretty sure I aced it and a couple of days later, Luna received an email confirming my place and the approval for financial aid. We celebrated by watching another romcom, followed by Luna animatedly describing the political climate in France while Karlie yawned and I struggled to keep up.

The weekend passed quickly and, soon enough, it was Sunday night. I lay in bed as my nerves wrangled my stomach into knots over and over, making me toss and turn between highs of excitement and anxiety.

Eventually, I flung off the duvet and made for the kitchen.

'You can't sleep?'

My eyes shot to the right. Karlie was standing behind the corner wearing her matching pyjama set, her afro awry.

I shook my head. 'Anxiety. Why are you awake?'

'Too many thoughts.' She frowned. The fridge hummed in the background, the little blue light shining off her eyes in the dark. 'Plus, I was too hot with my cover on, then I took it off and I was too cold. D'you like poetry? I've got a book we can read.'

We curled up on her bed, turning on the fairy lights and the salt lamp on her bedside table. The book was small and thick, filled with sweet, deep poems that struck something within me.

I leaned my head on her shoulder as she read them out loud and eventually, I stopped reading the words as she spoke them and closed my eyes. Her voice was rich in the stillness, like melted chocolate.

I don't know how many poems she read, or how long it took me to fall asleep – all I know was that I was still in her bed when her alarm went off the next morning.

'What the hell is that?' I cried, lurching upright.

'Mm, that's some strong shit right there,' Karlie murmured as she slammed snooze on her phone and headbutted the pillow again.

I stared at her, open-mouthed. Waking up to hardcore rap music was not something I appreciated.

Since Karlie wasn't getting up, I decided to take advantage of the empty bathroom, brushing my teeth and splashing my face with cool water to wake me out of my sleepy daze.

I'd just started making breakfast when Luna marched into the kitchen.

'I didn't know it was wear-your-pyjamas-to-school day.'

I stopped pouring my cereal. She smiled warmly by the kitchen doorway, wearing black trousers and a light blue shirt that matched her eyes.

'Chop chop! You have ten minutes.'

'Great,' I muttered, ditching the cereal and sliding past her. I'd almost forgotten it was school at all, but seeing her dressed for the occasion drilled it home.

Once in my room, I dug around my clothes drawer, throwing them all across the floor until I found my yellow dress. It was what I had worn to the interview at the hotel; the nicest thing I owned. I pulled it on, barely pausing to breathe until I smoothed it down in the mirror. It would have to do.

I grabbed my empty bag off the floor and dropped my phone inside, before pestering Luna about paper and pens.

'Why didn't you do this the night before?' she asked, digging around in her pencil case for spares.

'Luna, please, I don't wanna be late – what time is it? Do we have to go?'

She rolled her eyes and handed me a pen. 'Relax. I only said you had ten minutes to make you get dressed.'

I squinted at her in disbelief.

'That being said,' she pulled out her glossy phone and touched the screen, 'we should still leave. Now.'

'God save me.'

'Karlie, get your fat bum in here. Let's go!' Luna bellowed, loud enough for the neighbours to hear.

# CHAPTER 9

The slam of the car door echoed through the misty morning as I stood in the dirt car park. On the drive over, I had been drawing circles into my damp palms over and over, trying to take deep breaths without anyone noticing how damn nervous I was.

My friends had tried to distract me by singing to pop music, which only worked until we reached the twisting lane that led directly to the school.

I drew in cool air, watching the clouds gathering above.

'First impressions?'

I glanced at Luna, but she was looking ahead at the two-storey brick building with gigantic stone pillars sunk into the steps. It must've been three times the size of my last school and judging by the number of people hanging around the steps and the brick walls, the student body was probably of similar proportions.

I chewed on my lip as we walked towards the white door, left perpetually open.

'I like the field,' I answered, unable to find anything else of note. 'Are those woods?'

Karlie smiled. 'Yeah, we know a lotta good places in there.'

I raised my eyebrows. 'And for what purposes, may I ask?'

'God, nothing sinister!' Luna snorted. 'Karlie just wanted to make us look badass.'

'Screw you, Luna! I'm a badass bitch.'

Luna rolled her eyes. 'You wish.'

We walked a short distance towards the steps before Luna stopped to dig something out of her bag. I glanced around, my eyes skirting across the tops of the student's heads so I wouldn't make unfortunate eye contact with any of them.

Suddenly, the wind slammed the door in front of us into the wall with a bang. I almost jumped out of my skin.

'Who's a little scaredy cat?'

'Karlie, I'm literally this close to smacking you right now,' I retorted, holding two fingers out barely a centimetre apart.

'Sweetie, I ain't done nothing to you.'

'Oh, yes, you have.' I flicked my hair back, glad to have something to argue over so I wouldn't have to feel my nerves. 'What was that stunt you pulled this morning with the rap music?'

'"Stunt"? It's my alarm clock, you dummy. It's not my fault you fell asleep in my bed.'

I rolled my eyes, about to protest, when I caught sight of a stone gargoyle, glaring down at me from the wall. I stared at it, wondering who in the hell had designed the exterior.

'Can we just go inside already?' I asked. 'That stupid gargoyle is giving me the creeps.'

'Aw, wittle Chiawa's afwaid,' Karlie said like a five-year-old, 'Did someone hwut yow fweewings?'

Fire burned in my chest as I glared at her, screwing up my fists in balls. She was laughing now, making me feel even more foolish. I spun on my heel and started towards the front door.

'But you don't know where you're going,' Karlie called after me.

I could still hear the mocking tones in her voice.

Stomping up the steps, I ignored the gang of boys under the "no loitering" sign who nudged each other and pointed at me. The building was taller from this angle, looming overhead in the murky sky like a dark shadow. If there was one thing that anger gave me, it was courage.

Luna was still telling Karlie to apologise as I pushed through the students, climbing up the steps.

A hard body collided with mine.

'Woah, I'm so sor—' started a blonde guy before interrupting himself. 'Hey, I haven't seen you around here before.' His voice was raspy, provocative. He rubbed a hand over his freshly shaved chin as he looked me up and down.

I really wasn't in the mood to entertain his advances.

'I'm Elijah.'

'I'm leaving.'

I sidled past him, making a beeline for the door before any other people could bump into me. But I was no closer to it when I heard a familiar chuckle. It rang clear through my ears, different from the gossiping girls in the corner and the myriad of chit-chat as students strolled past. I zoned in on *him*, leaning against the brick wall.

'What the—?'

Maybe he heard me or just read my lips, because he grinned in response, running his fingers through his immaculate dark hair. There was something wicked in those blue eyes.

*Get yourself together.*

I pursed my lips and with a great deal of self-control, I tore myself away from Kaelan and walked through the front door.

*What the hell is he doing here?*

I pulled all my hair over one shoulder, pressing myself into the wall to avoid the other students in the hall. He had to have been stalking me – there was no other way. I couldn't believe I was letting a guy screw with my emotions, especially when he himself didn't give a damn.

Gritting my teeth, I pushed off the wall and started walking through the crowd. He was always so calm – messing with me was like a game to him. He made me lose control, but it was only because there was something different about him. I couldn't put my finger on it. Something that made my heart race, that pulled me towards him.

Something addictive.

'Chiara!'

I looked behind me to find Karlie waddling towards me as fast as her heels and skin-tight skirt would allow.

'Listen, I'm really sorry—'

'Don't worry, we're good. I can't hold a grudge to save my life.'

She grinned and looped her arm through mine as we walked between students rushing every which way.

'I think we're in the same form room. Can I look at your timetable?'

I pulled out the handwritten note from my coat pocket.

'It's already wrinkled,' she told me as if I didn't know.

'Where's Luna?'

'She has a different form. But looking here, we all have English together,' Karlie said as we made our way upstairs and swung open the door to our form room.

'So,' the teacher announced a few minutes later, wiggling her head with an exaggerated grin, 'class, this is Chiara.'

I stared at the sea of bored faces.

'Say hi!'

There were a few mumbles.

The teacher gave a strained smile before raising her eyebrows at me through her bright red glasses. 'Would you like to tell us something about yourself, dear?'

*Not really.* 'My... favourite colour is green?' I said, my voice cracking a little near the end. I hated when teachers did stuff like this; it's not as if anyone in that room actually cared.

'Lovely!' her voice was jarring against the awkward silence between the five rows of desks and the barren walls.

She patted my shoulder, the fake grin still plastered to her thin lips, before guiding me into the seat right in front of her desk. Karlie shot me an apologetic look.

Waiting for further instruction, I watched the teacher as she settled down into her swivel chair and frowned at her computer. The noise levels in the room had started to rise from non-existent to a murmur and then to a loud chatter as if the students had suddenly reawakened and discovered what it meant to be alive.

I glanced at Karlie, who was talking to a girl I'd never seen before. I tried to peek at the girl's face, but her long curtain of hair made it impossible from this angle. She said something that made Karlie laugh.

I sighed and turned back towards the front. This school probably wasn't going to be any different than how it was normally. Dull, unnecessarily tiresome and long. The only difference was, here, I stuck out. I turned and casually cast a glance around the room. It was only a few moments, but it was enough to gauge everything I needed. The scent of wealth, privilege and arrogance clung to the air. I saw it on their snub faces as they laughed, how their branded clothes hung off their bodies and how they compared the things they owned as if having the latest model of something made them a better person.

I wiggled down into my seat and folded my arms over my chest. Of course, no one would want to talk to me. Who was I to them? Some random new girl who decided to come a couple of months before A-levels, someone with thin, cheap clothes whose favourite colour was green?

'Are you all right, dear?'

I looked up to find the teacher watching me, something akin to concern floating in her eyes.

I frowned and a little too harshly, responded with, 'Yeah?'

'You just looked a bit sad, that's all.'

I shrugged. I'd heard that one before.

'Do you know anyone in this class?' She leaned forward on her fake wooden desk, nodding like I'd already started speaking.

It would've been embarrassing to admit I knew Karlie, who didn't seem to remember my existence at the moment. I swallowed the hurt and pushed it to the place where all my hurts piled up, where I could ignore them until they were no longer ignorable.

'No.'

'Aw,' she said, scrunching up her nose, 'I'm sure you'll make friends in no time.'

With a quick smile, she returned to her computer. I sighed and watched the second hand tick by on the clock above the whiteboard.

'Not fair! Two frees?' Karlie exclaimed when we got out, running her eyes over my schedule.

'Yep.'

We squeezed between clumps of people pushing through the narrow halls in both directions, the incessant chatter rising all around us. Even with the threat my blood craving posed, there was something paradoxically safe about being in a crowd, something about the loss of identity that I liked.

Karlie led me up a flight of rickety stairs wedged into a dark corner, before turning the knob on a small door with the word "Library" printed on it. I ran my eyes over the rows of wooden shelves packed tightly together and the books stacked high up to the ceiling.

The silence was the kind of comfortable that you wanted to melt into, the kind you wanted to wrap yourself in.

'Are you sure you're good here?'

'Yeah.'

Karlie's eyes looked around, but they didn't see. Not what I saw.

'See you later? I'll come back with Luna and we'll go for lunch.' She pouted. 'I hate that you gotta be here alone on the first day!'

I smiled. I didn't mind being alone when I could simultaneously get lost in another reality.

Karlie left, and I turned to notice the librarian watching me from her desk. She looked like she was about to start a conversation, so I dove behind a shelf.

I ran my fingers across the spines of the fantasy section, the genre I liked to read the most. At random, I pulled out one and almost gagged. How classy. One about vampires.

I glanced around but no one was there to notice the uneasy

smile that had crept across my face. I flicked to a random page as my blush crept higher, embarrassed for being embarrassed. What was I trying to look for anyway, advice? It all sounded so romantic, the whole notion of drinking another's blood. As if it wasn't monstrous.

I skimmed the paragraph the book had opened on, one about life and death. The weight of realisation pressed down upon my chest. I shut the book and pushed it back onto the shelf before I was tempted to read any more. It was fiction anyway, useless to me. Besides, I knew who I had to talk to if I wanted real advice. Not that I wanted his help. In fact, now that I was thinking about it, I didn't even need advice in the first place. It would be fine.

I would be fine.

Abandoning the fantasy section, I turned to the romance aisle instead. I wondered which of these books Luna had read... probably all of them.

A girl slipped between the shelves and stopped next to me. The scent of her blood leapt out, causing a now familiar wave of nausea to rile my stomach. I dug my nails into my arms as she reached for a book near my head, my breaths coming out ragged. Before I could do something I'd regret, I pulled out a book at random and forced myself to leave the aisle.

I sat on one of the beanbags littered beside a large window, putting my head in my hands. This couldn't keep on happening. Relying on Kaelan for blood was out of the question; I'd have to find a way to get it myself, preferably without committing homicide or theft.

Remembering I still had the book, I turned it over in my hands. I almost choked on my spit when I saw the cover. Some naked guy with abs was leaning on a bed, staring seductively at a woman whose single thigh was in the frame.

I glanced up to make sure no one was watching. This definitely qualified as a steamy romance novel, and I probably would've put it back if I weren't scared of bumping into any more humans. It was best I kept to myself until the craving went back down again.

Flipping to the first page, I began to read, trying not to smile whilst contemplating my existence. I was so lost in the plot that I didn't even notice the two girls creeping up on me.

'Whatchya reading?'

'Shit!'

Having jumped out of my skin, I looked up to find Karlie and Luna giggling, before Karlie swooped low and whipped the book out of my hands.

A wail died in my throat.

'Chiara!' she whispered, drawing my name out. 'I never realised you were that kind of girl.' She winked.

I was burning up... it must be a vampire thing, either that or the librarian had turned up the radiators.

'Okay, but, Luna, you've probably read that one, right?' I choked out.

'Me? Personally?' She laughed. 'No.'

I got up and snatched the book back from Karlie. 'It wasn't on purpose – I just grabbed the first book I saw!'

'And then you decided to read it.'

'That's not important.' I blushed. 'It wasn't even that good anyway. God, it's hot in here.' I fanned my face before narrowing my eyes at them 'Are you sure it's been two hours already?'

'Time flies when you're having fun.'

'Alright Karlie give her a break,' Luna said, looping her arm through mine. 'Let's get some lunch.'

# CHAPTER 10

The dining hall was a vast, cavernous space lined with tables in perfect rows and columns. But the inhabitants were anything but orderly.

The students were like wild animals, sitting on the tables and on the floor, wherever they could find a spot, some hurtling their food at their friends.

I looked around in disbelief. The jarring noises blurred into one incessant, monotonous roar and the air smelt of sweat and body odour.

And blood.

*Food, not blood*, I reminded myself, suppressing the instinctual urge that made me salivate. *You're hungry for food.*

I turned towards the lunch queue again.

'What is that?' I asked Karlie, pointing towards the pile of multi-coloured mush they were dolloping onto the plates.

Her eyes gleamed as she turned to me. 'Vegetable surprise.'

I wrinkled my nose. 'Sounds appetising.'

By the time I got my food, Luna had already left to find us a seat. I looked around the packed room. An unlikely outcome. Then I looked again, this time searching for a very specific set of eyes.

He had to be here, right? Everyone was here. Was he watching me now, knowing I was looking for him? I inhaled and sharply turned to Karlie.

'Can we just eat outside?'

'In this weather?'

We both looked through the windows at the pouring rain. At least he'd have trouble finding me in this place. Not that he was even looking for me.

I followed Karlie as she expertly dove between the tables. The one Luna had found was miraculously empty.

'Don't. Ask.'

I raised an eyebrow as I sat opposite her. 'How did you know?'

'She has psychic powers.'

I grinned, which immediately turned into a frown as my gaze landed on the vegetable surprise.

'Can we not bring packed lunch?' I asked, shoving my plastic spoon into the goop.

Luna shrugged. 'School rules.' I watched in horror as she stuffed it cleanly into her mouth. 'What?'

I groaned. 'Oh God it's even worse when it's regurgitated!'

Luna covered her lips. 'Why are you looking in my mouth then?'

'Why were you eating with it open?'

'Can we sit here?'

We looked up to find three guys waiting with their trays; brothers, clearly. The two with hazel eyes – so pale they looked golden – appeared to be twins, identical apart from the fact that one had decided to shave off all his hair. My heart skittered when I noticed the last of the brothers, standing behind the other two: Blue Eyes.

Kaelan watched me in a way that made me feel like he could read my mind. I forced my attention back to the speaker.

'So,' he chuckled, 'is that a yes?'

'Yes!' Karlie squeaked.

I resisted the urge to slap my palm against my forehead.

'Um, I mean yeah, c-cool.'

She pulled a kinky strand of hair out before letting it bounce back into place. Kaelan had his characteristic smirk and I could only guess that he also thought it was a nice save.

I pushed my tray to the other side of the table where my friends were and stood, angling my body as far away from Kaelan as possible. Not that it made a difference; his magnetic field was still interrupting mine, making it go haywire against my will.

He pulled the bench out and I was glad when Luna tugged on me so I could avoid watching his arm muscles while he did it.

'They're so hot,' she whispered as we huddled together.

Karlie raised her chin. 'I call dibs on Goldie over there.'

'Wait, which one?'

'You idiots,' I hissed. 'They can hear everything we're saying.'

'They can't. We're whispering.'

I knew what the three of them really were. They could hear everything we said even if we whispered quieter, even if we were across the room. I glanced at the twins, who seemed to be covering their smug expressions by shovelling down their food as fast as possible. My food looked even less appealing now that Blue Eyes was sitting opposite me. It was agony, the fact that I was acutely aware of every inch of my skin, scared of the thought that he was watching me and scared to check if he really was.

Karlie and Luna were starting to converse with the two other guys, who seemed more friendly. I listened as the one with the shaved head introduced himself as Nico, extending a steady hand for each of us to shake. The other was Rheo, who made wild hand gestures as he talked and whose eyes seemed to take in everything at once while he did.

Kaelan was seemingly not in a talking mood. The girls and the twins were all bouncing off one another now, while he and I sat in uncomfortable silence. To distract myself, I scooped up some of my food and sniffed it.

*Ugh.*

It must've shown on my face because I heard Kaelan chuckle.

I set my spoon down. 'Stop staring at me. How am I supposed to eat?'

'Don't flatter yourself, doll,' he responded cooly, regarding me. 'It's a little difficult to block you out of my peripheral vision.'

I glanced at Karlie and Luna for backup, but they were too heavily engrossed in conversation.

'Well, why the hell did you decide to sit opposite me then?'

He shrugged. 'Seemed like a good idea at the time.'

His nonchalance was starting to get to me. 'Why are you even sitting with us? The amount of times I've seen you in the past week is ridiculous – you've gotta be stalking me at this rate.'

His eyebrows shot up for a split second before he recovered.

'Stalking you?' he said in a low voice. 'In that club, Chiara, you were the one who came up to me. When I recognised you while driving past that street, I did what anyone with a moral compass would have done. Oh,' he added as if the thought had just occurred to him, 'and now you're going to my school. So, please, if there is any way I can avoid you, I'd love to know.'

I swallowed.

Kaelan leaned back, then pulled out a sandwich from his jacket and bit a chunk off.

I ran a hand through my hair, deciding once and for all not to even bother with the vegetable surprise. Having nowhere else to look, I hazarded a glance towards the rest of them.

Rheo was clearly the clown of the group, making flirty innuendos to Karlie that sent her into fits of giggles and Luna into eye rolls.

Nico, on the other hand, was different from his brothers. Whenever he spoke, he systematically explained things, like he was sure of himself and of what he knew. He was business-like. Polished.

I sighed at my plate. My stomach was in turmoil, rolling over and over in on itself. But whether it was out of hunger or Blue Eyes sitting less than a metre away, I didn't know.

I didn't like him.

He was too arrogant, not to mention rude twenty-four-seven. And I seriously doubted he had a "moral compass". Forgetting myself, I eyed him, wondering why he had bothered to help me now that I knew he didn't like me either. His eyes swayed back and forth between my friends, the deep blue in them dancing. Now that I looked closer, he wasn't even that attractive. I didn't know why my bodily reactions were making such a big deal out of someone like him, when every real sense, AKA my mind, was telling me to stay far away.

His eyes were on me.

*Shit.*

He watched the emotions play out on my face like it was the most interesting show he'd ever seen. The corner of his mouth twitched.

'Alright, we'd better go.' Rheo clapped Kaelan's back as our eyes slid away from one another.

I watched him slip effortlessly into the crowd without a goodbye, becoming one with the humans as if he had known how to belong his whole life.

'That has never happened to us before,' Karlie stated breathlessly as we emerged into the busy hallway moments later.

It was lit in falsely yellow tones, the walls pasted with bright-coloured posters about computer safety and anti-bullying.

'I think you bring us luck,' she yelled into my ear.

'Or maybe,' I muttered, 'they sat with us because it was the only free table in the whole lunchroom.'

The bell rang, making a shrill, high-pitched noise that cut through the chatter like a double-edged sword. Somehow, in a couple of seconds, eighty percent of the students in the hallway had managed to slide into a classroom, leaving only a few stragglers behind.

'Come on!' Luna cried. 'We'll be late for English and the teacher is horrible.'

'Wha— I can't run with this bag!' I cried, but Karlie and Luna were already halfway down the hallway.

I started hobbling after them, holding my bag into place on my back to stop it from bouncing up and down.

'You look like a troll!' Luna called back.

We had not even made it one step into the classroom before a shriek rocked our eardrums.

'You three! You're late,' screeched our English teacher.

The old woman stood behind a desk, her remaining wispy hair pure white, like snow. She had a cardigan wrapped around her and a heater by the board. The room felt like an inferno.

'Sorry,' all three of us whispered together.

'Eh?'

'We're sorry,' Karlie stated in a louder voice, tinged with impatience.

I gave her a look.

The teacher swung one side of her cardigan over the other and said, 'Well! Take your seats then, ladies. We'll continue.' She turned to the class, crossing her arms. 'Can someone tell these troublemakers what they've just missed?'

I looked around the classroom as one unfortunate soul had to repeat the contents of the last few minutes. Of the available seats, one was next to the flirty blonde guy from this morning, another next to a girl with lips painted dark red. Her smile could only be described as nasty.

'That's "The Witch",' Karlie whispered, following my gaze. 'You should watch out for her.'

Before I could ask what she'd done to earn the nickname, the teacher told us to sit down. Karlie and Luna hastily chose the two other available seats, leaving me standing in front of "The Witch's" desk. She was chewing gum, looking at me with a bored expression through liquid-lined eyes.

'Chiara, is it?' the teacher said harshly. 'Take a seat next to Viviana. Today, please.'

I mumbled an apology, sitting hurriedly and taking out my things.

'Now that we have briefly recapped *The Bloody Chamber*,' the teacher started, 'let us revisit the work of one of our favourite writers, William Shakespeare.'

The entire class groaned.

'I'll have none of that,' she tutted, wagging her finger. 'Shakespeare was revolutionary.' She paced back and forth, her hands clasped behind her slightly hunched back. 'Born in 1564, as I'm sure you'll have remembered, his work is still relevant hundreds of years later.'

'You would know,' muttered Viviana.

I couldn't help but smile a little.

'This term, we will be focusing on *The Tempest*, and as homework you will be working on an analysis project with the person sitting next to you.'

The teacher continued to jabber on, before letting us get on with our classwork. I turned to the girl next to me. Maybe she wasn't as bad as everyone thought.

'You're Viviana, right?'

Her eyes cut to me. 'It's Viv.'

'Sorry.' I looked down at my highlighted page. 'Um, when did you want to start working on the project?'

She let out an exaggerated sigh. 'Listen, new girl. While you may be willing to sacrifice several lunch hours for this pathetic project, I am not.' She glanced down at her perfectly sharpened black nails. 'Meet me by the gates next Wednesday after school.'

'Next Wednesday?' I frowned. 'That's the day before it's due in.'

'And?' Viv sat back. 'Do you have a problem with that?'

Her dark eyes glittered with a challenge.

'I-no. No problem.'

'Good,' she said smoothly, as the bell rang. She picked her black handbag up from the desk and turned to me, lips parted. 'Oh. One last thing.' She leaned in close, a threat in the air. 'Stay away from Kaelan.'

# CHAPTER 11

I collapsed against my bedroom door later that evening, the girls and I having screwed around with makeup for the last hour and a half. Going out tonight was exactly what I needed.

I stared at the dark beyond the window. The quiet was comforting, like a soothing balm that elapsed across my mind.

Thinking back to Viv's threat, discomfort settled in my stomach. Blue Eyes had apparently forgotten to mention he had a psychopathic girlfriend who preyed on new additions to the student body.

I rummaged through my clothes, trying to find something to wear tonight. The more I thought about it, the worse I felt. If they really were together, that meant that what I'd taken as flirting had all been in my mind. I frowned, recalling the way he had looked at me, that day in the car.

He was probably just being nice to me. Why had I been so slow to get it? He even made it clear today when he basically told me to piss off at lunch.

I hated how much I cared, when I barely even knew him.

My hand stopped on a black bodycon dress, basic, but still cute. I picked it up, about to shut the drawer when I caught a glimpse of smooth green cloth. A skirt I'd worn on

101

my eighteenth birthday. I didn't remember much from that day, only that the night ended with black tears rolling down my cheeks. Sophie had thrown me a party, but despite being surrounded by people, I had never felt more isolated.

She'd always told me to "be more confident" and "stop caring what other people think" without ever realising that the more she said that, the more she reinforced my lack of confidence and how she had the upper hand in our relationship.

It was just another bitter reminder that Sophie didn't love me as much as I loved her.

I pulled on the dress, fluffing out my hair in the mirror. My eyes were lined with kohl and my lips were a deep red wine hue.

Karlie slunk into the bathroom, four shots of rum in. 'You look hot,' she slurred.

I adjusted my dress in the mirror. I just wanted to forget.

We stood at the front of the queue outside the club, Karlie attempting to look sober enough to pass through. My palms were sweating even though I'd brought my ID with me this time. The same bouncer as before, Gabriel, turned it over in his hands.

'I'm afraid I can't accept this.'

My heart hammered through my dress as I stared back in disbelief. It took me a second to register the joke in his eyes.

'Man!' Gabriel hooted with laughter, shoving me playfully, so hard he almost knocked me over. 'You should've seen your face!'

'Lighten up, Chiara, he was joking,' Luna whispered, rubbing my arms as she led us inside.

I looked back to see Karlie and him already engaged in some serious eye fucking.

Karlie joined us ten minutes later with three drink discount bands. Luna rolled her eyes and Karlie gave her an unapologetic shrug.

'You love me,' she said as she gave us each one. 'You do.'

It was less packed than before, and given that the craving had swollen up again, I was glad for it. I sucked in the musty air and closed my eyes for half a millisecond. It was enough to block out the metallic, earthy smell the tinge of blood provided and enough so I could forget that I was anything more than human, even for a little while.

Luna came back with drinks, and I sipped my vodka and coke while dancing half-heartedly. I wondered if Kaelan was here again, although thinking of him was a shitty distraction from the old wounds laying open in my chest.

'Let's get shots,' Karlie exclaimed, trying to drag us to the bar.

Luna pulled away. 'You've had too much already, give it a rest.'

Karlie pouted, before grabbing my arm. 'Chiara will come with me, won't you Chiara?'

Before I could answer, she was already taking me through the crowd to the bar, where she ordered two shots.

'Come on, drink up,' she said, taking my half-empty cup and replacing it with the shot.

'Luna was right, you shouldn't have any more. You're gonna be sick.'

She laughed and threw it back. Her hair and eyes were wild, lit up with life. I looked at the plastic shot glass in my hand and downed it without another thought.

We danced, hands floating above our heads in the stuffy room. Some guys who had started dancing with us bought us more drinks, and the minutes blurred into one, mingled with perfume, sweat and vodka.

Karlie stumbled into me, and the two of us almost fell over. We held onto each other and giggled. One of the guys started wrapping his arms around Karlie's waist, pulling her into him.

I straightened up as Karlie whined, her grip tightening on my wrist. The music was suddenly loud in my ears. My smile faded. I yanked her back to me, and before he could do anything about it, I pulled her back through the crowd.

More sober now, I remembered.

'Karlie, we left Luna!' I cried, scanning the bodies. 'I can't see her anywhere!'

Her eyes widened dramatically. 'Oh no! Lun-lun!' she called, cupping her hands around her mouth.

Guilt and panic welled in me. I couldn't believe we had forgotten about her. What if she was in danger? She might have walked back without us, but that was probably even more unsafe. There were monsters out there.

Karlie gripped my arm again, doubling over. 'I'm gonna—'

Before she could finish her sentence, I'd dragged her outside into the smoking area. She bent over by the wall and puked. I leaned against the wall nearby, fixing my eyes on the few stars the city lights couldn't drown out.

When Karlie was done, she sat on the ground. I sat down too. The floor was cold tarmac, littered with cigarette stubs. She leaned her head on my shoulder.

'You're not gonna puke again, are you?'

She gave a sleepy laugh. I noticed her phone peeking out of her pocket and pulled it out. I'd been so drunk I'd forgotten that I could call Luna. She answered on the second ring, and within five minutes she found us, bringing two guys with her.

I squinted up at them through bleary eyes. It was the twins from lunch. Kaelan's brothers. My gaze shifted behind them, but he wasn't there.

'Where were you?' I asked Luna as she bent down to hug us.

The twins had sat down now too, Rheo close to Karlie.

'I'm so sorry, I found these two and we got a bit carried away. We did try to look for you guys, but it was so crowded in there.'

I nodded, vaguely aware of Rheo asking Karlie if she was okay. She was already slumped across his lap when I turned towards them.

'She's had too much to drink,' I explained to Rheo, as if he couldn't already tell.

He looked down at her, his hand resting on her head. I felt a spring of jealousy shoot through me. It was so easy, that simple affection. Why was I always attracted to complicated things?

I tuned into the tail end of Luna and Nico's conversation, hearing something about twins. A thought struck me. If we really were immortal, they could've just turned at the same age. Maybe they were brothers after all.

'Are you two really twins?' I asked.

Nico wagged a finger at me. 'I know what you're thinking.'

I blinked at him, his face haloed in the street lamp.

'Spare her the dramatics, brother,' Rheo exclaimed. 'We are twins.'

'And what about Blue Eyes?' My heart stopped. *Fuck.* 'Kaelan,' I said quickly, hoping to cover my mistake, 'I meant Kaelan.'

Rheo and Nico smirked at each other, while Luna frowned.

'You gave him a nickname already? Didn't you two just meet?'

I groaned internally, willing the ground to open me up. Why did she have to make it worse? She still didn't know that Kaelan and the kidnapper/club guy were the same person, but now I'd probably never tell her.

Rheo and Nico were biting on their tongues to stop themselves laughing.

My palm dug into the tarmac. 'Don't you dare tell him.'

The twins looked at each other, and that was when they lost it.

I waited, gritting my teeth. 'Are you done?'

Rheo wiped a fake tear out of his eye as Nico held his belly.

'I'm sorry, I'm sorry,' Rheo cried. 'That was... unexpected.'

'I'd say,' Nico choked out, punching Rheo's arm.

'Okay, it really wasn't that funny, so I don't know why you're making a big deal out of it.'

'Ah,' Rheo grinned, 'then you wouldn't mind us sharing this info with our big brother, would you? Let him know about your little crush?'

Heat rose in my cheeks. 'Absolutely not. You will not do that.'

'Hmm,' Rheo said, stroking his chin playfully, 'and what will you give us if we don't?'

Anger shot through me, though I didn't know what to do. Luna looked like she was about to intervene when Nico spoke.

'Let's make a deal.'

'A deal?' I asked.

'Yes. A proposal, of sorts.' He glanced at Rheo, who looked just as confused as I was. 'You see my brother here, he's a ladies man. But he hasn't been on a date in years.'

Rheo nodded, catching on. 'It's true.'

'He's had his eye on this one girl for a while, but I'm afraid to say he's failed to make any moves.' Nico leaned in. 'He needs some advice.'

'I don't understand. Which girl?'

Rheo looked pointedly down at Karlie.

'Ah. And how would I help you with that?'

His eyes widened. 'Are you kidding me? She'll laugh in my face if I ask her. What if I'm not her type?'

I glanced at my sleeping friend. Her hair was falling over her eyes, her expression soft and peaceful. Should I be helping this boy? We barely even knew him, although she had been drooling over him at lunchtime, and now she felt comfortable enough to fall asleep in his lap. Not that being drunk out of her mind had anything to do with it.

But it wasn't just that. He wasn't human. He could hurt her.

As if sensing my thoughts, Rheo pressed his palm to his chest and smiled. 'I'm a good guy, I swear.'

I laughed. The way he said it made me believe him enough to concede. 'Alright, let me get this straight. You two will keep my secret if I give Rheo dating advice.'

The twins both put their heads in their hands. 'No! Not just any old dating advice,' cried Rheo, 'it has to be *specific* to her. Insider stuff, you know? I need to be confident that I won't be rejected.'

'So!' Nico added. 'Have we got a deal then?'

I quirked my mouth to the side, before extending my hand to shake Rheo's.

'It's a deal.'

# Chapter 12

My days had begun to follow a rhythm, things flowing smoothly besides the occasional blood craving. We'd drive to class while playing old school R&B, meeting up with the twins during our break times. In the evenings, we'd paint our nails and watch a romcom, snuggled up in fluffy blankets on the sofa.

Luna had already started revising for her A-levels, while Karlie declared she'd give it another month. I'd been using online study materials, following the detailed revision plan Luna had made for me. I figured since she generally seemed to have her shit together, I'd better do whatever she told me to.

When it came to Rheo and our "deal", things had turned out better than I'd expected. It had started off with me phoning him after school, smoothing over his doubts and talking him through his insecurities. "Just focus on Karlie," I'd tell him. "If you want her to trust you, you need to be loyal. Now's not the time to mess around with other girls, Rheo."

He wouldn't tell me why he was scared to get to know a girl, or why he hadn't apparently done it in so long. Even though I didn't fully trust him to keep my secret, I had to admit, he was growing on me.

Rheo had a nice voice and there was something pleasant about him that I couldn't put my finger on. I liked his laugh and it made me feel good to make him laugh. In fact, I'd decided he and Karlie might even be a good match for one another. I could practically feel him beaming through the phone when I told him so.

He started to give me blood, during our free periods. He kept it in a silver thermos and passed it to me as we sat against the radiator in the girls' bathroom. We would laugh at our stained teeth, giddy, until some year 7 would happen in, see us and bolt, thinking something bad was going on, but not knowing exactly how bad it really was.

If anything, the "deal" was a godsend. The nausea hadn't returned since I'd started taking blood regularly, and I was no longer scared of losing control around humans. The craving was manageable, as long as it wasn't ignored.

The only slight hiccup in my days was Chemistry. It was the worst lesson I had by a mile. As soon as I'd walked in that first time, the scent of smoky wood and lemongrass – his scent, Kaelan's – tumbled into me and I knew I was in for trouble.

'Hello there,' the teacher had greeted me, scooting forward in his chair. 'Welcome to Chemistry. My name is Mr Kalip.'

He looked only a couple of years older than us, but something about his grey eyes made him seem far older. He'd winked at me and I'd looked away, trying hard to suppress the embarrassed smile on my face. It wasn't because I found him attractive, but because the whole class had seen him do it.

He'd run his finger down his laptop screen. 'And you must be... ah, Chiara. Sit next to the lovely lady, Willow, on the right.'

I'd stepped down the aisle, pulling at the tight fabric of my leggings. My eyes had locked with Kaelan's of their own accord, against my will. It was only half a second, but it had felt as though time had stopped, stretching out. His eyes had shone when he looked at me. I'd wondered if he had been holding his breath too.

'Wrong row, Chiara,' Mr Kalip had said loudly, sending some scattered laughs throughout the room.

I'd torn my eyes from Kaelan, feeling my face heat up as I spotted Willow waving to me by the wall.

I'd sat down quickly as Mr Kalip started the lesson. Kaelan had been sitting in the next row over, one seat behind. The back of my neck had prickled the whole lesson, as though his eyes were tracing my outline. He probably hadn't even been looking at me at all, but I'd still tensed at the possibility, Viv's warning to stay away lingering in the back of my mind.

To distract myself from him, I'd glanced at Willow. She had dark braids piled on her head, red strands woven throughout. She'd caught me looking, so I'd whispered that I liked her hair.

'Thanks,' she'd smiled, 'I like your...' She'd trailed off, unable to find anything noteworthy.

I'd laughed, feeling slightly hurt. 'It's fine. You don't have to compliment me back.'

'Willow and Chiara? This is not speed dating.' Mr Kalip had tapped the board with his finger. 'Pay attention.'

I'd gripped my pen hard, focusing on the chemical equations his veiny hand had written across the board. The silence in the room had been palpable, underlying the monotone of his voice as he spoke nonsensically.

There had been no point trying to concentrate, or even pretending to. I'd drawn circles on my paper, Kaelan's presence loud behind me, though he didn't speak a word. It was almost unbearable.

Sneaking a glance at Willow's notes, I'd realised I had spaced out again. 'Do you understand any of that?'

'If you paid attention, you would as well,' she'd answered, continuing to write.

Kaelan laughed under his breath.

Mr. Kalip had turned back around, looking between Willow and I through slanted eyes.

'Chiara,' Mr Kalip had purred silkily, 'pray outline the nucleophilic addition mechanism for reduction reactions?'

My classmates had suddenly grow alert as he stood with his pen, ready to write. He obviously didn't expect me to explain anything from the gleam in his eye.

'I'm not sure how to.'

'And why are you "not sure" when I have been discussing the subject in great detail for the past half an hour?'

Someone had let out a low whistle.

'I'm sorry?' I'd ventured.

Mr Kalip had made a show of shaking his head, sitting down on the edge of his desk.

'This is the only time I will allow behaviour such as this. Next time, you'll find I won't be so tolerant.'

There had been no reason for him to single me out. I couldn't have been the only person not paying attention, and he certainly didn't need to humiliate me for it.

I'd nodded sharply, looking him in the eye so he would know I wasn't fazed. I never respected those who abused their power.

For the rest of the lesson, I'd tried to focus on the PowerPoint even though it made little sense to me. We had been covering a new topic and Mr Kalip was going through it like it was simple enough for a child to understand, which it wasn't.

Kaelan's eyes were definitely on me. I had felt them on the tips of my hair, lingering on my bare shoulders, my hands as I wrote. I'd steeled myself, waiting for the moment Mr Kalip faced the board before I turned my head and darted my eyes to the side, finding Kaelan's. He'd held my gaze, a small smirk tugging at his lips.

'Chiara!' exclaimed Mr Kalip.

Kaelan had broken first, looking down at his paper. Was he blushing?

I'd snapped my head towards the teacher, who had malice gleaming in those soulless grey eyes.

'That's one too many times now, young lady, and I did warn you.' He'd paused for a moment, as if relishing the final blow. 'Detention.'

I'd stared at him in shock.

The bell had rung then, releasing us from the claustrophobic room.

Willow had given me a pitying look before packing away her things, making a quick exit as if to sever any kind of association with me. I'd sighed and thrown a glance over at the window, gazing at the woods I'd spotted on the first day, the ones I now felt I wanted to hide in.

Kaelan had turned to see where I was looking and I'd quickly returned to packing my bag.

After that first Chemistry lesson, I'd half expected the boy to apologise; it was his fault that he was staring at me, making Kalip lose his shit and hand out the detention. But even though we always hung out with his brothers, Kaelan never joined us. It wasn't like I saw him enough for him to be able to apologise, even if he wanted to.

Whenever I did happen to see him, he was always alone. I

stopped thinking him and Viv were a thing; perhaps she only had a crush, nothing more.

He was the reason I looked forward to Chemistry, where although we ignored one another, I was pretty sure we listened to each other's conversations. He was good at speaking, good at words. Kaelan's voice was different from Rheo's, it carried more grit, something that was heavy and light simultaneously. I wanted to melt into it and wrap myself in its melody. I caught myself more than once lamenting over the fact that he never talked to me – at all.

When I came in early I had to sit and pretend not to notice as he strode in through the door, his presence gleaming brighter than any other student. He made sure to walk past my desk every time, so closely my stomach fluttered as he passed. He grazed my arm on more than one occasion, like he knew what he did to me, like he wanted to tease me.

To distract myself I would slip into my work, focusing on the handouts that Willow and I completed together. I'd be damned if I let some boy affect my grades for the worse.

# CHAPTER 13

It was a cold, sunny Saturday when I turned up at the garden centre for my first shift. My manager floated over to greet me in a cloud of floral perfume. I stood awkwardly as she began to rant in her native tongue. Her shrivelled lips were shamelessly decorated with hot pink lipstick and her shrewd brown eyes looked sharp as an eagle's. She clicked her tongue at my blank face before taking off my coat and pushing my shoulders towards the outside area.

'Marie?' Her voice rang crisp in the afternoon air.

I followed her gaze behind the potted plants towards the woman walking calmly towards us. The manager started explaining something rapidly in French as the woman came to a stop. Her eyes were small and round, a mix between blue and green. Long, dark hair streaked with grey framed her face.

Her gaze landed on mine, held mine, and I had the strangest sensation that she could read my soul.

I shifted on my feet, turning back to the manager, who was still talking.

Marie held up her hand. '*Je comprends.*' She tilted her head out of respect to the other woman before smiling at me. It reached up and tugged at the corners of her eyes. 'Come,' she said, 'you have much to learn.'

Over the next few hours, Marie showed me how to take care of the plants. She showed me which ones liked more water and which less, how to cut branches that were dying and to strap them to a stick if they were too heavy for the plant to carry their weight. She showed me what the different colours of the leaves meant and what I had to do to make them turn to green again.

She had an essence about her that was tender, gentle. It was how she held the leaves and touched the flower petals. The way she would hum softly as she watered, handling the plants as if they truly were living. She respected them, and I respected her for it.

'You must learn French,' she told me as we sat on a little round table that looked out on the plants, sipping lavender tea during our break.

I laughed. 'Languages aren't exactly my forté.'

'I teach you.' She sat up straight, held her head high and then motioned for me to do the same. '*Comment puis je vous aider aujourd'hui?*' She smiled. 'It means, "how can I help you today?". Say.'

The words that came out of my mouth sounded more like a string of "bleh" than anything else. She laughed, a rich sound that echoed throughout the garden. I listened more carefully the second time she repeated it, before she told me to write it down so I would remember.

Spending time with Marie did something to soothe the ache in my heart. She reminded me of what I'd pictured my mother, my real mother, to be like.

My mother had given me up for adoption after my father had died, but I'd never been told why. It was a game I liked to torture myself with, thinking of that great unknown. Over the years, I'd begun to believe it was simply that she didn't want me. It made sense; nobody wanted me.

Karlie and Luna seemed to be the exception.

'There she is!' Karlie yelled when I got in from work.

I smiled as I kicked off my shoes and flopped on the sofa next to my friends.

Luna nudged me. 'So, how was it?' she asked, folding over the page of her book.

'Amaz— Hey!' I stole the book. It was the same one they'd caught me reading in the library on my first day of school. 'What the hell, Luna! I can't believe you're reading this after roasting me about it.' I threw it down in her lap as her cheeks bloomed pink. 'Unbelievable.'

'Don't you worry, Chi-chi. I gave her hell for it already,' Karlie informed me as she braided her hair.

I watched as she reached for a new section, adding in long store-bought pieces to her own hair. 'How long have you been doing that for?'

'Four hours.'

My mouth dropped.

'She's not kidding,' Luna added. 'I've read most of my book in the time it's taken her to do that.'

A high-pitched voice sounded in the room. 'Hello, girls!'

'Muuhum!' Luna wailed, throwing her head back.

'How did she get in?' I whispered to Karlie.

'She has a key, you idiot.'

'I didn't hear the door squeak.'

Karlie leaned in. 'What? Why would it squeak?'

'What do you mean, it always—'

'Sorry to intrude on your evening.'

I looked up to find a tall, broad woman with thick black hair curling around her chin. She took off her fur coat and hung it next to mine before coming over. She walked like a queen.

'Karlie! Good to see you,' she cried, kissing her on the cheeks. 'Ooh, I love the braids – they make you look splendid, darling.' Luna's mum turned to her daughter. 'Hello, my angel. Any news? Any boyfriends?'

'Mum, we've had this conversation a million times before; no, and I don't want one.'

Luna's mum sighed dramatically. 'Oh well, I suppose it doesn't matter.' She reached out and pinched her daughter's cheek. 'You've been feeding them well, munchkin?'

Luna grunted and tried to push her mother's hand away. 'Yes. All they do is eat.' Her face broke into a beam. 'Chiara likes my macaroni, though.'

Luna's mother took that as the green light to acknowledge my presence. 'Oh! I didn't even see you there!' she exclaimed.

I swallowed down the comment to where it wouldn't hurt. This close, her presence was huge and overbearing.

'It's fine. I'm Chiara, Luna's friend.' I held out my hand, and she broke into loud belly laughs before pulling me in for a hug so tight I was having trouble breathing.

'I know, darling, Luna's told me all about you.' She wrapped her fingers around my wrist. 'Very skinny, though. Like Karlie. My, what have you girls been living off, love and fresh air?' She nodded at Luna. 'We'll need to fix that.' She burst into laughter again when she saw my face. 'Oh, no, don't worry, dear, I won't get poor Luna to force-feed you! Karlie's been living with her almost two years now and we didn't get very far, did we?'

Karlie shrugged, reaching the end of yet another strand. 'I have a high metabolism.'

Luna's mother sighed. 'Yes, I wish I had one of those. Oh, well. Why don't your parents come around sometime? We haven't talked with them in, gosh, I don't even know how long!'

Karlie sighed and scrunched up the empty plastic hair packets in her palms. 'I'll ask them. They're probably too busy, though.'

'Nonsense!' Luna's mother waved her hands, although her smile looked tighter than it had five minutes ago. 'Tell them it was a personal invite from me. They can't refuse that, now, can they?'

'You'd be surprised,' Karlie muttered through gritted teeth.

'I think that's enough, Mum.' Luna stood up and started ushering her mother towards the door.

'What? But I've hardly said hello!'

'I'm sorry, I love you, but it's late and we're all tired.' Luna took the fur coat off the hanger and helped her mum put it on. 'Maybe some other time.'

'But—'

''Bye! Sweet dreams!' and she shut the door on her.

We all let out long exhales.

'Sorry,' Luna started, walking back towards us, 'she can be a bit much. If I hadn't made her leave, she would've been talking all night.'

'I hate when she brings up my parents,' Karlie mumbled.

Luna glanced at her. 'I know.'

Though I was also relieved by the absence of her presence, I couldn't help but feel a familiar pain cut through my chest. If I were Luna, I wouldn't be complaining.

At least she had a mother.

# CHAPTER 14

It was earlier than usual when I woke up the next morning. The sky was bloodshot, scraped through with streaks of grey as if a tiger had clawed it. I sat in the quiet room, feeling the old lingering pain in my chest. I'd come to Paris on a childish whim that I might meet my real mother. She was from here, after all.

I stared at the chipped paint on the windowsill. *I'll probably never meet her.*

Grabbing some clothes and the door key, I left the flat. Paris was in a lull at this hour, which I liked. I inhaled deeply as I walked, the cold air kissing my cheeks. I just wanted the past to leave me alone.

My feet had taken me to my destination without my realising. The abandoned park, the willow tree. There was nothing here, just broken equipment and forgotten memories.

I sat on the willow tree's roots, leaned my head against the trunk and closed my eyes. Bird song filled the air, sweet against the clean scent of earth.

This place was special to me, like finding a crystal amongst pebbles. When I pressed my face against the bark, I imagined I was listening to the rhythm of the earth, the same way that I could hear the rhythm of my heartbeat in the stillness.

Something shifted in my periphery.

I pulled away from the tree, watching the rustle of a nearby bush. A rabbit leapt into the clearing.

All the blood rushed to my feet.

Its tiny heart was beating fast, but there it stayed, unaware of what I could do to it. I pressed my thumb into my palm, drawing in a shaky breath. I wouldn't do it. I couldn't, could I? Rheo had been giving me blood, but this was different. It was still warm.

I wanted to know how it tasted.

The rabbit was on its haunches, ready to leap and—

Blood.

It was everywhere.

I looked down at my shaking hands and the carcass lying by my knees.

'Oh God,' I whispered, touching its slick fur. 'Oh God.'

I didn't even know what had happened until it was too late.

*It wasn't me; it wasn't me.*

I wiped my hands on the grass as my eyes pricked. The blood wasn't coming off. I spat on my hands and rubbed them again. It did little. I let out a sob, burying my head in my arms.

I was just as bad as the man who attacked me, who turned me into the same creature as he was. Whatever was left of my humanity had died back then. I hadn't understood that I'd had something so beautiful and fragile until it was stolen away.

'You know, it's weird that I never saw Rheo before, but now I see him everywhere,' Karlie mused through a full mouth.

The lunchroom was as crowded as ever and the plates and

chatter clattered straight through my chest.

'It's a frequency illusion,' Luna stated, earning an eye roll from Karlie.

I said nothing and continued pushing my food around on my plate.

Thanks to me, Rheo had the guts to talk to her alone, stealing moments of privacy in the library during our frees. He was thinking about asking her out, but he didn't know if she felt the same way.

Luna smiled, putting her hand over Karlie's. 'He's a nice guy – I'm really happy for you.'

'It's not like they're together or anything,' I muttered.

'Yeah, it's not really like that, see?' Karlie shrugged. 'He's jokes.'

I coughed to cover my laugh. Friend zoned. I'd keep this one a secret since Rheo wouldn't survive the blow to his confidence.

'Anyway what's goin' on with you and Nico? You two been getting awful cosy recently.' Karlie winked.

I'd noticed this too. When they were together, Nico and Luna were usually having some kind of deep, existential debate, which ended in intense eye contact and an observably uncomfortable amount of blushing.

Luna smacked Karlie's arm. 'Shut up, we are so not! He just has an interesting mind – it's not like we're canoodling.'

I sniggered.

'Yes, missy?' Luna raised her eyebrows at me. 'Do you have something to add, or are you planning on sitting in silence for the entirety of lunch?'

The insides of my stomach pinched together. I wasn't exactly in a talking mood after what happened this morning.

Luna sighed. 'Chiara, what's wrong? You can tell us anything, you know?'

I almost laughed at that one. How could I tell my friends I'd murdered a rabbit and drank its blood?

That I wasn't even human.

'I'm just tired,' I said instead.

She didn't buy it and I knew it, but she didn't push it further. I watched as they turned to each other for conversation. Karlie laughed and her face lit up like a sunbeam. Luna's eyes held depths complex as ocean currents.

My heart ached when I looked at my friends. It would break into jagged shards if I ever lost them. They would find out eventually what I was, when I didn't age. They would know and they would hate me.

I chewed on my lip, wondering if I should finish my meal, when a voice bellowed across the room.

'FIGHT!'

The silence lasted about a second before everyone started roaring, leaping out of their seats.

Karlie stood up and pulled on my arm. 'Let's go!'

I let them drag me into the harsh sun, thinking this would distract me from the turmoil in my mind. We pushed past the smaller students on the outside of the circle, who tried unsuccessfully to weasel their way through. I felt wholly out of place, grimacing at the mass of students so readily jeering and chastising, screaming and shouting. They were a pack of wild animals, thirsty for blood. If only they knew what that was really like.

I found myself at the centre of the hurricane, looking it in the eye. It was not peaceful.

My hand flew to my mouth. Glossy hair behind her, Viv's

black nails clawed at the cheeks of another girl. She dug them in, drawing blood. The crowd winced. The other girl writhed free with a yell and tore at Viv's hair, grabbing manic fistfuls.

'Man, it's way more entertaining when girls fight,' some low-IQ twat said beside me.

Things started to heat up. Viv punched the other girl in the face with a cheer from the crowd. The girl stumbled, then swung blindly at Viv, who dodged and gave her a swift uppercut to the abdomen.

'Fight, fight, fight!' the crowd chanted.

I looked around me, nauseated. Their eyes were glossed over, many with cruel and jeering smiles. Karlie and Luna seemed to be immersed, Karlie clutching my arm for support.

Viv swung her leg around and kicked the girl in the lower back. She crashed to the ground. Viv walked over as the crowd fell silent, wiping her mouth with the back of her hand. The girl lay whimpering on the grass as Viv circled her.

Part of me wanted to intervene, before it was too late. But the other part of me wanted to shrink into the nameless mass and pretend I hadn't seen anything at all.

Before I could decide what to do, a boy with deep blue eyes stood between Viv and the girl.

'That's enough,' he said calmly.

Viv's eyes were locked on the girl on the ground. 'Get out of my way, Kaelan.'

'Viviana.' He stepped closer. 'Look at me.'

His voice was beautiful, the voice of reason.

'Look at me.'

Her eyes broke away from the girl and bore into his. There was a moment of silence as they stared at each other.

Viviana, he'd called her.

I felt sick. I wanted to leave.

Some idiot broke the silence by making a loud kissing noise, triggering a cascade of rude laughs across the crowd. Kaelan turned away to glare at them while Viv looked back down at the girl. I watched Kaelan, until his eyes landed on mine.

There was something in his expression. It was gone so fast I almost didn't catch it before it disappeared.

Almost.

'Girl, that was insane,' Karlie commented as the crowd dispersed and we drudged back to lessons.

'I didn't know Kaelan knew Viv that well,' Luna frowned. 'Come to think of it, I've seen them in the hall together before, but—' she stopped and glanced at me. 'I'm sorry.'

The sun was starting to burn my skin. 'Sorry for what?'

Luna gave me a soft smile and, grabbing my hand, said, 'I know you like him, that's all.'

I glanced around us, pulling away. 'Luna, stop. It doesn't matter – I don't care!'

Karlie and Luna exchanged glances.

'Can we just forget about it, please? I don't want to talk about this.'

Karlie crossed her arms over her chest. 'Fine, we don't have to talk about it. Let's add this topic to the list.'

I frowned. 'What?'

'You can't expect us to sit on the side and watch you go through stuff alone. You haven't told us *anything* about your past, why you are here, or what's going on in your head when you have your mood swings, like today at lunch.' Her eyes flashed. 'I'm sick of your behaviour.'

It felt like she'd punched me. I didn't know Karlie was capable of being so cruel. I watched her walk off, tears pricking my eyes.

It was true that I hadn't told them anything. I didn't know what made me think it was okay to live in their flat, eat their food, go to their school and keep secrets all the while.

I looked at Luna, standing there with pain in her eyes. 'You guys should've said something,' I said quietly. 'I didn't know she felt like that.'

She gave me a small smile. 'Karlie's just hurt you don't trust us enough to share what's happened to you, but we both understand it must have been difficult. She'll calm down soon enough. Take your time, Chiara.'

With that, she too began to walk away from me. I sucked in a breath, holding the pain in my chest tight so it wouldn't overflow. I didn't want to even think about what had happened, let alone tell them.

I swiped away the few tears that had escaped, taking out my timetable with shaking hands. Art. At least I'd be left to paint in peace.

A warm hand wrapped around my arm, startling me.

'Chiara.'

I turned to face Kaelan, glancing at him briefly through my hair, before looking at the ground. Why did he, of all people, have to be here when I was in this state?

Whatever he had come to tell me had clearly gotten stuck in his throat. I tucked my hair behind my ears, looking him in the eye. Let him see me and run. Then I'd be alone again, exactly how it should've been this whole time.

'What do you want.'

He smiled, embarrassed. 'I-I was gonna say something, but it seems stupid now. Are you okay?'

'Do I look okay?'

'Sorry.' He scratched the back of his head. 'I mean, if you wanna talk about it, we can. I don't mind missing my next lesson.'

I stared at him, confused.

He stared back, a sheepish smile pulling at his lips.

'What did you want to tell me?'

His eyes glistened. 'Oh, that. I... the thing with Viviana? I just wanted to say it's not what it looks like.'

My heart was pounding far too loudly.

He searched my eyes. I hoped he wouldn't find what he was looking for.

'Why would I care?' I managed to ask. 'I barely even know you – it's not my business who you get with.'

He shrugged. 'I just thought that maybe it would matter to you.'

'What are you saying, Kaelan?'

His cheeks went strangely pink as a grin spread across his face. 'You had to make it harder for me.' He rubbed the back of his neck. 'I guess I shouldn't be surprised.'

I frowned. What the hell was he talking about?

'Look, I gotta go. If you... ever need anything to do with, you know, you can come to me. Even if you just need someone to talk to.'

His eyes rested on mine. I liked the way he looked at me.

I felt a smile creep onto my face and tried to bite it back, but he'd already seen it. His eyes were fixed on me, like I was the most interesting thing he'd ever seen.

'I'm late for Art,' I said, remembering myself.

I turned and walked away.

Viv was waiting for me by the gates after school. I'd agreed previously to do our Shakespeare project at her flat, but that was before I witnessed her going ape mode on that poor girl.

I walked towards her uncertainly. Her sharp black nails scrolled on her touch screen, the same nails she'd used to make the girl bleed. I wondered what kind of ulterior motives she had in store for me. Poison my water? Slit my throat on the sofa? She was the definition of polished; perfect. She was the last person I expected to bust out kung-fu moves. What had that girl done that was so bad anyway?

'You can come closer than that.' Viv lifted her gaze from her phone and fixed her steely eyes on me. 'I don't bite.'

'Actually, you do.'

She laughed and flicked a curl over her shoulder. 'That bitch had it coming. Let's go.'

After a Metro ride to the outskirts of the city, I stood beneath her block of flats. This looked like the part of Paris the tourists didn't see. I followed her inside without a word. Cracked, peeling paint lined the graffitied walls and the concrete stairs had wet clumps of fallen plaster crumpled over them. I looked up at Viv. She had a certain kind of grace, with her elegant appearance and mannerisms. Even if they were a mirage of what lay underneath. Still, it wasn't the kind of place I expected her to live.

We climbed up the steps in silence, her heels echoing throughout the building. Viv came to a stop on the sixth floor. The door opened without a creak, making me think of Karlie and Luna's squeaky door. I wondered what they were doing without me, if they were talking about what had happened between us. Maybe they'd want to kick me out, now that I'd been a shitty friend.

I swallowed the lump in my throat as I stepped inside. I'd never deserved anything they'd given me. I'd taken it selfishly and spat it back in their faces without a thank you. They should've left me on the streets.

'Feel free to move away from the door,' Viv said sarcastically from behind me.

I mumbled a "sorry" and shuffled further inside, looking around the light open space. An old, worn-in sofa sat in the corner opposite a box TV, and an alcove in the back wall stored an enormous amethyst crystal. Golden figurines stood around it, the area littered with incense sticks, black candles and various card decks.

The alcove carried a rich, intense energy. It lit the room.

I stepped forward tentatively, eyes swinging to Viv for guidance. She unceremoniously dumped her bag on the circular table and, without recognition, went into another room.

'You can leave your stuff there too.'

I unhooked the straps of my bag and set it down next to hers. Taking one last look at the alcove, I followed her, parting the hanging beads in place of a door.

Viv stood with her back to me as she poured water from a glass pitcher. The kitchen was tiny, with only a three-tile thick space between the cabinets on both walls.

'Would you like some water?'

I wrapped my fingers around the beads. 'No, thanks, I'm good.'

She turned around, clutching her crystal glass with her painted talons. Her eyes glistened darkly. 'Or would you prefer blood?'

I froze.

She set down her glass and leaned back against the counter, her arms spread to either side. 'You've been in my visions, recently. It was a most unwelcome surprise.'

I sucked in air, trying to stop my body trembling. She would attack me if I ran, I was sure of it.

Her dark red lips tilted upwards. 'Don't look so scared. I only wanted to tell you what I know, so I can be done with it. I've seen how you became like this, and I've seen why. You were always meant to follow this path, Chiara. Your ancestors were vampires, your parents included. You were turned at eighteen, as is customary for generational families. It was not chance, it was your fate.'

I stared at her. My parents were like this? My ancestors? It was strange to think of being part of a family when I'd been alone my whole life. Why couldn't I have been turned by my mother, why had it been some stranger? How could fate have been so cruel?

'What more do you know about my parents?' I asked her.

Of all the questions I had, it was the most burning. I knew next to nothing about the people who should have been there for me.

Viv shook her head. 'I'm done. I've said what I had to for the visions to cease. If you are meant to find out more, you will.'

I opened my mouth angrily, then shut it as she gave me a warning look. It was clear that it wasn't as if she *couldn't* find out more, rather that she wouldn't.

Another thought came to my head.

'You didn't seem surprised to know vampires existed. You know Kaelan. You know what he is.'

Her eyes gleamed in a way that made me feel naive. I was a child, putting together a simple puzzle for the first time.

'Very good. Yes, we are friends, of sorts. I caught him hunting, he caught me in the midst of my craft. We keep those secrets to ourselves.' She regarded me carefully. 'The respect I hold for him is the reason I told you to stay away. There was one more thing I saw.'

I leaned in, trying to keep my face straight. 'You've got it wrong. I'm not the one initiating things.'

'Because he doesn't know what I do,' Viv snapped. She paused, looking out of the kitchen window. 'There is no avoiding what will happen, I know that now. All I wanted was to protect him. From you.'

My heart skittered. 'What do you mean, what is going to happen?'

Viv turned around, putting her glass in the sink. 'I do not know. But whatever it is, it will hurt him deeply.' She faced me again, letting out a gentle sigh. 'So, Shakespeare?'

# CHAPTER 15

I had a dream that night.

The ground beneath me was deep purple, glittering in the light, its texture smooth yet jagged. Though my feet were bare, it was as if I was stepping on clouds.

I recognised the crystal: amethyst. Crouching down, I tried to feel the cool stone. But my fingers could never touch it.

Frowning, I stood again, glancing around the cavern. Shrouded in darkness was a sleeping figure, not more than twenty metres away. Or maybe it was the figure that was dark. They pulled me in, driving my steps.

A boy.

I floated closer, unable to stop; not wanting to.

I gasped. The amethyst ended and I stood on a cliff, looking into a smoky valley, where a river lay, deep inside. The boy was on the opposite cliff, a wide chasm between us.

His features were noticeable now and I gazed at him longingly. I knew what colour those eyes were when they were open.

And I knew what they looked like on me.

I woke, remembering every detail. The darkness settled on each surface in my room, lingering like silence in the air.

I stepped over to my window and cracked it open softly. Moonlight poured across the sky, dripping down into the dark foliage below. I stuck my head out and inhaled deeply.

My dream was a mirror of my mind. Kaelan was there always, in the background, out of reach. There was something undeniable about our connection. Judging by how he'd behaved yesterday, he must have felt it too.

As they had done before, Viv's words echoed in my mind. "Stay away". "I wanted to protect him. From you".

What could I possibly do that would hurt him so deeply? I wondered if, when she talked about fate, she also meant that mine and his were intertwined. "There is no avoiding what will happen," she'd said.

It sounded like it would be best if I did stay away. The problem was... I didn't want to.

I was curious now, intrigued as to what lay inside him that made me care more than I should. I wanted to know what hid buried inside myself that was capable of hurting someone enough to incur a vision in Viv.

I wondered if she would have any more. About my mother, perhaps? I wondered if she'd even tell me if she did.

Crawling back into bed, I closed my eyes and waited for sleep. Something else was bothering me. I'd got back late last night after finishing the project, and Karlie and Luna had already fallen asleep. Unsaid words lingered on my tongue. I couldn't sleep because of their weight.

'Karlie?' I knocked on her door. A shaft of light seeped out from underneath. It took her a moment to open it, and when she did, I saw her hands were covered in paint.

'Why are you up?' she asked.

'I can't sleep, what about you?'

'Me neither.' She smiled. 'Come in.'

We sat on her carpet, painting in the dim light. I painted a forest, and she painted three girls holding each other. She said it was the three of us. Karlie's skin glowed, her braids falling over her face as she painted.

'I'm sorry. About not telling you guys anything.'

She looked up. Her expression was open, urging me to continue. I put down my paintbrush and wrung my hands. Only Sophie knew the things I was about to say. And we didn't talk anymore.

'I grew up in the foster care system,' I began. 'My foster parents weren't the kind of people that should have been taking care of a child.'

Pausing, I dug my fingers into the carpet. I didn't really want to say more. But I needed her to understand.

'Sometimes they... would leave me alone for a few days. I was too young to work. When there was no food, I went to the corner shop, since the owner, Mr Becksworth, would give things to me for free. I had to learn how to do everything by myself. I was too young for that.'

Karlie was holding my hand. It made everything worse.

'How could they leave you by yourself?'

I shrugged. 'They had lots of friends; they were always at a party somewhere. I liked it better when they were gone. They always argued and I'd get yelled at if I got in the way. When I was little, I didn't know any better. I'd yell back.'

Squeezing my eyes shut, I let out a shaky breath.

'He lost his temper sometimes,' I whispered. 'He'd hit me and my head would knock into the wall.'

I heard Karlie inhale. Her arms were around me in seconds, and I buried my head into her hair. My cheeks were wet. I tasted salt on my lips.

'You ran away, didn't you?'

I nodded. They must've guessed it before, but now at least she knew it for certain. I'd laid my heart on the table for her to see, bloody and broken. She held the pieces in her hands.

'Thank you for telling me,' she said softly. 'Can I tell Luna, or do you want it to be a secret?'

I pulled away, looking her in the eye. 'Tell her everything. I won't talk about it again.'

The hallway was packed with students, noisy and hot. The lights overhead burned my eyes. I pressed myself against the wall as everything spun.

Last night shouldn't have happened. I should've just laid in my bed until sleep came, given Karlie less detail. I'd said too much. She'd probably told Luna already. What did they think of me? That I was attention seeking? That I was going to bring more trouble than I was worth?

I forced myself to breathe. Karlie had been kind. But what if they were only being friends with me out of pity?

*They're good people*, I reminded myself.

But someone like me didn't belong in their world.

I weaved through the crowd, going to a place where I could put my mind at ease. There was an empty art classroom that anyone could use in their free periods. I needed to catch up on my coursework anyway.

There were a few people there already, headphones on, spread out around the room. In here was better than out there. The whitewashed walls lined with prints were comforting. I was wondering where to sit when a low male voice broke the silence.

'You can work next to me, if you want.'

Blue Eyes.

He looked up at me through his hair, his expression almost sweet. The same pull I'd felt before tugged at me again, and I obliged.

I sat, our arms almost touching. The air between us was charged, electric. Every inch of my skin was on fire being this close to him.

'What are you doing?' I asked, noticing the piece of wood in his hand.

His voice was mocking. 'What does it look like?'

Shreds of wood fell to the table as he scraped them off with his knife. I watched his hand move, his fingers caressing the wood and smoothing it down after each cut.

'I assume you have better things to do than watch me the whole hour?'

My heart hammered as I responded hotly, 'Well you were the one who wanted me to sit here in the first place.'

'Hey, no need to get feisty,' he grinned, glancing sideways at me. 'You can walk away anytime.'

I glared, then pushed myself to standing.

Kaelan raised his eyebrows, looking up at me. 'Are you really leaving?'

'What if I am?'

He studied me for a moment, looking as though he wanted to say something, then thought better of it. He shrugged and turned back to his carving.

I walked to the cupboard to pick out a few brushes and some acrylic paints, then returned and dumped them on the table next to him.

Kaelan grinned. 'Miss me already?'

'You wish.'

I tried to block him out of my periphery, opening my sketchbook to brainstorm my final piece. It was going to be bright, like a lightning strike, with birds and open skies. I picked out a few complementary shades to work on a colour scheme.

It was hard to think productively when I was half occupied by the fact he was this close. I watched him from the corner of my eye. His head was bent over his work, his movements smooth and precise. Like him.

His hands were like burnt sunshine, and annoyingly covered what he was carving. I leaned forward, squinting as if I might suddenly develop X-ray vision.

After a few moments, he sighed. 'I'm not a monster, Chiara. It's okay to ask.'

I gave him an awkward smile as he held up the carving, which although not finished, was clearly identifiable. A wolf.

'Stop distracting me. I haven't done anything yet,' I said, giving him a dirty look before squirting some paint onto a plastic pallet.

He laughed, sending heat fluttering through my stomach.

'You're the one distracting me, *koúkla mou*.'

I glanced sideways, my heart beating loud in my ears. Kaelan watched me with curiosity, though amusement also played in his eyes.

'W—' I coughed. 'Where are you from?'

He leaned his head on his hand. 'Greece.'

*Jesus.* I nodded, turning back to my empty page before he saw the blush creeping onto my cheeks. I knew he had an accent but would never have placed it.

Greece. It fitted him perfectly.

I stared at my blank page. Kaelan was finishing his carving, probably feeling pleased with himself at my reaction. I scowled, hating the way I had no control over myself around him.

Knowing it was useless trying to brainstorm further, I flipped the pages backwards, going through my old work. I liked nature; I'd used the concept of it being deathless, its existence expanding past human timespans.

'You're better than I expected,' Kaelan's voice whispered in my ear.

I jumped, before rounding on him. 'You dick! Don't scare me like that!' I smacked his shoulder while he just laughed like a devil.

'Chiara!' he cried, eyes wide. His fingers lightly skimmed the inside of my arm. 'You have paint everywhere – it's toxic, isn't it?'

I snatched my arm away. I must've leant it on the pallet without realising. 'What are you on about? It's not toxic enough to hurt me. And even if it was, it still couldn't kill me.' I leaned closer, whispering, 'I'm immortal, aren't I?'

I stood, walking to the sink by the wall.

'That's not how it works,' he called.

'Then how?' I muttered as I washed off the paint. 'Enlighten me, Einstein.'

'For one,' he said, suddenly in my ear again.

I felt the warmth of his chest pressed against my back as his fingers ran down my arms.

'You can die any one of the millions of ways a human can. All except for old age.'

His fingers were tangled in mine under the running water

until he turned off the tap and was gone.

I looked around the silent classroom and blew out a sigh.

'I hate French,' Luna huffed as she walked over to me and Karlie. 'It makes no sense!'

It was breaktime, and we were sat on the beanbags in the library. I stifled a laugh as the librarian shh-ed us from the next shelf over.

'Good thing you live in Paris then,' I noted.

Luna looked at me guiltily, then crouched to hug me. 'God, I'm so sorry Chiara. I've barely seen you today, but I wanted to tell you I think you're really brave and I'm sorry that we put pressure on you to tell us anything when you clearly weren't ready.'

I looked at Karlie over her shoulder. News had travelled fast then. Luna pulled away, her face wrought with worry. It made me want to bang my head against the wall. She shouldn't have cared, and neither should Karlie.

'It's alright, it's all in the past now,' I said to calm her, even though it wasn't fully true. I would carry the pain with me for the rest of my life, however long that would be now that my body wouldn't shut down.

Luna smiled at me warmly, then curled up beside me on the beanbag. She leaned her head on my shoulder as she flipped through her French textbook.

'I can't believe I have to take this bloody useless exam on it as well. Can you imagine writing whole essays in another language?'

'Pft, I can barely write one of those in English,' Karlie exclaimed.

'I could probably help you with your French, if you like,' I told Luna. 'Marie has been teaching me some at the garden centre.'

She considered it, agreeing it would help.

French was the only tangible connection I had to my real parents. The least I could do was learn their mother tongue.

Sometimes I wondered what my life would have been like if my mother hadn't given me up. Would we have lived in a nice house, like one of those cottages in the south of France? Maybe I would have been raised on croissants and the ocean, smiling at the stupid simplicity of things.

Luna dropped her textbook and pulled out the infamous romance novel. 'I think it's high time for something a little more appetising.'

Karlie and I laughed as she began to leaf through it.

'Oh, how was detention with Mr Kalip?' Karlie asked.

I'd just come back from it, forty minutes of silence and boredom. Thankfully, I caught sight of the twins approaching, sparing my answer.

'Hello, ladies.' Rheo grinned as he leaned on a bookshelf. It started to roll forward and the smile was whipped off his face as he stumbled along with it.

We all burst out laughing as Nico thwacked his back.

'Dumb fuck.'

Rheo flopped down on a beanbag, stretching his body out long and crossing his arms behind his head. 'So, who here thinks I should bribe the dinner lady for some real food?'

I grinned, but it slowly faded when my gaze shifted behind his head. There was Kaelan, walking with his hands in his pockets around the library. It was clear he'd never set foot in it before. There was something childlike about his eyes, wide and observing.

'Yo! Look who showed up!' Nico called out, pointing at his brother.

The librarian shh-ed him.

'You're an idiot,' Rheo exclaimed to his twin, 'pissing off old ladies. Didn't *Mamá* tell you not to yell in the library?'

Kaelan crouched by Rheo. 'Considering there was no library in our village, probably not.'

'Hey, at least I have more manners than Rheo,' Nico argued.

Rheo looked highly offended. 'I beg to differ.'

'I agree with Nico,' I said. 'Rheo wouldn't know what a manner was if an angel slapped him in the face.'

Kaelan's laugh was the loudest and I turned to look at him in surprise, hoping I was better at concealing how happy it made me than he was at his attempts to stop.

Rheo lifted a sassy hand to his chest. 'Ouch. I am deeply wounded. Although, I wonder, why would an angel slap me if it was supposed to be angelic?'

'What a truly profound question, Rheo,' Nico said before I could respond. 'It takes such deep intellectual understanding to wonder such things.'

'What can I say, brother?' Rheo grinned. 'Deep down, I am a philosopher.'

'Hey, what book are you reading?' Nico swooped low and swiped the steamy romance book from Luna's lap.

This time I started laughing so loudly Kaelan turned to me in question, his eyes bright.

Nico's face did something strange as he saw the cover. He dropped the book like it was hot and ran his hand over his shaved head. Unfortunately, it was now in prime position for Rheo to lean over and take it. Karlie bit into her smile.

'Woo!' Rheo let out a low whistle. 'My, my, look what we have here.'

'Let me see.' Kaelan leaned over and I watched his eyes as they danced over the cover. He tried to suppress his embarrassed smile, but it spilled onto his face anyway.

'Is this the kind of shit you girls read?' Rheo flicked through the book. 'Ahem. "I ran my hands over the contours of his chest, feeling the planes of his torso. I licked his abs"...'

Luna and I screamed and held onto each other.

'... "as hard as boulders. He tasted so good".'

Kaelan and Nico were laughing now, so hard I thought I saw a tear glisten in Kaelan's eye.

'Wow, that's priceless,' he exclaimed once he had calmed down.

'This stuff's great,' Rheo agreed animatedly, flicking through the pages again.

Luna, by now, was bright red.

'You done with it?'

'W—' She laughed. 'What?'

'I said, are you done with it? I wanna see what this whole romance novel thing is about. See, I'm kinda jealous. Girls, they get to read all that stuff and learn all the secrets. Whereas us guys,' he motioned to his brothers, 'we have to learn the hard way.' His face was suddenly pained. 'Personal experience.'

I laughed. 'It's a tough life, Rheo.'

# CHAPTER 16

## KAELAN

### *SIROS, GREECE – 1911*

'Kaelan, *mátia mou*, help your *mamá*. Take this jug, fill it with water and bring it back to me quickly. You know where the well is, don't you?'

My *mamá* sat down hard in her chair, similar to the women in the village who were much older than she was. She smiled at me warmly and her suntanned skin creased near her brown eyes.

'But, *Mamá*, why can't you get it?'

She clicked her tongue and shooed me out of the weathered wooden door, out of the kitchen and into the street.

My bare feet were small, stepping expertly on the cobblestones to avoid the cracks. *It's not fair*, I thought. My brothers were out playing by the rocks on the beach with all their friends and here I was again, the one doing all the chores. I ran up the hill, passing carts towing hay for the animals, passing the taverns and the church where my *mamá* went every Sunday to say her prayers. I climbed to the top, the jug swinging wildly in my tiny hands. Like most things in the village, the well was made of cobbled stone and stood on a platform overlooking the rest of the buildings below. Beyond it was the sea.

I clutched the handle of the wooden wheel and turned it to pull up the bucket of water. I poured it into the jug as several women came up with jugs of their own, the water splashing all over.

'Do you need some help with that?' one of the younger ones asked. I held it with both hands close to my chest, watching the top in case it spilled.

'No, I'm strong.'

She laughed and told me I was.

I walked back to my *mamá*, pausing outside our stone house with the terracotta roof. I took a breath and unhooked the handle with my foot. *Mamá* clicked her tongue at me from inside.

'How many times have I told you to keep your dirty feet on the ground?'

'Sorry, *Mamá*.' I put the jug on the wooden table and poured it into an oven-baked clay cup.

She brought it to her lips and prayed over it, before drinking it down fast.

'Can I go play now?'

'One last thing.'

I frowned at the dirt floor.

'Go fetch the small basin and pour the water in there. I want to soak my feet.'

I did as she told me, setting the basin underneath her stool, before pouring the remaining water from the jug into it. She sighed, pulling her skirt up higher onto her lap. I wondered what all the blue and black marks were on her legs, but I didn't ask.

She caught me staring and swatted my head. 'Go. Go play with the others now. Have fun, *mátia mou.*'

# CHAPTER 17

I loved everything about the water. Always. I loved how wide it was and how long it stretched on for. I loved how it changed colours with the sky and moved all on its own. My brothers and I used to play on the rocks at the end of the beach and go swimming in the bay. I remember how we used to beg the fishermen to let us help them so we could see the proud look on our *mamá's* face when we brought home free fish.

I was standing in the water now, although this wasn't the sea and it wasn't my home. I hadn't been home in many years, and it was driving me crazy. I'd go back the next chance I got. *Mamá* would still be there, like she always was, waiting for us to come back to her.

I turned away from the lake and stepped up the muddy bank, running my hand across the rough bark of a tree. There was a small branch that was broken and dying. I dug around in my pocket until my fingers found the smooth handle of my knife, putting it to the branch and cutting until it came clean off. Holding it in my palm, I felt it out for weight. Light. Useful. I stepped out from under the leaves and sat down cross-legged.

It wasn't the lake that I liked the best, it was that no one else knew about it. I'd discovered it the first time we came to Paris, a decade ago. No one knew about it then, either.

A red kite flew in a circle in the sky and it gave me an idea. I began to scrape off the bark of the branch. It fell back to the earth, exposing the raw white and red underneath. Little by little, I carved out the wood until it looked more and more like a bird.

It reminded me of Chiara.

I sighed, running my thumb over the wing. The sun had fallen to the west by now, casting shadows across the smooth water.

I slid the knife and the bird into my pocket.

'Yo, Kaelan, get your fat ass up here,' Rheo yelled from upstairs. 'I need help!'

I groaned, slamming my head into the back of the sofa. I hadn't even been back five minutes. What was he doing now, painting his nails?

His voice had come from my room and, sure enough, that's where I found him and Nico, right in front of my wardrobe. My shirts were lying all over the floor.

'Think again,' I said.

'Look, Kaelan,' Rheo turned to face me, 'have you seen my wardrobe recently? Nothing in there is good enough. If I'm going to ask Karlie on a date, I've gotta at least look the part.'

I shrugged. 'Whatever. Take what you want, just don't ruin it.'

'Brother! When have I ever?'

Nico made eye-contact with me and from the smirk on his face, he was apparently finding this whole exchange amusing.

I raised an eyebrow. 'Think, Rheo. The last time you borrowed my clothes, they washed up on a beach in the Indian Ocean.'

'That was not my fault.'

My eyes widened. 'The turtles were wearing my Calvin Klein underwear as a hat!'

Rheo yawned. 'Does it look like I'm in charge of the turtle's desires?'

Nico snorted, eyeing the clothes on the floor. 'Imagine if, after all this effort, she doesn't even say yes.'

My smirk faded when I saw the look on Rheo's face. I knew my brother; he didn't usually do the whole dating thing. Rheo clearly liked her more than he wanted to admit.

'Come, Rheo,' Nico thumped his back, 'everyone knows you're a *kamáki*; I don't see why this one should be any different.'

Rheo pulled off his shirt and threw it on my floor before putting on one of mine.

'Look, ever since we came to this school, I knew there was something different about her – Karlie. I would've gone up to her...'

'But you were too scared,' I finished.

He shrugged before flopping onto my bed.

Nico scoffed. 'The only point of going back to school, besides getting our A-levels so we can actually get degrees, was for you to potentially find your mate. If you recall, you were the only one out of the three of us who wanted to try again. If you knew it was her all along, you should have told us sooner.'

Rheo sat up and ran his fingers through his hair. 'Yeah, but I don't know, do I? Yet.' He looked at me and narrowed his eyes. 'How come you have it so easy? Chiara's a vampire, after all.'

Her green eyes flashed across my mind.

I shrugged. 'I wasn't supposed to find anyone.' I glanced out the window, watching the trees sway against the sunset. 'It just feels too soon after... you know.'

Even Nico sobered up.

'Yeah, but Kaelan, here's the thing. Chiara isn't her, she's...' Rheo paused. 'I don't know, she's genuine. I just don't see her capable of betraying you in the same way. Besides, she's really struggling with the whole vampire thing. She told me she killed a rabbit the other day and I think she's traumatised herself, honestly.'

I laughed. 'Sounds like her.'

# CHAPTER 18

## CHIARA

We rolled up to school twenty minutes late. I slammed the car door behind me and its echo sounded throughout the empty morning air.

'Girl, move!' shouted Karlie, already halfway across the car park.

I ran to catch up to her and Luna before we parted ways in the hallway.

'Meet at lunch on the field!' Luna called back.

I ran as fast as I could to Chemistry, cursing Karlie for taking her sweet time eating her breakfast that morning.

'Miss Beaufort! How nice of you to finally join us.' Mr Kalip leered at me from behind his desk.

I ignored him, looking around the room at the papers my classmates had their heads bent over.

'Did you forget, I wonder, about the test?'

*Shit.*

Kaelan lifted his head to catch my expression. Mr Kalip turned and Kaelan shoved his head down, leaning it on his arm as he scribbled.

'I did, sir,' I whispered. 'Sorry.'

Mr Kalip's grey eyes shimmered in the fluorescent lights as

he shook his head in mock pity. 'Well, since your classmates have already started, you will have to complete the assessment after the lesson. Can you do that for me, Chiara?'

I gritted my teeth. 'Of course.'

'Good.' He smiled. 'Now sit and wait for the rest to finish.'

I didn't dare look at Kaelan as I took my seat, burying my head in my arms so I wouldn't make eye contact with Mr Kalip either. I was ninety-eight percent sure that Mr Kalip had not even told us we had a test in the first place because, if I had known, I would have revised for it. Which I didn't. So, I was going to fail either way. This was just prolonging my inevitable doom.

'Alright. Pens down.'

I lifted my head, glancing at Willow's paper.

'No cheating, Chiara,' Mr Kalip said as he took it. 'You're walking a fine line, young lady.'

Hurt seared in my chest. What did he have against me anyway? It was clear from the moment I walked in that first day that he hated me. I traced the lines on the desk with my finger while he collected the rest of the papers.

As he started the lesson, I tucked my hair behind my ears and did my best to focus, even though I knew none of it would help me for the test. The class was especially silent today, even though the air outside was settling into the kind of comfortable warm that signified the approach of summer.

'Psst.'

I glanced at Kalip. His back was turned, so I turned my head warily to Kaelan.

'What?' I mouthed.

He threw me a ball of paper, but it rolled off the edge of my desk before I could catch it, landing on the floor. Kaelan bit his lip in apology.

Kalip was still going on about alkanes and alkenes, so I slid down in my chair, sticking out my foot to bring the ball towards me.

'If you get caught...' Willow whispered under her breath beside me.

I picked up the ball with both feet and grabbed it, my eyes on Kalip.

I wondered what could be so important that it couldn't wait until later. Kaelan knew Kalip hated my guts. Why would he have risked me getting caught? *Unless he wants me to get in trouble?*

I sucked in a breath as Kalip turned around, addressing the class.

'Who can tell me some properties of alkanes?' His eyes skimmed the faces and I pretended to read the board so he wouldn't pick on me.

'Chiara?'

*Well, that worked.*

'Colourless and odourless,' I said.

'Good.'

He looked about to move on when he noticed the ball on my empty desk.

'Where are your notes?' He frowned at the piece of scrunched-up paper. 'Are those your notes, Chiara?'

'I—'

But he was already walking towards me.

The class was silent as Kalip picked up the paper. Kaelan swore under his breath.

'Test notes!' Kalip exclaimed, his face lighting up like a child on Christmas day.

My heart sank to my feet.

His eyes narrowed as he struggled to keep the smile off his face. 'Thought you could cheat, did you, Chiara? I see everything. Count yourself lucky that this won't be taken up with the head.'

I would have laughed if I wasn't terrified of him. Kalip mistook my expression to mean that I was seriously affected by his change in tack, nodding to himself before throwing the ball in the bin and continuing with the lesson.

I swallowed hard. Kaelan had been trying to help me.

The lesson ended, and I stayed in my seat while everyone else packed up. The commotion was enough for Kaelan to accidentally drop his pen by my feet. I watched him crouch to pick it up and suddenly his hand found my loose one hanging at my side. My pulse quickened, but his fingers were gone almost as fast as they had come, leaving a slip of paper in my hand.

*Meet me by the rowan tree afterwards.*

The rowan tree was in the corner of the courtyard, where students notoriously bunked off their lessons to hang out beneath it, smoke and sometimes do other, more interesting things. Its leaves were dark green and small; the gaps in between filled with budding white flowers.

Under it all, he stood, waiting for me.

'Hey,' Kaelan said once I reached him. 'I just wanted you to know that I'm sorry.' He held my gaze. 'I mean it.'

I scoffed. 'You must've known Kalip would find out.'

'You think I did it so you would get in trouble?' His eyes

were wide. 'I knew you weren't paying attention when he told us about the test – I was trying to help you!'

The heat in me faded and I took a step closer. He looked so lost, as if he were drowning.

'It's okay,' I said quietly. We were face-to-face now. 'By the way, I'm pretty sure I aced it.'

The breath he drew in was shaky, like he was nervous. 'Rheo told me you haven't been feeding as much anymore. It's because of the rabbit, isn't it?'

I looked away from his eyes. Here was another person who cared, and I couldn't stand to see it written on his face.

It was true; I had been declining the blood Rheo offered me. It had already been difficult to live with myself before I became this monster, but my own flesh disgusted me now. This was an easy way to hurt what I'd become.

'Chiara,' he whispered, tucking a strand of hair behind my ear carefully, as if it were the most precious thing in the world. His deep blue eyes were rimmed with indigo; something I'd never noticed before.

Like the amethyst in my dream.

'I know you hate it, but you have to try. You'll starve yourself.'

I drew in a breath, letting it out slowly. He was right.

Kaelan lifted my chin. 'Promise me you will look after yourself.'

His eyes were set on mine, holding me. They dropped down to my lips.

'I promise,' I whispered.

My heart was pounding so hard I knew he must be able to hear it.

He swallowed, taking back his hand and stepping away. My

lips parted slightly in question as he turned, giving me one last look before disappearing under the leaves.

'Guess what I brought!' Luna cried, jiggling her handbag in our faces.

The three of us had found a place to sit on the field, which was cast in bright spring sunlight.

'Please, please, please be pizza,' Karlie whispered, crossing her fingers.

I laughed. 'It's not pizza.'

'How would you know?' Luna looked offended, clutching her handbag close to her chest.

'One,' I started, counting my fingers, 'because it's not vegan and, two, because... I mean, you can't fit a twelve-inch in your bag.'

'Well, I'm only vegan for a week, and cheese is practically vegan anyway.' Luna folded her arms. 'It doesn't count.'

'It does.'

'Potato tomato,' Karlie exclaimed, sticking her hands into Luna's handbag.

'Oi!' Luna smacked them, then pulled out several sad-looking sandwiches wrapped in clingfilm.

'What are those?' Karlie wrinkled her nose.

Luna dumped one in my hands, and I unwrapped it tentatively, peeling back one of the slices of bread. 'Maybe we should've gotten school lunch?'

Karlie had already eaten a mouthful, nodding her head. 'It ain't bad.'

'It's vegan cheese,' Luna said.

Karlie stopped chewing, her eyes wide. 'What's that?'

'Eh, primarily coconut oil.'

Karlie opened her mouth, letting the half-chewed mush fall out.

'Hello, ladies.'

We all turned in sync to find the Greek brothers hovering above us. Their eyes trailed down to Karlie in horror, who had a long strand of spit swaying from her mouth. Nico nudged Rheo, who looked embarrassed as Kaelan chuckled with laughter. Karlie pulled her fingers through her spit to dislocate it from her mouth.

I hadn't been able to focus during English because of what had happened under the tree, and I didn't dare look at Kaelan now; I'd seriously hoped he would skip lunch with us today.

'What's up with the sandwich?' Rheo asked, sitting next to me.

'Vegan cheese.'

'Ah.' He nodded, eyeing Karlie as she blushed so hard I thought her head might burst.

'What am I supposed to do now, eat only the bread?' Karlie huffed.

'Here, take mine,' Rheo said. 'No vegan cheese, promise.'

Karlie's skin deepened to a new shade of crimson as she accepted his sandwich. She acted so differently around him; all it took was one look for her to be consumed by nerves.

'So, what do you think about aliens?' I asked the group.

Kaelan glanced across at me, a smile playing on his lips.

Karlie threw up her free hand. 'Oh, not this again!'

'I, for one,' started Rheo, 'think there's no question about it. The government hides stuff all the time.'

'And what do you think, Kaelan?' Luna asked, to my surprise.

I went still. I tried to keep my expression neutral, relaxed. He didn't need to know how my feelings for him writhed within my stomach, creating chaos.

Kaelan shrugged. 'I think anything is possible,' he said, looking straight at me.

As students started leaving the field, we stood up along with them. Rheo hung back, eyeing Karlie with intensity.

'Just do it,' I whispered to him.

Rheo jumped up and down, blowing out air. Nico thumped his back before pushing him forward, so hard he almost collided with Karlie.

'Aaand that's our cue to leave,' Nico exclaimed, swaggering off behind Kaelan, who was already halfway across the field.

I could hear Rheo making his pathetic offer in the background as I watched Kaelan moving, his arms swinging in a controlled but loose way. He was so full of opposites.

I would need an eternity to figure him out.

# CHAPTER 19

The afternoon breeze picked up, swaddling me in a soft cocoon as I waded through the long grasses of the abandoned park. Kaelan was right. It was time I started to accept what I'd become. It had been a while since I'd killed the rabbit, and my will was on its last legs. Better an animal than a human.

I paused as a small deer scuttled through the branches, hidden behind clusters of holly and other brambles. Her blood ran swiftly.

I crouched in the earth, digging my fingers into the dirt for support.

Another rabbit, I could deal with. But a deer? I tore my eyes away from her, scouring the scene, looking for something, anything else. I needed blood and I needed it now.

But there was nothing else.

Something desperate pushed my despair sideways and warped it into strategy. I snapped my head back to the deer.

She paused.

Her eyes were liquid black, lined by long, delicate lashes. She looked straight at me, unafraid. Maybe she knew she was going to die. Her eyelids blinked slowly, as if savouring her remaining moments.

I took a shaky breath.

Before I could process what was happening her dead body was in my arms. Bright, thick blood oozed from the vein I'd pierced with my teeth. I pressed my lips to the wound, feeling the liquid running through me and mixing with my own, replenishing me.

It tasted like heaven on fire.

As my thirst began to ease, I pulled away and watched her blood running down my arm. Dread seeped into my chest.

I stared at the streaks of death, burning into my flesh. The deer's eyes gazed in terror somewhere into the distance. Eyes that would never see again.

*I'm a monster.*

I stroked her soft coat, wiping my mouth with my hand, finding even more blood. Even my t-shirt was soaked in it. Choking on a sob, I picked up the deer and carried her to a more secluded location.

'I'm sorry,' I whispered, laying her down in the dirt.

I closed her eyes gently before crawling a couple feet away to lay on the ground. Killing an animal felt bad enough, but it was even worse that I didn't eat the meat or use the bones. It seemed like such a waste.

My back was pressed against the earth and I looked up at the sky through the trees. I wanted the blue to go away. It seemed to be smirking at me, like it thought my life was one big joke.

The red was still seeping into my flesh as if it was becoming a part of it.

This couldn't be how it was done. I wondered what my mother would think of me, if she saw me now? Viv had said that this was my fate, but if that were true, why did it feel so wrong? The leaves above me rustled softly in the breeze just as a blackbird swooped between them.

I stood, left the deer and started to walk deeper into the woods. The trees whispered to me as I brushed my hand along their bark. I wondered how long the forest had stood here for. It was a miracle it was even here in the first place, when so much of the land had been lost to the city.

Silence lay heavy in the air as I stood between trees that had been here for centuries, no doubt. When one fell or was cut, another would grow in its place. There was a certain permanence about it, something more solid than the fleeting reality of modern life. To think that I could outlive this tree... it seemed wrong. Unnatural. Life and death came in cycles; there was never one without the other.

I gazed at the treetops, wondering if I would ever get bored of life, or if it would get any easier. Would there come a time when I wouldn't want to live anymore? Walking back through the trees, I emerged into the clearing where the playground was. My shirt was stained, I realised. This time, I didn't have a coat to hide under.

*How am I supposed to walk back when it looks like I murdered someone?*

I peeked my head around the corner, looking towards the street. Only a few people were about. Maybe if I ran fast enough, they would think the red was part of a tie-dye shirt?

I started to sprint, keeping my head down. It was a bad idea, but I couldn't have called Luna to pick me up. It would've been a difficult explanation. My feet pounded hard on the pavement as I rounded the corner.

Black hair, tan skin.

My eyes widened.

Kaelan.

I threw myself behind a bush before he noticed me.

# Chapter 20

## Kaelan

*Siros, Greece – 1917*

'Wake up, *mátia mou* – we must leave. I have done something terrible,' *Mamá* whispered as she shook me.

'What is it? It's dark outside, *Mamá*!'

'Come, Kaelan, we do not have time for this. Rheo, Nico!' she murmured.

I laughed. 'That wouldn't wake the faeries.'

I kicked Rheo in the side and he sprung awake.

'You fool!' he screamed, launching into me.

I laughed again, sidestepping as he rammed into Nico's bed and fell on top of him.

'Kaelan! You must set a good example for your brothers!' *Mamá* stabbed her finger in my chest.

I grinned back.

'Wipe that smirk off your face, young man, or else I shall have to do it for you.'

She waved her hand in the air but I knew it was an empty threat; she wasn't the one who did the hitting. It was only then that I noticed she was wearing her travelling clothes.

'What is this about, *Mamá*? Where are we going?'

She picked up Nico, who was half asleep, and propped him to standing.

'Rheo, hold your brother. And put on some clothes.' *Mamá* turned back to me, guiding me by the arm through the doorway to the kitchen. 'I have done something terrible. We must leave before your father gets home because he will kill me. I know it.' She glanced around the kitchen, her face as pale as the whitewashed wall.

I frowned as she stuffed fruit and several flasks of water into a bag. 'What have you done?'

'Rheo, Nico!' She clapped her hands together.

Rheo was now fully clothed, wearing a sheepish look as he dragged Nico across the dirt floor. 'He fell back asleep.'

*Mamá* clicked her tongue before splashing the last of the water from the jug onto him. 'Up, up! We must leave.'

Nico made a sound like the dead coming back to life, blinking the water out of his eyes.

'Such a drama queen,' Rheo tutted, kicking him for good measure.

We lay down in the back of a horse-drawn wagon and covered ourselves with straw.

'You never answered my question, *Mamá*,' I whispered as it set off.

'Oh, *mátia mou*, I don't think I can bear to speak what I have done aloud.'

'We are covered in straw and it smells. No one can hear you here.'

It was silent apart from the roll of the wheels on the cobblestones and Nico's snoring. Rheo, for once, was keeping his mouth shut.

*Mamá* sighed. 'I fell in love, *mátia mou*, with another man.'

'But what about father? How could you be so stupid!' I cried.

'Do not make me feel worse than I already do! You know as well as I that we all would have died if we stayed any longer in that house. It was the only way to make him angry enough to break our bond.'

I stared at her. 'You mean, you broke the soul contract?'

She nodded, wiping a tear away from her face so fast I wasn't sure if it had been a trick in the dark.

'*Mamá*, does it hurt?' I curled my hand into a fist. 'This is my fault, I should have protected you!'

'*Mátia mou*, easy, there was nothing you could have done.' She offered a weak smile, unfolding my fist with her calloused hands. 'Go to sleep, now, it is almost midnight. We will be several villages over by morning.'

She started to sing then, a lullaby her *mamá* and all their *mamás* before used to sing. She sang it to us almost every night.

After she had finished, I whispered, 'Where are we going?'

'Hush! You must sleep. And what have I told you about asking so many questions?' She stroked my hair. 'Listen and watch, and you will know the answer.'

# CHAPTER 21

I went on runs to clear my head. Something about the rhythmic thud of my feet soothed me, like the rhythm of the songs my *mamá* used to sing. Runs usually helped me to forget stuff for a while, but right now, this one wasn't working out like they usually did. Green reminded me of Chiara and it was everywhere.

*She's not Tasha*, I reminded myself again. I ran harder *You should be over it by now. You should've been over it years ago.*

Some wounds dug so deeply that healing them would be miraculous. And I didn't believe in miracles.

I turned the corner into a residential area. A branch snapped to my left.

'Crap.'

I knew that voice.

I skidded to a halt. 'Chiara?'

Sure enough, Chiara stumbled out of the undergrowth, managing to look graceful and clumsy at the same time. She looked up at me with wide eyes. It was impossible to hold my laugh in.

'Shut up,' she grumbled. 'How is this funny?'

I shrugged, still grinning until I noticed the state of her t-shirt.

Without thinking, I pulled the hem closer so I could get a better look at the stains. My fingers grazed her stomach by accident. I felt her body shiver, and heat surged through me. It was difficult to stop thinking about all the things I wanted to do to her.

Breathing deeply, I stepped back and dropped the fabric. 'You can't walk around like this. Someone will call the police.'

Chiara moved closer to the bush in a poor attempt to hide herself.

I followed, unable to stop.

She pulled her hair over one shoulder as she glanced around warily. 'I was running so people wouldn't see. It's not that noticeable, right?'

I held back a wince. She looked like a murder victim.

Without a second thought I pulled off my shirt and handed it to her. 'Just take mine. You can give it back later.'

She stared at me like I just suggested we fly to Mars.

'Sorry, it's kinda sweaty.'

She nodded and took it anyway, biting her lip. I lost track of what happened after that. Her lips looked soft, full. I wondered what it would feel like to kiss them.

'How am I supposed to change with you watching me?'

I snapped my eyes back to hers. There was fire in them.

I turned around fast, my heart beating rapidly at the thought of her changing behind me. Her blood-soaked t-shirt landed next to my feet. I stared at it before picking it up. It was still warm.

I swallowed, trying to push down my desire for her 'How did you get so much blood on it?'

'Shut up. Not everyone is an experienced murderer.'

I chuckled. 'Just so you know, we don't usually kill the animal, my brothers and I.'

'Oh.'

'Yeah, you just have to stop yourself before.'

She didn't say anything for a while. I wondered if I'd offended her. I was about to ask if I could turn around when she spoke.

'I'll remember that.' Her voice was rough.

Was something wrong?

I felt a light tap on my shoulder. Her touch did something to me that I hadn't felt in a while. I turned to find her standing there, my shirt a little baggy on her. *Damn.*

'I—' my voice sounded strangled, so I coughed, glad she was too busy staring at the ground to see my face.

'You don't have to make fun of me; I know it looks bad.' A small wrinkle formed on her forehead.

All I wanted to do was wrap my arms around her.

'It really doesn't.'

She looked up.

I didn't think, I just spoke. 'Do you want to go somewhere with me?'

*What am I doing?*

Surprise flashed in her eyes. 'Like where?'

I shrugged. 'You'll see.'

'Okay, Mr Mysterious.'

I gave her a look. 'Please never say that again.'

A grin bloomed across her face. God, she was beautiful.

Balling up her t-shirt in my hand, I carried it over to the nearest rubbish bin.

'I wonder what the bin men will say,' Chiara chastised.

'It's Paris. They've seen worse. As long as the police don't get their hands on it, you'll be fine.'

She looked at me with wide eyes and it took everything I had not to smile.

'Kaelan, this isn't funny! That's real blood! If someone did find it and decided to investigate...'

'Look, I swear nothing bad will happen,' I reassured her. 'No one will even look twice at it.'

'You better be right or else I'll kill you.'

I raised my eyebrows. 'I'd like to see you try.'

'What, you think I'm not strong enough?'

I scoffed, looking ahead at the houses all the way down. 'That's an easy yes.'

'Race ya.'

'Wha— Chiara!'

But she was already twenty paces ahead of me, practically kicking up dust. I glanced back at the street for a split second before following her. She laughed at me as I caught up, speeding down the pavement. I had to hand it to her, she was faster than she looked. I pushed harder, but she must have done the same because the two of us were now sprinting at top speed and neither could outmatch the other. My muscles hadn't moved this fast in a long time. It was exhilarating.

'Slow down. We have to take that path,' I panted, pointing to a gap in between a wall and a fence that led up the hill. I knew she wouldn't slow down until I showed her I wasn't competing anymore, so I slowed first.

'That was amazing!' she breathed, holding onto my arm for balance.

My skin tingled where her fingers were. When she let go, I had to stop myself from grabbing her hand.

'Wait till you see the view from the top.'

We started to walk up in silence, accompanied by the sound of birds chirping. I glanced at Chiara. Her eyes were alive, searching the trees. I knew it wasn't only the running making my heart race.

'This is it,' I said as we entered a clearing. The view I had seen a hundred times before, but it never ceased to amaze me. The Eiffel Tower stood below us, so close yet so far. Everything else was just part of its shadow.

I turned to Chiara to catch her reaction. Her cheeks were flushed and her hair was wild as she looked out over the city.

'It's beautiful,' she breathed.

*Like you*.

We were silent for a while then, just taking it in.

'Do you ever get bored of life?' Chiara asked. Her eyes were set in the distance where the sky met the furthest building. 'I mean, I guess it's hard to get bored in a place like this.'

'Sometimes I do.' I caught myself staring at her again, against my will. 'But over the years, I realised something.'

She fixed her eyes on mine.

'You can't be anywhere else but in the moment. Thinking about the future all the time... you'll get depressed. The past is interesting for reflection, but at some point, you have to let it go.'

She sighed. 'I've heard that before. It's just difficult for me to let my past go. ' She raised her head, shifting her gaze once more to the horizon. 'I guess all I can do is try.'

The wind picked up and blew her hair in her face. I laughed and reached out to help her, tucking the strands carefully behind her ears.

Her green eyes were sparkling and her lips formed that

embarrassed smile.

*I think I'm losing my mind.*

She was everywhere, in everything I saw and did. I liked it. A lot. Her eyes searched mine as I leaned in, my fingers sliding into her hair, cupping her head in my hands.

The moment our lips touched, I knew.

# CHAPTER 22

'What's up, Kaelan?' Nico yelled from the kitchen. 'You were out late.'

I caught myself smiling at the ground like an idiot.

'What happened to your shirt?' he asked as he rounded the corner.

I'd completely forgotten about giving it to Chiara, since I was still caught up in what had happened.

'Whatever you're thinking, it's not that.'

'You're right, brother,' he winked. 'It's probably worse.'

I pushed past him as I rolled my eyes and opened the fridge. 'I'm guessing you didn't make anything for dinner.'

'You know me too well,' he grinned. 'Hey, don't look at me like that; I had the decency to order pizza.'

An hour later, we were lying on the sofa playing Mario Kart. I leaned back all the way, the controller loose in my hands. Nico, *au contraire*, was leaning forward and slamming his fingers against the buttons – as if that would help him win.

I couldn't stop thinking about Chiara. *When am I going to see her again? Damn. Chemistry.* I groaned, forgetting Nico was right there. Chemistry was bad enough before; she did all kinds of hot things that distracted me. Like when she played with her bottom lip absentmindedly while she was thinking. I wished Mr Kalip had put me in a different seat, maybe somewhere Chiara wasn't practically in my direct view. It was getting harder to control myself around her, and I was scared I'd end up taking things too far.

Especially now that I knew what those lips tasted like.

I ran a thumb over my own. Today had been a mistake. I didn't want to get her hopes up when I wasn't sure I was ready to be with someone again.

Out of the corner of my eye, I saw Rheo stroll in.

'What's got you so smitten?' Nico asked, barely glancing in his direction.

'Where've you been? He went on a date.' I looked away from the game for a few seconds to find Rheo smiling stupidly at his feet. It was probably a similar expression to the one I'd had earlier.

Nico's character caught up to mine and I glanced over to see him sticking out his tongue in concentration like he'd done since he was five.

'You know,' Rheo muttered, 'I can't help but think... maybe I'm being stupid, but... hey, would you cut that out?'

I sighed and dropped my controller, then pulled Nico's out of his sweaty palms and turned off the TV.

'What'd you do that for?' Nico shouted.

'Calm down. Rheo looks like he's got something important to say.'

'Brothers,' Rheo exclaimed 'I think she's the one. I just feel this... this pull towards her.'

'Sounds like she's definitely the one then,' Nico joked.

'Can you actually be serious, for once?' Rheo ran his hands through his hair. 'I don't have a single fuck of an idea what to do!'

I pushed myself to my feet, offering my hand to help Nico up. He looked at it for a second, then took it.

'We're happy for you Rheo, really.' I started. 'It's just that Karlie's a human and you're not, so be careful, okay?'

'Oh God, what would *Mamá* say?' He looked up at the ceiling. 'I should stay away from Karlie; this can't go anywhere without me taking away her normal life.' Rheo ran his hands through his hair and looked at me. 'What should I do?'

I sighed. Rheo might be annoying at times, but he was still my little brother, and I didn't like to see him like this.

'Take it from someone who knows, Rheo. If she really is your mate, it doesn't matter how hard you try and stop yourself.' I took in a shaky breath, the reality of my own situation setting in. 'You won't be able to stay away.'

# CHAPTER 23

## CHIARA

I could still feel his lips on mine.

His rough, gentle hands running down my cheeks, weaving through my hair. The sheen of his bare chest in the evening light.

It didn't seem like he'd realised his impact on me, just being. One look, one touch, and my instincts were set on fire. I hated how much power he had over me and the way he dominated my thoughts. I lost control when it came to him.

And that scared the shit out of me.

I had difficulty falling asleep that night, my thoughts spinning around in circles. The days had been steadily getting warmer, the clouds building up so high that they looked ready to burst any second.

I wasn't sure what would happen between him and I going forward. Would we go back to the way it was before, stealing glances and concealing our feelings? He was unpredictable, like a storm in summer. He kept his cards well concealed at all times, but now that I'd seen a glimpse underneath, I knew he was full of unexplored dimensions.

I wanted to know them all.

Monday morning, I walked into Chemistry to find Kaelan sitting in Willow's seat. I opened my mouth, glancing at Mr Kalip to see how the hell he had condoned this, but he was intensely looking over some paperwork

Reluctantly, I walked over to my desk. It was difficult to focus at the best of times, but would be near impossible with *him* sitting next to me. Kaelan was leaning down, getting something from his bag under the desk.

I crossed my arms. 'Why are you sitting here?'

He snapped his head up, slamming it into the bottom of the desk.

'Ow,' he winced.

I couldn't tell if his face was red from leaning down or embarrassment.

When he saw I was unamused, he composed himself quickly. 'I can sit somewhere else, if you'd prefer.'

I narrowed my eyes before letting my bag drop to the ground and sliding into my chair. I'd never noticed how close the chair beside me was until now. Our legs were almost touching.

'Alright, class.' Mr Kalip stood, clapping his hands together. 'Let's start. Oh, and by the way, don't think I haven't noticed the change in the seating arrangement,' he stared pointedly at Kaelan and I. 'But if the two of you are good, I might let it slide.'

I ran my tongue over my teeth, staring at the floor ahead.

This was a terrible idea.

The minutes passed like hours, until it was halfway through the lesson. Kaelan had been strangely quiet, apart from when he answered the questions no one else knew. I wondered how many times he had completed A-level Chemistry, or A-level anything for that matter. It seemed torturous the first time around and I couldn't imagine why anyone would do a repeat even once.

I wasn't gonna lie though, his intelligence was kind of sexy.

'Now, who haven't we heard from yet...' Mr Kalip's eyes roamed around the room before landing, as if by a magnetic pull, on his usual victim. 'Chiara!'

I gritted my teeth, aware of Kaelan laughing in my ear.

'What is the answer to the question on the board?'

I was about to speak when I felt Kaelan's hand on my bare thigh. Completely surprised, I gaped at Kalip, unable to utter a word. Kaelan took his hand off almost instantly, but I could still feel the imprints his fingers had made.

'Chiara?'

Mr Kalip narrowed his eyes at me, but I could no longer remember the answer. I couldn't speak at all.

'Right. I'll be seeing you after school, Chiara,' he stated, before moving on with the lesson.

I felt sick.

Kaelan kept trying to get my attention, but I ignored him and focused on the lesson. I couldn't afford to get in trouble again. He eventually gave up, and after the lesson had ended, I left before he had a chance to say any more.

He knew Kalip hated me; he must have known the consequences his actions would have. My thigh prickled where his fingers had been. He'd touched me like he owned me.

I just couldn't understand why he'd done it.

The shadows were long by the time I returned to Mr Kalip's classroom. I'd avoided Kaelan the entire day, staying with the girls instead. Karlie had told us about her date with Rheo, which had apparently gone well. While I was happy for her, it only reminded me of Kaelan's kiss and the mess he'd now made.

'Come in, come in,' Mr Kalip exclaimed as I pushed on the door.

His elbow was leaning against his desk and he stroked his chin, staring at me. It was only him and I in that classroom.

I shifted on my feet. 'Um, should I sit down?'

'Oh, yes, yes, do that,' he replied hastily, as if he had just come out of a reverie.

I slid into the seat Kaelan had sat in earlier. The stale air was thick with silence and the afternoon's heat. The woods were still there, half covered in shadow and half gleaming in the light. I wanted to run through them with my arms out wide, feeling the air float through my fingers as if my arms were wings.

'I wouldn't get comfortable there, Chiara,' Mr Kalip's harsh voice sounded, breaking through my fantasy. He pointed to the old chalkboard on my side of the classroom. 'You will spend the next forty minutes writing the words "I will pay attention in class" on that board.'

I looked at him in shock. What was this, the Victorian Era? 'Sorry?'

His grey eyes were cold, leaving no room for argument.

I swallowed and reluctantly pushed myself out of Kaelan's chair. Mr Kalip was already back to reading his damn papers and a part of me wondered if it was a decoy. He clearly had nothing better to do with his life.

I took the chalk, gritted my teeth and began to write. I started at the top of the board, suddenly feeling self-conscious that my back was to Mr Kalip.

'Writing slowly will not make time go faster, Miss Beaufort.'

I whipped my head around to glare at him, catching his eyes trailing down my body for a split-second before they snapped back up, meeting mine with an unapologetic smirk.

I clenched my jaw and turned back to the board. My limbs were stiff as I continued to write the lines, the pit in my stomach growing deeper with the knowledge that his eyes were still on me. I wanted to leave. I wanted Luna and Karlie to hold me and I wanted to crawl into my bed and stay there until the way he looked at me like a wolf eyeing its prey left my consciousness.

After what felt like years, Mr Kalip proclaimed my forty minutes were up. He smirked at me, but it didn't quite reach his eyes.

'I trust you will behave next lesson?'

'Yes, sir.'

Without another word, I scurried out of the classroom.

The moment I stepped outside was bliss. The air was sun-soaked and swaddled me like a blanket. The forty minutes of torture seemed like a world away already as I threw my head back and stared at the calm, smoky-blue sky.

I took a deep breath in and sighed, then started along the dusty track that led to the car park, s hidden behind a group of trees. The birds sang sweetly from high up in their branches, out into the musty, hot air.

*When I die, I'll come back as a bird.*

'Oh crap,' I muttered as I reached the car park, fishing around in my bag for my phone to call Luna to pick me up.

'Hey.'

I lifted my head, squinting at Blue Eyes leaning against his brother's car. His face was illuminated in sunlight, making his eyes glow in a way I knew couldn't be human.

'What are you doing here?'

He exhaled, then pushed himself off the car to meet me. 'You've been avoiding me all day.' He gazed into my eyes with a soft intensity. 'I need to talk to you.'

I crossed my arms. 'I didn't like what you did today in Chemistry.'

His face dropped and my heart dropped along with it.

'Chiara, I-I'm sorry.'

'It's done now. I don't know what you think you're doing here, but you better go home. I'm calling Luna.'

'Wait—' His arm shot out before I could get my phone. 'I didn't mean to do it, okay?' He ran a hand through his hair as his eyes swam in circles. 'I just wanted to sit next to you so we could talk about what happened, you know, with the kiss. Then Kalip picked on you. I swear I was just trying to comfort you, but it ended up coming out all wrong.'

I looked him in the eye. 'You really don't understand, do you? Apologising doesn't fix what you've done. You have no idea, Kaelan, what being a girl is like.' I stepped closer, old anger seething under my words. 'You don't have to think about what you wear when you walk down the street, because creepy old men aren't going to stare at your ass or your boobs. You don't have to worry about being catcalled, kidnapped or raped. I bet you don't even have to cover your drink when you go to the club. I thought you were different,' I spat, tears welling, 'but the way you treated me in Chemistry proved me wrong. And Mr Kalip he—' I covered my eyes with my hand. My voice lowered to a whisper. 'He... God, I felt so unsafe.'

'Chiara—'

I glared at him. 'Don't.'

We were silent for a while as hot tears slid down my cheeks. He clenched his jaw, then his fist, like he was trying to physically restrain himself.

'Can I speak?' he asked finally. His emotions were written all over his face.

I wiped my cheek and nodded.

'You're right. You didn't deserve that, *koúkla mou*. I wasn't thinking.'

'Stop making excuses.'

'I'm not trying to!' His eyes were wide and I felt my heart crack. He swallowed, his voice rough. 'I care about you. I didn't mean to hurt you. At all. I know I was out of line and I'm sorry.'

I sighed. 'You're confusing me, Kaelan. All this time, you've left me guessing whether or not you like me back; you push me away, then pull me back in as if I'm some kind of toy you can mess with.' I avoided his eyes. 'Figure out what you want; maybe at least one of us can have some peace.'

He took a step closer. I could feel the warmth of his body.

'But I already know what I want.' He lifted my chin gently, making me look at him. 'You.'

My breath caught in my throat.

'I've always liked you, Chiara,' he said quietly, dropping his hand. 'Always. And it scared the hell out of me, which is why I acted like that. But I don't think I could ever be just friends with you. I want to be more.'

I began to play with his fingers. 'And what if I don't want to be more?' I asked, teasing him.

He broke into a grin and pulled me into his chest. I leaned my head against him and sighed, listening to the steady beat of his heart.

I liked the way he held me, as if he was holding the whole of me.

There was something sweet in that moment, in the realisation that I liked him and he liked me, and that there was no one else but the two of us in that dusty car park long after school had finished on a Monday.

# Chapter 24

The days melted into weeks as spring turned progressively to summer and exams loomed like a dark cloud over the sun.

The flowers at the garden centre were in full bloom, with bright reds, pinks and whites that sprouted from tiny dark green stems with full leaves. On my days off, the girls and I went to different art museums to get inspiration for Karlie and I's final exam piece.

Despite the added stress of Chemistry lessons with Kalip, I tried to make the most of the remaining time we had left in school before study leave started. While I still liked our conversations as a group, it was our conversations alone, mine and his, that I enjoyed the most. I found myself telling Kaelan things I didn't even know I knew about myself. Little things about me, like what I liked and my opinions on things. He seemed interested in stuff I thought nobody would care about and I swore he could make a conversation out of nothing. It seemed to me that he'd lived a thousand different lives all over the world, somehow managing to pack the wisdom of a one-hundred-and-fifteen-year-old man into the body of an eighteen-year-old.

He told me about when Nico had a spiritual phase and

decided to be a monk. They all did it with him, shaved their heads and went mute mostly – until they got kicked out and stranded in outer Mongolia. Kaelan had been lost too many times to count, with little more than the clothes on his back and a few coins in his pocket, but, somehow, he always figured it out. The way he spoke was enchanting, drawing me closer to him with every word to the point where I would forget where I was and what I was supposed to be doing, dropping into his past so fully it was like I was reliving his moments through him.

I liked how he laughed at the stupid stuff I did when I wasn't even trying to be funny. I liked how his eyes glistened when he got excited and that he rubbed the back of his neck when he was embarrassed. I liked how warm his eyes were when they looked at me, at odds with their deep blue. His laugh alone did something to me that reconfigured every emotion within my body until it was all shining, pure light. I caught myself staring at him sometimes without even listening to the words coming out of his perfect mouth.

He was truly beautiful.

'Woo, it's hot in here!' Karlie exclaimed as she threw open the car door.

We'd decided to go to the beach less than thirty minutes earlier, after Karlie proclaimed she'd had another of her ideas.

'Ugh, and the aircon doesn't even work properly!' I moaned, fanning the air out with my hands.

'You two babies.' Luna shook her head, starting the ignition. 'You'll live.'

A rap song played quietly as we drove with the windows

down. I stuck my head out to breathe better, making unfortunate eye contact with a dog doing the exact same thing.

'Okay, drama queen, the aircon's in full swing now,' Luna told me.

I rolled up my window as Karlie leaned through the gap in our seats, cranking up the volume so the rap song she was playing blasted out.

'Karlie, that's way too loud!' I yelled, making to turn it down.

She smacked my hand away and said seriously, 'That's the only way to listen to rap.'

'Karlie, turn it down! I can barely hear myself think!' Luna exclaimed.

I swatted Karlie's hand away from the dial and turned it down by a few notches. 'What even is this song?' I grimaced.

Karlie stuck her head between the seats again to glare at me. 'Just 'cause you live under a rock, Chiara Beaufort, does not mean I do.' She pouted and started bopping to the beat. 'It's my jam.'

'Karlie, put on your seatbelt,' Luna said as she changed lanes.

I laughed as Karlie stuck out her tongue at her. 'But it's way more fun up there with you guys. Why do I always gotta sit in the back like a toddler?'

'Maybe if you stopped acting like one, things would be different,' Luna said.

'Hey, I know this one!' I exclaimed as the next song started playing, cranking up the dial.

Luna groaned and Karlie cheered before she started belting out the wrong lyrics. I joined in. Soon, the car was filled with our out-of-tune singing as the beat reverberated through our seats and chests.

'Come on, Luna. You know you want to!' Karlie shouted.

'I'm driving. If I sing, I'll probably crash.'

But when that chorus hit, I heard her deep, melodious voice join ours and we were complete.

I could barely contain my excitement as we drove into the beach car park, throwing open the door once we'd stopped. The air here was different, sharper. Salty. I tuned in to the waves crashing against the shore out of sight, drifting out then sweeping inland.

'Alright, get your bags,' Luna called out, opening the boot.

Karlie already had her shoes off and had started running towards the beach. I laughed as Luna shook her head.

'She's bloody crazy, that one.'

Another few paces forward and around a stack of tall leafy trees, there it was. The blurred blue waters were dense and stretched out so far they blended with the sky. There was something about that, the power it took to lift its weight and send it crashing down and pulling back. I smiled, throwing my arms out to my sides, feeling the breeze stir through my clothes.

'Come on, you dummies!' Karlie cried, taking our hands.

We laughed, running down the steps to where the tarmac met the sand.

I broke free of Karlie's hand, dropping my things on the ground. Everywhere was golden as the sun's light bounced off each grain. I ran forward along the beach, feeling the ground slip between my toes as I sank and almost tripped over. I laughed at myself.

It was delicious, the freedom of it.

I stopped. The sun glimmered off the water's surface and I could practically smell its coolness, like a balm compared to the hot air pressing into me on all sides. The waves crashed, sending a frothy swash over my toes.

I heard Karlie suck in a breath next to me as Luna came up behind us. The three of us stood together in silence as the waves ceaselessly spilled onto the shore and were dragged out again.

'Can we go in?' I asked, turning to Karlie.

She had already started to pull off her clothes.

Luna glanced around. 'There's no lifeguard on this beach.'

'Don't you know how to swim?' I teased.

She looked at me for a moment, then shook her head with a smile. 'Sorry, I don't know why I'm so stressed out lately.'

Karlie threw her shirt on the ground. 'I bet it's exams. They make you more stressed than usual.'

Luna started braiding her long black hair. 'Thanks, Karlie.' She looked me up and down. 'Aren't you going in the water?'

Karlie eyed me now, too, standing there in her bikini. I played with the hem of my shirt. I didn't have a swimsuit, so I'd borrowed hers. It felt uncomfortable to wear it in public, the thought of all those eyes on my bare skin making me self-conscious.

As if she knew what I was thinking, Luna piped up. 'Chiara, there's barely anyone here.'

I sighed, glanced around, then stripped.

'See, that wasn't so hard, was it? You look lovely!' Luna exclaimed.

'Chi-chi, you need to have more confidence 'cause you're actually really pretty.'

I blushed. 'Shut up, Karlie.'

She winked and I rolled my eyes, then took my clothes and dumped them with theirs a couple of metres from the water, hoping to dump my anxiety along with them.

'Alright,' Karlie said, taking my hand and Luna's, staring deadpan at the ocean. 'Three, two, one, go!'

We ran straight into the water, screaming as icy waves lapped at our thighs.

'Holy shit,' breathed Karlie.

I laughed, splashing her face. She squealed, her eyes twinkling as she splashed me back.

I let the water lift my arms up to the side, relishing in the strange floating sensation.

'This is so nice after that car ride,' I murmured.

The air was charged with salt and the coolness of the water was energising. We waded in deeper, the water rising and falling around our hips. I fell back on the waves, feeling the sun on my skin. The sky was the kind of blue made for dreams and hopeless fantasies.

'What are we going to do after graduation?' Karlie asked.

'We should go travelling.'

Luna's clear blue eyes darted between Karlie and me. 'Where?'

'Anywhere,' I shrugged. 'I wanna see the world.'

Karlie's dark eyes glittered as she gazed into the distance, her lips spreading into a smile as she tucked her braids behind her ear. 'I can imagine. Just the three of us, right?'

My mind lingered on Kaelan. He probably wouldn't want to come if it was just us girls. 'Right.'

'I don't know – it's risky to travel,' Luna said. 'We could just find a summer programme here or back in England. Work...' she trailed off as she caught sight of Karlie's expression. She sighed. 'Okay. I'll start researching ideas.'

'Thank you!' Karlie leapt onto her, Luna laughing as she

almost got submerged.

I joined them, squeezing them tight.

We unravelled, sucking in air, giddy with excitement.

'Alright, lets head in and get some ice cream,' Luna suggested.

We ran up the seabed, managing to jump past the drag of the waves. The other two had gone farther ahead as I walked slowly, taking one last look of the ocean over my shoulder. I tripped up the sand, landing on my hands and knees.

'Hey, doll.'

I looked up. There stood Kaelan, barefoot, biting his lip.

'What are you doing here?' I asked, standing quickly.

'Luna told us to come.'

I raised my eyebrows at him. 'She didn't mention that to me.'

Kaelan shrugged. We stared at each other for a little too long before he coughed and I looked away. We usually never ran out of conversation. I didn't know why it was so awkward all of a sudden.

'I better catch up with the others,' I said, making to get past him.

He caught my arm. 'Chiara—'

Kaelan's gaze was heavy as he looked down at his hand on me. It was warm against my cool, damp skin. His eyes were full of words left unsaid.

I reached up with my free hand to ruffle his hair. He smiled and ran his hand through it after me as if to feel the trails my fingers had left.

Kaelan shifted his hand down my arm to interlace our fingers, and I pulled him towards the base of the rocky cliff at one end of the beach. I could just about make out the paths weaved throughout it. The question in Kaelan's eyes turned into a wild grin as he eyed the top of the cliff. Maybe he wondered what the view would be like.

We began to climb, me first, then him. Pausing halfway up, I looked out at the beach spread in a wide arc. I glanced down, expecting Kaelan to be far below me, but he was close by. He pulled himself over a ledge and looked up at me, panting. The sun shone on his face and beads of sweat formed around his hairline.

I chewed on my lip as I reached for the next rock. It came loose in my hand.

I gasped as it fell; I'd put too much weight on it, moving one of my feet at the same time. My arms flailed like useless wings as my body tipped back.

Kaelan reacted in a split second as I fell, grabbing my arm. I swung hard into the side of the cliff and whimpered. He didn't let go. Sucking in air over and over, I glanced down at the jagged rocks under my feet.

'Chiara, look at me.' His voice was low, determined. 'I won't let you fall.'

I held his gaze as strongly as I held onto his arm. He grunted as he hoisted me up enough that I could climb onto the same ledge he was on.

'Are you okay?' he panted, glancing quickly over me.

I nodded, still gripping his arms with my shaking, sweaty hands. Suddenly, his body was pressed against mine. I breathed into his neck, my exhales shaky as I listened to his heart. His beats were mine, a lullaby that soothed.

'I will always protect you,' he whispered. 'I swear.'

I tucked my wet hair behind my ears and traced the remaining path with my eyes. It wasn't as steep and would begin to turn into more of a discernible path nearer to the top.

'Do you want to keep going?'

'Yes,' I said. 'I didn't come this far just to go back.'

I began again, more carefully this time, and by the time I got to the top, I'd gained my momentum back. I almost cried in relief, and at the beauty of the view. The ocean soared out from all directions, shimmering, magnificent and never-ending. I ran towards the edge of the cliff and smiled before turning back to face Kaelan.

'It's beautiful, look!'

But it wasn't the ocean he was looking at.

'What?' I asked, taking a step closer to him.

He smiled to himself. 'Nothing.'

'Tell me!' I cried, smacking his shoulder.

Something flashed in his eyes then, like fire. Kaelan grabbed my waist and swung me low so we were both suspended above the ground.

'I'll show you.'

He kissed me so deeply, he drew out my soul.

All of the water had dried off my body by the time we wandered towards the grasses and trees in search of shade. I bent down at one point to inspect a clump of tiny white flowers, so delicate they looked like stars. I debated taking some back for Marie – she loved the simpler ones the best. She said the simple things in life were always the most beautiful, and usually the most underappreciated. She made an effort, always, to appreciate them. I wanted to do the same.

'Here?' he asked as we came to the base of a slope that was

large enough to shade us.

We lay on the grass, cool and dry under my bare skin. I rested my hands by my head and looked at the sky. It was endless, an ocean made of air.

It was the kind of quiet that was sweet, filled with the whirring of grasshoppers and the flutter of butterfly wings. I looked at Kaelan. A shadow cast under his cheekbones, a deeper hue than the rest of his golden skin. His expression was soft as he watched the sky and even softer as he turned to rest his gaze on me.

'It reminds me of my home,' he said, his voice a little rough. 'In Greece.'

'Do you want to go back?'

'Of course. I haven't been there since my father died. And even then, I didn't go back to the village I grew up in. I didn't want to remember what happened to us. What he did to us.' Kaelan's eyes were sad as he gazed at me now. 'But I miss it.'

'When was the last time you talked to your father?'

Kaelan didn't answer for a while, then rolled onto his back and fixed his eyes on the sky.

'When I was eighteen.'

# CHAPTER 25

## KAELAN

### SIROS, GREECE – 1923

I swung open the door of the local tavern and went straight for the bar. It was only 11 a.m., but I wasn't surprised to see my father getting drunk with his vile friends. I came to a stop behind him and crossed my arms. His laugh was cruel and took me right back to when I was a small, helpless boy.

I wasn't so helpless now.

'Father.'

I spat the word out, clenching my fists to prevent myself from swinging them too soon. *Mamá* warned me not to fight.

His friends stopped talking and eyed me.

My father grunted, turning slowly so I caught sight of his mangled face. He looked perplexed to see me and I wondered if he would recognise me now. But then he started to laugh. I reeled back as the alcohol from his breath hit me.

'You show up here now, boy?' He looked over my body. 'What are you, eighteen?'

'My God! He's the spitting image of you, Dinos!' barked one of his friends.

'I didn't come to talk,' I announced. 'I want to be turned.'

His eyebrows shot up, but his surprise quickly shifted back to amusement.

'I'd be careful, Dinos. That boy looks like he's ready for a fight,' one of his more intelligent friends simpered.

'Bah! And I'll give it to him if that's what he is after!' My father stood, puffing out his chest.

Suddenly, I felt small again as he looked down on me with those cold, black eyes.

'Do you want to fight, son?'

'How dare you call me that!' I shouted, then spat at his feet.

His growl turned quickly into a leering grin, meant to show me he was untouchable.

'How is my wife?'

*Fuck it.*

I lunged for him, making contact with his face before two of his friends grabbed my arms and held me back. I struggled. I could smell his anger.

When he next spoke, it was in a quiet, bitter voice. 'Then I shall turn you now.'

I ignored his friends, keeping my eyes on him as he walked up to me. His breath was filthy, like him. There was cheering as he sank his teeth into my neck in a way that was more painful than it should've been.

'He screams like a girl!' one of them shouted amongst laughter.

During the excitement, the ruffians had loosened their grip. I gritted my teeth and kicked my father in the balls, then dodged past them all, throwing open the tavern door.

'Kaelan,' Dinos grunted, eyeing me in the doorway, 'I expect to see your brothers here soon. Two years, no more.'

# CHAPTER 26

## CHIARA

Kaelan's expression was hard as he chewed on his lip. Without thinking, I slipped my hand into his. He sighed heavily. I felt the weight that came with it, the weight of the burdens he had been carrying from far too young, for far too long.

Kaelan rolled onto his side to face me. 'He treated us like shit, Chiara.'

I pressed gently against the lines of his forehead, wishing more than anything that I could take his pain away.

'My *mamá* said she forgave him long ago.' He shook his head. 'I've never been good at forgiveness. Why should I forgive him anyway? He doesn't deserve it.'

'It might give you peace if you do. He is dead after all, Kaelan; he can't hurt you anymore.'

I remembered something Mr Becksworth had once said. I used to hate my foster parents for what they did to me and especially for what they didn't do. But one rainy afternoon, as I was helping Mr Becksworth stock the shelves while ranting about how awful they were, he stopped and looked me in the eye and told me that there is always a reason behind how people act. He said that I needed to learn to understand my parents instead of hating them.

I realised I'd been drawing circles in Kaelan's palm. 'People... do things for a reason. It's rarely personal. Maybe something bad happened to him that made him like that. Maybe his parents were abusive towards him, so abuse was his natural instinct.'

'You think too well of people. Some people are just bad, Chiara.'

I frowned. 'That's not true. I don't think anybody's born evil. I think they become it through the wrong experiences and dealing with life the wrong way.'

He regarded me for a moment. 'Maybe.'

Now that I was away from my foster parents and had talked about what happened with Karlie and Luna, it was easier to have relative peace towards how they'd treated me. I had never been the issue, I saw that now. It was just the kind of people they were.

We were silent for a little while. A question came to my mind, but it was so sensitive I wasn't sure if I should ask.

'Just say it.'

I looked at Kaelan in shock. 'How did—'

'I know you.' He smiled. 'Ask. Please.'

I let out a shaky breath. 'How did he die? Your father?' I squeezed his hand. 'Sorry, you don't have to answer.'

He took a deep breath as he looked at me. When he finally spoke, his voice was quiet.

'My father got into a fight with another vampire at a bar – in France, actually – and he killed the guy accidentally. My father didn't see the man's wife coming from behind until it was too late.' Kaelan looked down at our hands, still intertwined. 'I'm glad it happened. My *mamá* lived in fear that he would break in at night and kill her in her sleep. His death set her free.'

Honesty broke his face open, exposing someone raw and imperfect beneath.

I traced his cheekbones, then his jaw as he gazed into my eyes.

*I understand you.*

Later that evening, the sky was set on fire, burnt coral and crimson bursting out from the sun. It was set so low on the horizon it made the water look like melted light. We sat on the edge of the cliff once more, our legs dangling over it.

The story of his past lingered in my mind, even after we had changed the subject to something lighter. Maybe I'd been successful in forgiving my foster parents, but I didn't know how to forgive someone I'd never met, who'd abandoned me at birth and who was supposedly my mother. Someone I didn't understand.

I stared at the ocean. I'd always felt a connection to this land, because of the blood that ran through me, the blood that connected me to her, to my father. But all this time I'd been walking upon her native land, not once had I tried to find my mother. I wanted to. Of course, I did, but how could I? I didn't even have a name. Finding her was a lost cause, even before the obvious other concerns. What if she didn't want to be found? What if the reason she had abandoned me was because she didn't love me?

I dug my fingers into the dirt. I wondered if she'd ever been to this beach before, if she lived in the south or the north of France, or somewhere in between. I wondered if she'd want to meet me, or if she'd forgotten she ever had a daughter.

I leaned back on my palms. At least the ocean was beautiful, constant. That was the thing about nature; left alone, it wasn't affected by humans and human problems. The ocean didn't care if my life was messy, no more than the trees cared. They just kept on being. Somehow it made my problems seem smaller like they didn't really matter at all.

'What are you thinking?'

I glanced at Kaelan in surprise; I'd almost forgotten he was there.

'That I could live here – by the ocean,' I responded. It was the truth.

I felt a tightening of the small space between our two bodies.

'How in the hell did they get up there?' a voice sounding like Karlie called from somewhere behind us.

I looked at Kaelan with wide eyes and we both got up at the same time and ran towards the edge.

'What are you doing? It's dangerous!' I yelled.

Luna was down on the ground with Nico, watching Karlie and Rheo climb. They were about halfway up.

'Hmm. I think that's the path there, isn't it?' Luna mused, before starting on a side trail we hadn't seen.

'You're telling us this now?' Karlie cried. 'Rheo, get your hands off my ass.'

'What? I was helping you up.'

'Did we ruin your moment?' Karlie asked sheepishly once she got to the top.

Rheo doubled over and wheezed like an old man.

Kaelan scratched the back of his neck. 'Well—'

'You two have been up here way too long. Have you seen the time?' Karlie looped her arm through mine and carried me towards the edge Kaelan and I had been sitting on minutes before. 'We've been trying to give you space, but Rheo and Nico say it's too late to go home cause they're too chicken to drive in the dark.'

'We had a bad experience!' Rheo shouted.

Karlie whipped her head around. 'And what made you think you could eavesdrop, Rheo Demetrius Costas?'

'Damn, she hit you with the middle name!' Nico hollered.

Rheo looked like he wanted to jump off the cliff.

'Wait, so you guys aren't going home?' I asked the brothers. 'What are you gonna do? Sleep up here?'

Kaelan raised his eyebrows at Rheo and Nico, who exchanged a glance.

'Kaelan, do you remember that time—'

'I remember.'

'Right.' Rheo splayed his hands out. 'Well, see, I don't particularly fancy doing a repeat, do you, Nico?'

Nico surveyed the grassy landscape, smothered in the shadows of dusk. 'I'll take my chances.'

'Are we going home?' I whispered to Karlie as Luna joined us.

'I can't be asked to drive home in the dark,' Luna answered. 'It's over two hours away. I'll probably fall asleep.'

I stared at her. 'You, of all people, are willing to stay the night on top of a cliff? What was in your cereal this morning?'

'I bet it's 'cause of Nico,' Karlie hypothesised, pointing a slender finger in his direction in case he couldn't hear what we were talking about.

Luna snorted. 'Yeah, right. Come on. I wanna see the view properly.'

The three of us stood at the cliff's edge, looking out at the sunburnt sky as the waves lapped softly against the rocks below.

'It makes you wanna fly,' Karlie breathed.

I sighed.

When I was with them, my heart squeezed differently than when I was with him, but I liked it just the same. I closed my eyes and listened to the ocean and the silence.

Breathing.

'Let's light a fire,' Rheo proposed as the waning sun cast us all in shadow.

Karlie smacked his arm. 'You dumbass, you'll light the whole cliff on fire!'

'Yeah, Rheo, the grass is too dry for that,' Nico said, holding Luna's head in his lap.

'But what if there are hyenas?'

A laugh bubbled out of me and I rocked forward into Kaelan's arm. He chuckled softly, grabbing hold of me and burying his head into my neck.

The moon was full, gleaming through the darkened sky. I stared up at it for a long time. I thought there had been stars in Paris, but out here, they lit up the black as far as you could see. Tiny pinpricks. I rested my head on Kaelan's chest as I watched them. Everyone was talking in whispers. Karlie laughed at something Rheo said and his eyes shone so brightly I could see them in the dark. Luna and Nico were already out, curled in on one another. I smiled to myself and turned my gaze back to the stars.

'I know their stories,' Kaelan spoke suddenly, so low I could barely hear him.

'You do?'

'See that one?' he whispered, pointing. 'We used to call the end of that constellation "Dog's Tail".'

I smiled, tracing the lines between the lights.

'And that bright star at the end is the North Star.'

'Wow,' I breathed.

'Can I tell you the story?'

'Sure.'

'It starts with a sea nymph called Callisto, who was assaulted by Zeus, the King of the Gods. His wife Hera, the Queen of Heaven, was furious when she found out, but instead of blaming Zeus, she turned Callisto into a bear in her jealousy. Hera tried to trick the boy Callisto gave birth to, Zeus' son, into killing his own mother, but Callisto turned him into a bear to protect them both and cast herself and her baby into the sky. See that bigger constellation over there? That's Callisto. That small one is her son.'

'The little dipper and big dipper, right?'

I could feel him smile.

Something warm tingled in my chest. I leaned into him further, nestling my head against his heart. The beats were rhythmic and steady. He stroked my hair, his fingers careful like they always were with me.

I closed my eyes as he began to sing softly in Greek, his beautiful voice carrying the lullaby from his heart into mine.

# CHAPTER 27

Something warm was around me.

I opened my eyes to find Kaelan's arms holding me. We were all still lying there on top of the dusty cliff.

I relaxed into him.

My mind had been working on an idea last night when everyone was silent and I was left to my thoughts. The words had started coming after that, but none sounded right. I wanted to write them down, to figure out how to spill my emotions onto a page. Even if it was just my own eyes that would see them.

Peeling his hand off my stomach, I wriggled out of his grasp into a cluster of white flowers.

No one else was awake.

Kaelan was clinging to the bare earth now, his chest rising and falling. He looked so different when he slept... softer. His messy, dark hair hung over his eyes and I'd never realised how long his eyelashes were until then. Their tips brushed his honey skin. It made me want to sweep away his hair and kiss his closed lids gently.

Instead, I tore myself away and started to dig around in Luna's bag until I found Karlie's sketchbook and pencil. She'd made some drawings of the beach and the sea, Rheo smiling all goofy at her, and the three of us girls. It was a depiction of what she'd thought we must've looked like, watching the ocean at sunset on the edge of the cliff. Three shadows, their arms wrapped around each other, leaning their heads on one another. She must've drawn it by the torchlight from her phone. My heart tingled and I smiled as I found a blank sheet.

I climbed down the path to the shore, smelling the salt clinging to the cool morning air. I was just wearing the t-shirt and shorts Luna had brought up in my bag and I had goosebumps all over me. Walking to the middle of the beach, I plopped myself down in the sand and dug my feet in as far as I could, rubbing the grains on my legs to warm them up.

I'd written poems on and off before, but they always took me a long time to get right. Words were trickier than pictures; they didn't tend to flow out of me as easily. Somehow though, this poem was different, probably helped along by the intensity of my feelings.

I wrote one line after the other before reading the whole thing back and cringing. *Screw it, I just won't show him.*

I changed a line, one that revealed too much of my feelings. I scratched it out so hard I burst a hole through the paper.

What if he didn't feel the same way?

I blew out a breath, running my fingers through my hair.

'Crap.' I looked down at my hands, realising they were covered in sand, which was now in my hair.

'What are you doing?'

I shoved the poem into the sand, my heartbeat in my ears.

'Luna, don't scare me like that!'

She laughed and kneeled in the sand opposite me, tucking a black stand behind her ear.

'Is that for Kaelan?' She pointed at the poem, barely hidden.

I nodded, but she was already reaching for it.

'No! Give it back.'

'Oh, come on, Chiara. As long as it's not a steamy one.'

I blushed hard. I really would have died if I'd written anything like that.

Luna smiled as she began to read. 'This is beautiful,' she said, putting her hand on her heart.

I threw my head back and groaned. 'It's so cheesy, he'll hate it and I'll embarrass myself. I can't giv—'

'You can. He will absolutely love it, I promise.'

'But...' Why did my heart hurt so much?

'But what?'

I sighed and brought myself up to face her. 'Oh, Luna. I couldn't find a clearer way of spelling it out if I tried.'

'Sweetie.' She laid down the poem, taking my hands in hers. 'Kaelan loves you. Anyone with eyes can see that.'

My heart pounded ferociously against my chest as I searched for the lie in her gaze. Did he?

'Here.' She tore out the paper and flipped to a blank page. 'Let's rewrite it a bit neater so he can read it properly.'

After I was done, we left our clothes on the sand and ran straight into the sea, even though it was cooler than yesterday. I squealed as she kicked water at me.

'God, it's cold,' I gasped.

We held onto each other, laughing and shivering like crazy.

'Look!' Luna pointed a shaky finger towards the cliff. 'They're awake now.'

'It's about time,' I said.

Secretly, I hoped it was only Karlie. That way, we could drive home and I wouldn't have to give Kaelan the poem, along with my heart.

  Although he already had the latter.

# CHAPTER 28

## KAELAN

When I woke up, she was gone. I sat up and listened. Rheo snoring, the light wind, the water... her laugh.

Two women down below were splashing water at each other. I smiled. I couldn't take my eyes off her.

*Koúkla mou.*

She had the face of an angel, but it was one of the most deceiving things I'd ever seen. The stuff she made me feel... I ran a hand through my hair, a little stiff from sweat and the sea. Only one other person had ever come close to making me feel this way. Every time I thought of her, I wanted to throw up.

But maybe she wasn't like Tasha.

No, I knew she wasn't like Tasha. But even with that knowledge, it didn't mean she couldn't break me like Tasha had. Was it too soon? It had been five years since then; that was nothing. Tasha was the reason I'd held back all this time – as if it had made a difference. Chiara was like one of those siren mermaids; once you heard her call, you were fucked. Still, the scars Tasha had left didn't feel raw, not anymore.

I looked back at Chiara.

*What are you waiting for, a special invitation?*

She watched me as I came closer, her eyes roaming over my body like she already owned me.

She wasn't wrong.

Luna smiled like she knew something I didn't.

'Show him,' she whispered, before leaving us and walking back down the beach.

'Show me what?'

Chiara's lips were purple and she was shivering badly. I wrapped my arms around her, breathing in the scent of the sea on her skin.

'I wrote something for you,' she muttered shyly, looking up at me. Her skin was darker than usual from the sun, and it only made her green eyes brighter. She pressed a folded piece of paper into my hands. 'Read it alone.'

'But we're alone now.'

She gave me a look as if it were obvious. 'Just... without me there.'

'Morning!' Karlie called out, making her way towards us. 'Man, can we get outta here? My stomach is growlin' really loud.'

'I second that,' Rheo yelled, hot on her heels. 'Hey, Kaelan, how 'bout McDonald's? Kinda in the mood for some shitty frozen pancakes.'

I ignored them both, turning back to Chiara. She looked so small then, like she wanted to run away from me. She couldn't meet my gaze.

'What are you afraid of?' I asked, searching her face. I wanted to tell her it would be okay, whatever it was.

Chiara laughed weakly. 'So many things.'

I watched as their car drove off a short while later, the sun glinting on the metal. Nico and Rheo were hanging around the Bentley after throwing open every door.

'Either get over here,' Nico bellowed, 'or throw us the keys.'

'Give me a second, will you?'

I sat down on the sand, facing the ocean. I was used to being alone, but something about this beach made me feel lonely without her. My heart beat wildly as I opened the note, full of her beautiful sloping writing.

The second I started to read, I stopped breathing.

*Maybe it was the way you looked at me that first time.*
*Maybe it was the way you smiled,*
*the way your soft lips grazed my skin,*
*your warm breath tingling up my neck like a cry for the wild.*

*Maybe it was the way you saw things no one else looked for;*
*knew things no one else wanted to know.*
*I knew you the moment we met,*
*even though*
*you were wrapped in different skin.*

*As I look at you, I realise the*
*perfection*
*in the imperfection.*
*With your hands rough like tourmaline,*
*your smile bright like sunlight.*

*And as the tides move in and out,*
*as the sun rises and sets,*
*I see you look at me*
*and I smile as you smile, because*
*we both know that some things*
*never change.*

# Chapter 29

## Chiara

All the way home, Karlie snored loudly in the backseat.

I focused my gaze on a bridge running over the motorway in the distance, pressing my hands into my thighs. As if that would stop them from shaking.

*If Kaelan's in school tomorrow, I'll cry.*

I groaned, leaning my head against the seat. My intestines felt like they were wringing themselves out.

'Why did I give it to him again?'

'I told you, he'll love it,' Luna insisted.

I winced, looking back out the window. 'Then why do I want to crawl into a hole for a million years?'

'Chiara Beaufort, surely you wouldn't want to die over a bloody boy? He'd have to be blind and an idiot to not already know your feelings, and we both know that Kaelan is neither of those things.'

I didn't answer, folding my legs underneath me so I was practically in the foetal position. Her words were not helping. My skin was sticky from the salt, and I stank like sweat. I curled in on myself. I felt disgusting.

I didn't want to look at my reflection in the side mirror. I didn't want to see what Kaelan had seen when he'd looked at me this morning. He was beautiful no matter what; his looks were effortless, like everything he did. He and the salt and the breeze moulded into one another as if they were always crafted to co-exist.

I, on the other hand, was constantly pulling myself back together, scraping up the bits that seeped from under the box of "I'm doing well" I'd made for myself. The truth was that I wasn't even good at that. All I did was try and it was never enough.

It never had been.

When we got back, I sat on the shower floor and hummed to myself as the water ran down my skin. The drops were like hot rain, drumming out a steady beat as they landed.

I stopped humming abruptly.

It was the same tune Kaelan had sung to me last night.

That was the end of my shower. Quickly I stood up and turned it off, as if to get away from the memory as fast as possible. I sighed, running my wet hand over my wet face, before slumping against the wall.

I was still disgusting.

Kaelan was perfect. He was everything.

I was nothing but an inconvenience.

I put on a towel, crawled onto my bed and curled into the foetal position again. In the silence, I listened. The only sounds in the room were my shallow, quivering breaths as my body fought with me to suck in more air.

I really wasn't looking forward to school tomorrow.

'Go on without me. I'll be there in a sec,' I told the girls in the car park the next morning.

They'd had to physically drag me out of bed, and when they cornered me about it at breakfast, I said I felt sick. It was technically the truth, though I couldn't kid myself into thinking Luna didn't know exactly what the cause of my "illness" was.

While the other students walked past the bushes and down the stone path towards the school, I walked around to the other side and sat on the grassy field. I felt completely idiotic in this dress, something Karlie had forced me to wear that morning because it would "make me feel better". It was tighter and shorter than my usual attire, which in the morning hadn't seemed like that big of a deal, but now made me look like I was desperate.

*Maybe I can just walk home.*

I laughed at myself. The sky was a mocking shade of deep blue, with indigo clouds hanging hundreds of feet away. I longed to run across the field now, to run far, far away.

'I'll do what I can. Given what you've told me, it seems he requires closer inspection,' came a voice as glossy as the hair it was packaged with.

Viv.

I froze, peeking through the branches. My heart gave a sickening jolt.

Kaelan was with her.

I could smell him, smoky wood mixing with Viv's chemical perfume.

'Good. Let me know what you find.'

His voice was rough like he hadn't slept. That made two of us.

I held my breath as they walked past and prayed he hadn't noticed me. When I was sure they had gone, I stood, rolling my shoulders. What was I doing, sitting behind a damn bush? I ran my fingers through my uncombed hair, which now ran down to my hips.

Kaelan and Viv had probably gone in by now, along with most of the other students. I swung my drawstring bag over my back and walked towards the school, trying to calm my racing heart.

I had just entered the hallway when I heard Kaelan calling my name.

I turned, my eyes locked on his as he made his way towards me through the crowd. My nausea rose at the sight of him, my heart pounding in my ears. He looked good today, wearing a shirt that matched his eyes. It didn't help the panic trilling through my bones. I swallowed hard, hoping to choke it down.

'I waited for you,' he told me. 'I knew you were behind that bush.'

My hands found the wall. There was only a metre between us, but it helped. A lot.

'How? You couldn't see me from the path.'

He looked at me then, with so much warmth I couldn't bear to return his gaze.

'Did you think I would leave you like that?' he asked softly. 'After what you wrote?'

His eyes searched mine, but I knew all he would find were walls and a drowning girl behind them. Kaelan reached out and stroked my cheek gently, carefully. I felt my face crumple at the way he was looking at me.

'I'm sorry, I can't do this.' My voice was barely a whisper as I ducked away from him and ran down the hallway.

I pressed my knuckles to my forehead as I entered the library.

*What's wrong with me?*

I stayed in the library all morning, until Luna and Karlie found me at lunchtime. Luna had smuggled me some bread rolls from the dining hall and I nibbled at them, my appetite nearly gone.

'What's going on, Chiara?' Karlie asked. 'You skipped English and you've barely spoken the entire day.'

I stared at the carpet and pulled at my fingers.

'It's hard to explain. No one's ever looked at me like Kaelan does. It makes me want to hide.' I took in a breath as Luna put her head on my shoulder. 'I think he knows me better than anyone and that makes me feel see-through. I hate it. It's not like he's ever that vulnerable.' I buried my head in my hands. 'And now he has my stupid poem. He knows he has my heart.' My voice was barely a whisper. 'Imagine what he could do.'

Karlie lifted my head up. 'Chi-chi, it's pretty obvious he loves you.'

'That's what I said as well,' Luna nodded.

'But even if he does, what happens next?' My thoughts flitted to Viv. 'What if he gets bored of me? Cheats on me?'

'Why would he—'

'Because he's perfect and wonderful, and I'm just—' my breath caught in my throat, my eyes stinging with tears, 'me.'

Karlie stabbed her finger at me. 'Now, you listen here, Chiara. You are a beautiful, gorgeous goddess, queen bad bitch, you hear me? Nobody can take that away from you.'

I laughed a little, wiping my nose.

'She's right,' Luna nodded. 'And, honestly, Kaelan's probably wondering how he got so lucky in the first place.'

'Let that sink in. You can't let stuff like this pass you by just 'cause you're scared it won't work out. Like, yes, hearts get broken, but how will you know how much you can love if you don't even try?'

I chewed on my lip and played with the lace on my trainer. 'I guess I'm scared there will be no one better than him. No one gets me like he does. That's gotta be one in a million.'

Luna took my hand. 'Sweetie, there's always another guy who will understand you. What's meant to be is meant to be. If you and Kaelan do work out, that's great, but if you don't, it was just a learning experience. And, one day, sometime later, you'll meet someone who is right for you.'

We were silent for a moment as I digested this information.

Finally, I looked up and smiled. 'Thank you,' I said to both of them, then rolled my eyes with a small laugh. 'You guys are like my therapists.'

'We'll always be here for you,' Luna informed me, 'until we're old and grey.'

My heart felt full. When I was with them, it was like nothing else in the world mattered, and I knew the three of us could be anywhere at all and I'd still feel at home.

Unfortunately, that feeling didn't extend to Chemistry.

The thought of Mr Kalip's class alone dropped a weight in my stomach. Still, a silent hour next to Kaelan was better than another forty minutes of after-school detention.

I shuddered and pushed open the sticky wooden door.

Kaelan wasn't sitting in the chair next to mine. My stomach knotted as I watched him get out his stuff in his normal seat. Had I hurt him? He probably thought I regretted everything that'd happened. I sat down next to Willow, who was drawing some intricate-looking skulls on her notes from the last lesson.

*Maybe he realised I'm not worth it after all.*

I rested my elbow on the desk and my head in my hand, grabbing a fistful of hair so tightly it hurt. It distracted me from the other kind of pain I was feeling.

Kalip droned on and on, but I successfully managed to block Kaelan out for the entire lesson, shuffling out of the classroom along with everyone else. I was about to make my way back to the library and—

A strong arm wound around my waist, pulling me to the side. I opened my mouth to retort, then abruptly closed it when I saw it was Kaelan.

'Don't do that again,' I grumbled.

He grinned, eyes glittering. Though the noise from the crowd in the hall was like thunder in my ears, all I could hear was the unnaturally fast beat of his heart and the weight of his arm still around my waist.

I swallowed hard and raised my voice. 'I need to talk to you.'

Kaelan looked down at me as though he could read my soul. But he nodded anyway and glanced across the hallway.

'I know a place.'

'The cleaning cupboard, really?' I muttered as I stepped inside. The room was tiny, filled with buckets and mops.

'Think of any better places, doll?' he winked, closing the door behind him.

The air was thick and heavy, and it didn't help that he was standing so close to me. Not that I could back up. The small lightbulb above his head cast a glow on his skin as he leaned against the door, watching me with a gleam in his beautiful blue eyes.

He broke the quiet first. 'You don't have to explain yourself.'

'But I want to.' I held his gaze for a moment before staring decidedly at his shoes, light trainers that drew no attention from the rest of him. 'All my life,' I started, but my throat caught and messed up the words. I coughed and glanced up at him. 'All my life, the people who should have been there for me weren't. My foster parents didn't care about me and the people who did... I was such a burden.' I dug my fingers into my arm as the pain from the memory welled up. 'I was too emotional for them to deal with. And I just...' I sighed exasperatedly, feeling the tears start to come back.

'Chiara,' he whispered, suddenly even closer.

I couldn't hold them back any longer. He looked pained as he wiped them away, but all that did was make them come down faster.

'I'm sorry,' I mumbled

He wrapped his arms around me, his breathing shallow, stressed.

I didn't understand him at all, why he was still here and why he didn't care that his shirt was getting wet. But he made me feel safe enough to cry completely. I never let myself cry like this. It felt good to release the ache in my heart, so good I realised I must have been withholding a necessity from myself all this time.

Kaelan pressed his lips into my hair. It was greasy and knotty, but he didn't seem to care about that. He leaned his cheek against my temple, still holding me. And though my heart still ached, I knew that somehow, it would be alright.

'Chiara?' he breathed after some time had passed. 'I love you.'

My eyes flung open.

I lifted my head, forcing myself to look at him. He held my gaze. His expression was serious.

'I love you too,' I whispered back.

He grinned and pulled a strand of hair behind my ear, his touch gentle and firm, like always. His expression sobered as his gaze dropped to my lips before he glanced back at my eyes to make sure. But this time, I didn't wait. I pulled his face towards mine, teasing his mouth open gently. I felt him smile as I took control, weaving my hands through his hair as my tongue slid against his. Our kiss was salty and warm, new and familiar all at once. He ran his teeth lightly across my bottom lip, tugging on it slightly.

Eventually, he left the terrain of my mouth and ventured elsewhere. He brushed away the hair from my left shoulder and planted his lips on my bare skin. I closed my eyes and breathed as he drew a trail of kisses up my neck, to my jaw, before finally planting a teasing one right next to my lips.

It made me smile. If I thought he was intoxicating before, it was nothing compared to now. I breathed him in fully, kissing him deeply as if taking a long, heady drink. I still wanted more. I pushed him up against the door as our breaths grew shallower, our mouths moving like the push and pull of the ocean; syncopated. Rhythmic.

Suddenly the door we were leaning on swung open. Kaelan lost his balance and fell, pulling me along with him. I landed on top of him.

'If you wanted to take it a step further, you should've just asked,' he smirked, breathless.

'What are you kids doing here, eh?'

I looked up to find a bald man with furry white eyebrows

staring down at us.

Kaelan sat up and ran a hand through his wild hair, flashing a wink at me. I bit my lip.

'Back to lessons with you two.'

Kaelan grabbed my hand and pulled me along towards the hallway. I smiled.

He was my medicine.

# CHAPTER 30

## KAELAN

I liked the view from up here. Even at 2 a.m, it was where I came to think. The row of stupidly perfect houses beneath me was dark, like the sky. Living here was nice, but Paris was nothing compared to our village back home. It was like this hole was in me; my brothers and I were on the run, living like we were being chased. Every few years, we moved someplace else. I was tired of this life.

I squatted, drawing a line in the dust.

It didn't matter where we lived – hell, we'd spent time in some of the most beautiful places on Earth. I would never be satisfied until I was back on Greek soil, feeling the sun and listening to *Mamá's* laughter.

I stayed crouched, staring into the darkness. I could go back if I wanted to. I would go back now, but something was holding me here. Someone.

After what had been said in that cupboard, I felt like I owed her the truth. I needed to tell her, today.

I stayed on the roof for hours, going over the scenario from every possible angle: where I'd do it, what I'd say and what her reaction would look like. At one point, I thought, fuck it, I won't tell her at all.

But she deserved to know everything.

Driving to school, I blocked out the sound of my brothers bickering in the back. All I could think about was what I needed to tell her. *What if I ruin what we have?* I thought back to yesterday, in the cleaning cupboard, when her lips were on mine, when she'd pulled me closer like she wanted me really badly.

I ran a hand through my hair. She made me insatiable. Every time we kissed, it was like it wasn't enough, only something to tide me over until the next time.

Chemistry was torture.

Sitting beside her again, I couldn't focus. We both had a free period next, and I was counting down the minutes until I'd have to tell her.

I bit my lip and glanced quickly at Chiara. She'd opened up to me. It was only fair I did the same, but the last person I opened up to had fucked me over.

Chiara was doodling in her notebook, apparently having given up listening to Kalip ramble. I nudged her gently and she shot up, glancing over at me questioningly.

I tried not to smile. 'Pay attention to the lesson,' I whispered.

Her eyes were on mine, and I couldn't look away. There was a genuineness about her that made me feel like I could trust her.

'Miss Beaufort!'

*Shit.*

I whipped my head to the front. 'Chiara was just asking me to clarify something, sir. She didn't cover this topic last year.

Kalip's cold eyes assessed me doubtfully. 'Well, Mr Costas, perhaps you can encourage her to ask me for assistance next time.' His gaze landed on Chiara. 'As for you, Miss Beaufort, we will have to arrange a one to one after-school tutoring session this Friday. Exams are coming up; we can't have you struggling, now can we.'

I clenched my fists. Maybe he'd look less like a lizard if I gave him a facial rearrangement.

Chiara wasn't the same for the rest of the lesson. I kept sneaking glances at her; it was the only thing that made me calm down. Her heart was beating unevenly, faster than it should have been. I wanted to hold her, and I wanted to kill Kalip.

It was clear from the start that he'd always had something against her. He was a bastard, but I reckoned there was something else going on. Viviana had told me previously that she'd had a bad feeling about him. I trusted her instincts; they were never wrong. If there was some reason for his behaviour, she would find out.

At the end of the lesson, I packed up slowly so Chiara wouldn't be alone with him. I slipped my hand in hers. It was damp.

'Kaelan, I don't want to go,' she whispered once we were out in the hallway.

'I know.'

'He'll get me expelled if I don't.'

'I know.'

We were silent for a moment while everyone else around us was loud. Her hand was still in mine, fitting so well it was like it was always supposed to be there. I glanced at her, but she was staring up at the window, watching the blackbirds outside.

'Hey,' I said softly, 'it's going to be okay.'

She looked at me. 'That's what I keep telling myself.'

'I won't leave you alone with him. I'll stay with you, and if he doesn't let me come into the classroom then I'll stand outside the door and wait for you, okay?

She buried her face into my chest and I held her tightly. 'Thank you, Kaelan.'

I took a deep breath. It was now or never. 'I have to tell you something.'

Taking her hand, I led her over to a bench by the old rowan tree. The summer air was warm and the courtyard was empty. Chiara leaned against the tree and regarded me, her dark curls framing her face.

I cleared my throat. 'Do you know what a "mate" is?'

She tilted her head, waiting for me to explain.

'Every vampire has one, and only one. Some wait their entire lifetimes to find them.' I looked down at the bench beside her. 'It happens when two souls make a contract in the other realm, so when they incarnate into their physical bodies in this realm, they eventually find each other so they can spend their lives together,' I glanced back up at her, 'in a romantic sense. It's like fate.'

She squinted.

I shifted so I faced her more. 'You know it the moment you meet them. They feel familiar, even though you've never seen them before. I thought you might have known because of one of the lines you wrote in your poem: "I knew you the moment we met, even though you were wrapped in a different skin".'

She blushed, trying to hide her face behind her hair. I laughed softly, pushing it aside so I could see those eyes. She seemed to be nervous like I was. It made me feel better about this whole thing.

'You're my mate, Chiara. I know that now. Sometimes it's hard to know for sure when you first meet them, and I had a more difficult time than most because...' I looked down at my hands, swallowing the lump in my throat. '... because I thought I'd met her before.'

After a moment of silence, I forced myself to look at Chiara. What I saw in her eyes surprised me, but then again, it usually did. In them I saw a wide-open space; not judging, not on guard, just open.

'Do you want me to tell you the story?'

She nodded, taking my hand.

I blew out a breath as I watched the leaves of the tree, struggling to word it now that I was telling her for real.

'Her name was Tasha,' I said finally. 'We were in Australia at the time, Melbourne, and the first time I saw her I knew she was someone special. I thought I had it all under control. But I was wrong. All it took was a few months and she had me wrapped around her pinky finger.' I laughed bitterly. 'I was completely head-over-heels for her. Blind. I never even noticed until it was right in front of me.'

'I went out with my brothers to a bar one night, and Rheo looked around and said "hey, isn't that Tasha?". I turned and, sure enough, it was her, kissing some guy I'd never even seen. I got angry. I pulled the guy away from her and started punching him over and over. She was begging me to stop.' I paused. 'After that, there was nothing I could do to save our relationship.'

*'We can work this out! I swear I'll do anything – I'll be better, I'll spend more time with you.' I grabbed her hands, lowering my*

voice. '*Just tell me how to fix it. Please.*'

Tasha sighed. When she looked up at me, something in me broke.

'*Kaelan, there's nothing you can do to fix us. I led you on; it was wrong and I'm sorry.*'

I stared at her in disbelief.

Tasha ran a hand through her wavy blonde hair. '*Look, I don't want to hurt you, okay? I know I should have cut things off a long time ago, but I kept convincing myself that I would learn to love you. I'm sorry, but I just can't bring myself to feel the same way you do. I realised what I truly wanted was to find someone else.*'

My chest felt like it was being ripped open. '*Someone else.*' I swallowed hard.

She said it like it was no big deal. Like it hadn't just turned my entire existence upside-down. Like she didn't give a shit about my feelings.

I shook my head, failing to compute. '*No, that doesn't make any sense...*'

'*Kaelan—*'

I spread my arms wide. '*You moved in with me, Tasha!*'

I couldn't believe it. I didn't want to. The woman I loved, from whom I had no secrets, who I'd taken the time to get to know every single fucking detail about, down to the beauty marks on her body, might as well have been a stranger.

'*You said you loved me,*' I whispered.

The apology in her eyes told me everything I needed to know. I put my head in my hands. Where was yesterday morning, when I was so blissfully ignorant?

'*Kaelan,*' she said softly.

I felt her hand on the nape of my neck.

*'Get out,' I choked out, my voice thick with oncoming tears.*
*'I'm sorry—'*
*'Get out!' I screamed. 'Get out, please, just get out!'*


Chiara looked like she was about to cry.

I chewed on my lip. 'Looking back, it was so obvious. It was all wrong from the beginning, but I was desperate to find my mate. I was looking for her everywhere. That desperation messed with my better judgement, and somewhere down the line, I convinced myself Tasha was my mate when she wasn't.' I looked down at my hands.

'You're not over her, are you?'

I paused. 'I think I'm over her as a person, but it's taking me a while to get over what happened.' I looked up at Chiara. 'You've helped without knowing it. A lot, actually.'

She looked like a fallen angel, her hair surrounding her like a dark halo. I brushed it away from her face as carefully as I could. She caught my fingers in her shaking ones and brought them to her soft lips.

'Chiara,' I breathed. 'I meant every word—'

'I know.'

'I love you so much.'

She kissed my fingers, then let them go.

'How do you know I'm your mate? You were so convinced with Tasha and—'

I shook my head. 'Being with you... it's the opposite to what it felt like with her. I know what my mate feels like because I know what she doesn't feel like. I don't have to put on a show for you.' I smiled. 'I love that.'

The look in her eyes switched now, glinting mischievously.

'Are you saying you want to spend eternity with me, Kaelan Costas?'

I trailed my thumb down her smooth cheek and traced her lips. The answer to the question I'd always thought about was on the tip of my tongue. It came easier than I had expected.

'Yes.'

# CHAPTER 31

## CHIARA

When Karlie, Luna and I returned to the flat that evening, Karlie dragged us into her room and belly-flopped onto her bed.

'Ugh, I'm so done with men,' she moaned into her pillow.

Luna and I sat on the bed next to her and wrapped our arms around her.

'Did something happen with Rheo?' Luna asked, once we'd let go.

Karlie sat up and pushed her braids out of her face. 'I ended it.'

'What?' I spluttered. 'I thought it was going well between you two?'

Karlie shook her head, leaning it on my shoulder. 'It was all so messy. One minute he'd talk about being with me forever, and the next he'd go all distant. He's got a lot of shit he needs to sort out, I mean, I can't be fixing all his daddy issues twenty-four-seven. And don't even get me started on his ex.' Karlie rolled her eyes. 'This girl was like his true love or something. He still thinks about what could've happened. I told him if he wasn't ready to be in a relationship, he should've put on his big boy pants and stayed away from me. He was all "but I tried". Please.'

I remembered Kaelan telling me about Rheo's first love. She was his best friend growing up, and as they got older, that friendship evolved into romance. Kaelan told me that most people in his village came from a long ancestry of vampires and it was one of the few pockets left in Greece of its kind. The girl didn't want to be turned at eighteen as was custom; her parents viewed it as a curse and brought her up to believe she should protect her humanity. She made a pact with Rheo that they would both stay human; that they would grow old and be together. But days before Rheo's eighteenth birthday, Dinos, his father, returned to the island. Kaelan was long gone by then, so it was just the twins and their mother. Dinos broke in during the dead of night, clamped his hand over Rheo's mouth to stop Nico from waking, and turned him. Nico was next.

Rheo never got over it.

'Do you love him?' Luna asked softly.

Karlie's face fell. 'That's the worst part,' she whispered. 'I fall in love too easily. Always with the wrong people.' Karlie rested her cheek on the back of her hand. 'I don't think he's good for me. Just like I'm not good for him.'

'You're not what each other needs,' I said.

'Exactly. He needs somebody willing to listen to him, somebody with much more patience than I've got. What I need is a man who's got his life together.'

I sighed. 'I'm so sorry, Karlie. You wouldn't be in this situation if they weren't brothers.'

'Nah, it's cool. It's my fault for catching feelings.'

'But it's not like you could have ever helped that.'

'Yeah, well, it worked out for you and Luna.'

Luna blushed, bowing her head. Her relationship with Nico wasn't exactly a secret, but she didn't really talk about it either.

'You'll find the right guy for you someday.' I patted her knee. 'Here, let's do some painting. Maybe it will help take your mind off things.'

What painting actually did was help take *my* mind off things. I wasn't sure exactly how I felt about Tasha, but I didn't like the idea of him being so head-over-heels for anyone else. It made me feel less significant, like one day I could be just another one of his stories for his next "mate".

The thought made me feel sick.

If he had been so sure at first that Tasha was his mate and then so sure she *wasn't*, what was stopping him from realising that I wasn't either? How was I supposed to know if he was mine or if someone else was?

I swiped my paintbrush across the top of the canvas, frustrated. I had never felt this deeply about anyone, but that didn't mean I was ready to spend the rest of my life with him. Maybe for Kaelan it was different; he'd already lived so long after all. But I was still somewhat shocked that he claimed to have chosen me as his life partner.

It made me wonder, was he serious?

I stepped back from my painting and ran my eyes over it. There was a girl with light olive skin and waist-length waves. Her bare feet were tangled in thorny vines, but her face was pointed towards the sky. Her arms were wings.

'She looks like you,' Luna said.

Karlie rested her chin on my shoulder. 'She's trapped.'

I twisted my mouth, drawing a little circle in the air with my paintbrush.

'She always is.'

Butterflies ripped at the insides of my stomach as Kaelan and I made our way to Kalip's classroom. It was Friday evening, and the rest of our year had just gone on study leave. I gripped Kaelan's hand tighter as I thought of Kalip's cold grey eyes, his mouth curved upwards in a way that made my flesh crawl. I hated him.

We came to a stop in front of the classroom door.

'Are you sure you don't want me to go in with you?' Kaelan asked.

I took a deep breath. 'I'll be fine. I don't want him to send you home.'

He pulled me in to kiss my forehead. 'I'll be waiting here.'

'Sorry to keep you in on the last day, Miss Beaufort,' Kalip simpered from behind his desk as I entered.

I dug my fingernails into my palm so hard I almost drew blood. The heat in the classroom was stifling, with the sun beating ceaselessly through the windows.

He motioned for me to take a seat, suddenly feigning incredible interest in the pieces of paper lying on his desk. I wondered when he was going to start giving me revision strategies on the topic we'd covered. I kept quiet as he continued to ignore me. Sitting in silence would probably be better than a one-to-one lesson filled with his chastising remarks.

I wanted to look out of the window, but the sun beamed

down in rays so strong it was easier to look away. I shut my eyes.

In the darkness, I began to imagine what life might be like in the future with Kaelan in it. I imagined him taking me to all his favourite places, telling me stories from each one. Maybe we would go to Greece, and I could finally meet the mother he'd talked so fondly of.

My skin prickled and I snapped my eyes open. Mr Kalip had been watching me, something like hunger dominant on his face.

'Chiara,' his low voice rumbled. 'Mm, what to do with you.'

I froze. I wanted to scream.

He stood and took a few steps in my direction. My entire body was on fire. But I couldn't will it to move.

'You know, I've been watching you for a long time now.'

Something was wrong. My muscles were leaden and no matter how hard I strained, I could not move a single inch.

I tried to scream for help, but it came out as a throaty whisper. I thought of Kaelan waiting in the hall. He'd have no way of knowing what was going on unless he came inside, and I'd told him not to. Tears stung my eyes as Kalip sat upon my desk and leaned in, so close his musty breath was the only air I could inhale.

I trembled in terror as he rested his mouth against my ear, inhaling deeply against my skin.

'You're a very pretty girl, Chiara,' he murmured, retreating enough to run his long fingers down my cheek.

Tears were streaming down my face hot and thick.

'Get off me,' I choked out.

'It's a shame that I can't do much more than look at you.' His eyes trailed down to my lips. 'Though I suppose they'd never know.'

I summoned all the strength I had and screamed.

Kalip laughed. 'There's no need to worry your pretty little head. We're going to have so much fun together.'

Before his words could sink in properly, something dragged Kalip off the desk and slammed him into the ground. I blinked my bleary eyes, finally able to breathe as Kaelan punched him. The spell Kalip had put over me was broken and I stood, wiping my mouth with shaking fingers.

'Viviana's coming,' Kaelan said to me through gritted teeth, pinning Kalip down. 'She was in the library, she'll be here soon.'

Kalip's eyes locked on mine and he smiled. His mouth was full of blood.

Kaelan shoved down his head and choked him. 'Don't fucking look at her.'

I stood rooted to the spot, fear paralysing my body. Viv came running in and joined Kaelan in holding Kalip down.

'This... is only the beginning,' Kalip managed to say. 'I'll see you soon, little bird.'

Then he was gone.

I stared in horror at the place where his body had been milliseconds before. Kaelan and Viv looked at each other.

Neither seemed surprised.

'What do you think he is?' Kaelan asked her.

Viv wiped her hands and stood. 'An illusionist. Perhaps some other creature that plays tricks on the mind, but obviously not human.'

I stared at her. 'What do you mean "not human"?'

The corner of her lip curved up. 'Did you really think vampires were the only ones?'

I was silent, trembling as I stared at the place Kalip had been.

An illusionist.

Viv turned back to Kaelan. 'You should take her home. He can't hurt her there.'

I felt his hand close around mine. He started to gently pull me away, but my legs wouldn't move. Fear continued to course through my veins. Kaelan lifted me, one arm sliding under my legs, the other around my back. He carried me to the car and put me down in the passenger seat. I could feel his warm gaze on me, but I couldn't bring myself to meet it.

Instead, I closed my eyes. It was a mistake. In the dark behind my lids, Kalip was there and I couldn't move. His hands were on me and I couldn't scream. He disappeared into thin air and I was scared he could appear anywhere.

Like in this car. Right now.

I jerked up in a panic and Kaelan's arms were around me in seconds. He lifted me again, then sat himself down in the passenger seat with me in his lap. He shut the door.

Kaelan stroked my hair as I cried, my body shaking against his.

'He can't hurt you anymore. You're safe, okay?'

I sucked in breath after breath, trying to soothe my racing heart. 'Y-you don't know that. What if I'm sleeping and—'

'Koúkla mou.' Kaelan nestled his face into my neck. 'He won't, I promise. I won't let him touch you again.'

My breathing began to slow. He pulled his head back to look at me and his gaze was steady, calm.

'Kalip is an illusionist. He can't actually teleport, he just manipulates your senses to make it look or feel like he can. He can't just appear out of thin air.'

Kaelan smoothed the crease between my eyebrows and planted a kiss on my forehead, squeezing me again.

'Do you wanna stay over tonight?' he whispered into my hair.

I nodded.

I'd feel safer with him than alone in my own bed.

The sound of running water filled the room as I rifled through his clothes. He'd gone to take a shower, but told me to borrow a shirt to sleep in. Slipping on the largest one I could find, I was about to shut the drawer when I saw something nestled between the fabric. I frowned and pulled it out, tracing my fingers across the woven leather that bound the creamy pages together. A photo album. It was only slightly bigger than my hand, and when I opened it, I found a photograph of a woman, suntanned and deeply lined, sitting on a stool. Her wide lips were tilted upwards towards the camera.

I looked over the photo in detail, wondering who the woman was. I didn't hear when the water stopped or when Kaelan opened the door. I only heard the breath he drew in when he saw me.

I gestured to the photograph. 'She's beautiful,' I said softly, glancing at him.

Only then did I realise he was only wearing joggers. I suddenly felt the urge to abandon the album, run my hands through his messy hair and plant kisses along his chest. Something in his eyes made it hard for me to look away.

He walked over to me, taking the album from my hands. 'My *mamá*. I want you to meet her, *koúkla mou*. We'll do it this summer. I want you to see my home.'

'Oh yeah?'

He grinned. 'Yeah.'

'I would love to see where you grew up. I imagine it will be one of the most beautiful places I've ever seen.'

He looked at me with the kind of intensity I would've shied away from a week ago. But at that moment, I didn't. In the space it took for me to suck in a breath, his lips were on mine.

He lifted me up and I wrapped my bare legs around his torso, warm skin on cool skin, never breaking our kiss. He laid me down on the bed and his hands were gentle as they explored my body. His fingers caught the bottom of the shirt I was wearing, and I nodded when he looked at me in question. He pulled it slowly over my head, his eyes travelling across my bare skin as it was exposed. His lips were on mine again, our warm bodies moving against each other. He sucked on the dip in my neck, making me moan, before kissing his way down my body, lingering on my breasts, my stomach, lower. My lips parted as he pulled down my underwear and pressed his hot mouth to my centre, my hips tilting upwards involuntarily.

Pleasure came rhythmically, sweetly, building up within me as he explored with his tongue, making me breathe faster until what felt like an explosion of pleasure erupted inside me. I was shuddering as he raised his head to look at me, grinning wickedly.

At that moment, I truly felt like a goddess.

We lay in bed holding each other afterwards and I stroked his hair in the comfortable silence. I was tired, but too scared to close my eyes. I knew Kalip would haunt my dreams.

'Kaelan?' I whispered. A gentle glow shrouded the room, falling upon his golden skin. I traced his jaw lightly, moving to the edges of his lips. 'Can you tell me about the photos in your album?'

I felt them curve upwards. 'Like what?'

He smiled softly, groaning as he stretched and rolled out of bed, returning with the album.

He propped up on his pillows and I curled into him, pointing at a photograph on the second page. Rheo was sitting on Kaelan's shoulders as they splashed in the ocean, and a boy I'd never seen was carrying Nico.

'My *mamá* took this one. That's a boy from our village – our friend. I never saw him after that; this was right before I got turned.' Kaelan laughed. 'Look at my brothers. They're only sixteen here.'

'What? Let me see.' I shoved my face in closer. 'Wow. You look pretty young too. Even though you haven't actually aged.'

'So, you're saying I look old now?'

I laughed at him. 'Definitely, Grandpa.'

'Grandpa?' Kaelan recoiled. 'You think a grandpa could kiss you like I just did?'

I coughed, blushing hard and peering back at the photo to distract myself. A thought came into my head.

'How come Rheo can be so immature when he's, like, a hundred years old? It makes no sense.'

Kaelan laughed. 'Actually, it kind of does make sense if you think about it. The brain changes because of experience, but in a way, ours are basically frozen as the brain of an eighteen-year-old. It can still change, obviously, but it doesn't develop or mature like a human brain.'

I considered this, looking back down at the photograph, wondering if the way I'd see the world would change, or if I'd always feel trapped. I glanced to the side and met Kaelan's eyes. We stared into one another, time stretching.

Though, I didn't think I could be trapped in a world where he existed.

We looked through a few more photographs before turning off the bedside lamp, and to my surprise, I slept deeply until morning.

Kaelan's arms were around me, sure and strong. I nestled into him deeper, breathing in the smell of his warm skin. I couldn't imagine being with anyone else, not when he felt akin to the air I breathed or when loving him was an intrinsic part of me, something woven into my soul.

In the days that followed, study leave began. My fear of Mr Kalip slowly eased between long hours of studying and being held in Kaelan's arms. Revising for Chemistry wasn't easy though, and sometimes I would freeze and space out, but in those moments, Kaelan was always there, or Luna, or Karlie, and they would help talk me through it.

The girls and I ended up spending more time at the Costas' house, studying during our days and hanging out in the evenings to relax. Though I liked the cosiness of Luna's flat, I found something equal in the spaciousness of their house. It was the way the air hung in the open rooms, the sound of laughter that was always in my ears.

The way I was never alone.

Though Karlie and Rheo studied in the dining room with

the rest of us, it was as if an invisible wall divided them. Neither of them talked about it. Nobody talked about it. I caught them glancing at one another sometimes and then looking away so fast it was as if nothing had happened.

One day they were forced to sit next to each other at the table and the entire room held its breath to see what would happen. Neither of them acknowledged it until we struck up a conversation, and that's when the passive-aggressive comments started. It escalated until they practically shouted at each other through gritted teeth, with Rheo clenching his fist on the table until it shone white.

I walked out of the room.

That was the day I told Karlie to talk to him, for real this time. What was the point of the rest of us having to walk on eggshells, checking our tongues so we didn't say something that triggered one or both of them?

Karlie was silent for a long time. And Karlie was never silent. Finally, she agreed. I came home from the garden centre the next day to the symphony of their jarring voices bouncing off the walls, hurling accusations at one another.

'I just don't understand what you want from me!' Karlie cried. 'I'd rather you act like a man and tell me how you really feel.'

'How I really feel? Babe, I've *told* you how I feel, I just need a little time to—'

'Don't you go calling me *babe* when we ain't together. Listen up, 'cause I'll only tell you this once: I do not give a damn about your ex-girlfriend, daddy issues or any of your other problems. I'm not your mummy or your therapist or a rubbish bin you can dump all your shit into, and I will not be sticking around here anymore, you can count on that.' Her voice was hot as she added, 'I'm done with you.'

The room was silent for a long time. When Rheo next spoke, it was the bitterest thing I'd ever heard come out of his mouth.

'Well, if that's all, then kindly get the fuck out of my house.'

Karlie appeared in the kitchen then, barely acknowledging me as she stormed past, her face flushed and springing with tears.

'Karlie!' I shouted, following her out of the door.

'Leave me alone!' she screamed back as she ran down the road.

I sprinted to catch up with her, tugging on her arm to get her to stop. We were both panting, the sun beating down on us relentlessly.

'Just leave me alone, Chiara, please,' Karlie said once she'd caught her breath.

'I won't. You're not okay.'

She rolled her eyes, wiping away a tear with the whole palm of her hand. 'I don't need your help. Miss Look-at-me-and-my-perfect-boyfriend.'

I winced. 'Karlie listen – you're my best friend, okay? I want to be there for you, just like you are for me. Please, let me be.'

I watched her expression morph from anger into surrender as her face crumpled.

'I don't know what to do,' she sobbed.

I hugged her and didn't say a word. I'd never seen Karlie cry like this before.

It was horrible.

We were quiet for a long time, standing there in the middle of the road. The only noise was the occasional obnoxious whirring of somebody's lawnmower and the murmur of parties gathered in back gardens.

Karlie cried until she choked, her tears soaking into my hair and running down my back. But, still, I didn't let go, remembering all the times she'd held me.

'I'm sorry,' she said finally. 'Rheo just gets on my nerves so badly, Chi-chi. He doesn't care about me.' Her voice was muffled against my shoulder. 'Sometimes, I think the only people that do care about me are Luna and you.'

'Karlie, that's not true!' I frowned. 'Rheo does care about you, and so do your parents, and Luna's parents. Even Nico and Kaelan.'

Karlie scoffed and pulled away. 'My parents don't care. Why do you think I'm living with Luna? They were always too busy with their jobs to take care of me.'

She looked at the ground, scuffing her shoe on the tarmac.

'If they knew you at all, they would love you,' I said. 'It would be hard not to.'

Karlie glanced up at me and smiled, then flung herself into my arms.

# Chapter 32

## Kaelan

I returned home to find Rheo slumped in a chair, his head in his hands. Luna and Chiara were standing in the kitchen, taking turns yelling at him. I wasn't really sure what I'd walked in on, but I decided not to intervene.

'Well, what did you expect?' Chiara was saying. 'She's done giving you third and fourth chances.'

Luna nodded in agreement. 'Honestly, Rheo, what were you even thinking? How could you play with her emotions like that – does she not matter at all to you?'

At this, Chiara fixed her gaze on him and flung back her hair. I cast a pitying look at Rheo, who already looked ready to cry for *Mamá*.

'He wasn't thinking, I can tell you that. I swear to God, Rheo, do you even know what Karlie's feeling right now?'

Chiara's eyes were lit up with passion. I couldn't look away.

'You made her *cry*, Rheo, a lot.'

My brother made a strangled noise as if the fact physically hurt him. Come to think of it, I couldn't remember having seen Karlie cry before.

'I—' Rheo started, but Luna held up her hand.

'Don't speak.'

I'd have actually preferred it if he did because the silence was terrifying. I then shifted my gaze to Nico in the background, who was giggling into a pillow.

I choked on a laugh.

'Kaelan!' Chiara cried.

I held up my hands. 'I'm sorry! Hey – fuck you, Nico!'

Nico grinned, then flipped me off.

Luna sighed so loudly that the neighbours probably heard it. 'I get the impression that you three aren't taking this very seriously.' She cocked her head. 'Well, maybe Rheo is.'

I looked at my brother, his face tired and defeated. Still haunted by his past, he lived in peace that was relative to how successful his coping mechanisms were on any given day. But I knew his feelings for Karlie were more than just another coping mechanism, no matter how badly he'd treated her.

I knew my brother, and so I knew that what Rheo really wanted, what he was still searching for, was the love he was robbed of.

# CHAPTER 33

## CHIARA

'Hold still.'

We were sitting on the floor of my room as I squinted at him in the lamplight, trying to figure out which colours to paint him in. We talked to fill the space, both laughing and serious by turn.

The good thing about painting was that you could go over it again and again, but where Kaelan was concerned, this proved to be problematic. His smile was so beautiful, I was having trouble getting it right. After an hour, I'd barely done anything, but the low lighting was starting to hurt my eyes, so we called it a night.

It was the last time we would see each other until after exams.

I was surprised at how clear my mind was going into them, and a weight I didn't even know I was carrying finally lifted on the afternoon of my last one. I sat in the school hall afterwards, the paper finished and taken away. I stared at the sky and the wisps of white clouds outside the high windows, anticipation for summer tingling in my chest.

I couldn't wait to see Kaelan again. We had been calling each other every day and the sound of his voice was just enough to curb my craving until the next time we spoke. It was not as sweet or rich as being with him, but now, we had the entire summer to ourselves.

He'd called me after that last exam, saying he had a "surprise" for me. As if spending time with him wasn't enough of a gift in itself. My lips spread into a wide smile the moment I saw him. I couldn't help it. Maybe I was smiling because he was smiling too.

Our bodies gravitated towards each other as if we were the sun and the earth. When he kissed me, I felt every structure within me crumble to the foundations, only to be rebuilt again by the ecstasy his lips and tongue evoked within me.

When we broke away, I ran my fingers down his arms and interlaced my hands through his.

'I missed you,' I whispered.

He held me with his eyes. 'I missed you too.'

It was a beautiful day, one of the best that week, with a clear, deep sky and a mild Parisian sun. We got in the car and drove with the windows down, singing along to the *Bon Jovi* CD Kaelan had put in. My heart felt light and lighter still as I opened my eyes, my face full of the sun. I cupped my hands in my lap, pretending I could contain a little pool of golden light just for me.

I fell in and out of sleep for the rest of the journey, with Kaelan shaking me gently when we arrived. I opened my eyes to find tall, straight oaks surrounding us.

'Where are we?' I asked, my voice muffled with sleep.

'The woods.'

I smacked his arm. 'Wow, thanks, Einstein. You're really not gonna tell me where we're going, huh?'

He grinned. 'Nope.'

The air was sweet and clean, and I filled my lungs with it before following Kaelan towards the beginning of a narrow, winding trail. It was well-worn and we managed to walk side by side at the start, talking until we got too tired from the exertion of climbing uphill. Kaelan took off his shirt and carried it and I decided to do the same, leaving me in a sports bra.

'This better be worth it,' I panted as we stopped for a break.

'We're almost there,' he said, squinting through the trees as if he could make out the final destination through all the foliage.

His torso was covered in a sheen of sweat, glinting in the light that filtered in.

I tore my eyes away, starting on the path before he noticed me staring.

When I reached the top, where the woods and their coolness fell away, I was heaving in the air and ready to collapse into a pile. But the sight that greeted me made that thought and all others fly straight out of my mind.

Ten metres of sheer rock reached up to the heavens, with a stream of jewelled water tumbling over in sheaths. The waters fell into a pool at the bottom and even from this angle, I could tell it was so clear you could see the rock bed beneath it.

When the light hit the waterfall, tiny rainbows sprung up from within. My mouth parted in awe; it was only when Kaelan slipped his sweaty hand in mine that I remembered how to breathe.

'How did you find this place?' I asked, turning to him.

His eyes were alive. 'The first time we came to France, we did some exploring – do you like it?'

A laugh bubbled out of me. I tugged on his hand and started to scramble down, only letting go when I reached the pool. I peered into the crystal water, perfectly still apart from a slight ripple here and there. The rush of water from above filled my ears.

'Can we swim in that?'

Before he could respond, I took my shoes off and stuck a foot in.

'Kaelan, it's freezing!'

When I turned around, he was already down to his boxers. He bit his lip, taking my hands. There was no mistaking the mischievous glint in his eye.

'What are you doing?'

He yanked me into the water and I fell, nearly on top of him.

'Kaelan!' I cried, splashing his stupid, laughing face. All that did was make him grin wider and splash me back.

'How am I supposed to put my clothes back on now?' I asked, wringing out the drenched t-shirt I'd still been holding.

'It's fine, Chiara – look at the sun. It'll be dry in no time.'

I tackled my shorts next, sticking my leg out of the water to retrieve them from my right ankle as Kaelan watched, amused. I smiled widely at him, then wrung them out over his head before he could swim away.

'Enjoy my sweat.'

He puckered his lips and spat, wiping the water out of his scrunched-up eyes. 'I'll get you.'

I flung my shorts onto the bank too. 'And how will you accomplish that?'

We circled each other, crouching so only our heads bobbed above the surface. He flashed me a wild grin and launched himself at me. Before I knew it, his arms held me up and my legs wrapped around his torso.

'You're such an idiot,' I whispered with a smile. The drops of water on his cheeks were clear, but his eyes were even clearer.

'I dare you to call me that again.'

I glanced down at his lips, lingering close to mine. 'Idiot?'

His kiss consumed me, each pull deeper than the last. He took his time with me, savouring every moment. It somehow made me even more drunk on him, the way I had to go slowly.

My mate. My only.

Nothing else existed then. Not the sound of the waterfall or the blackbirds twittering from the forest. Not the sun and the stars or the moon and the sky.

Only him.

It was always him.

'*Eisai tóso ómorfos*,' he murmured, a little breathlessly.

I was breathless too. 'What?'

His fingers traced my wet hair, tucking it behind my ear. 'You are so beautiful.'

I felt my lips turn up involuntarily as I gazed at him, at the tiny water drops on his dark gold skin.

'I like it when you speak in Greek,' I whispered.

'Really?'

I nodded, then pulled his face towards me again, easing his mouth open. We were moving closer into the magnetising swirl at the base of the waterfall, pulled in towards the hammering sound.

I shifted us both so the water was hitting my back, gasping at the feel of the cold torrent drumming on my skin. 'Kaelan, you have to try this.'

He moved next to me and groaned. My stomach flipped at the sound.

'Imagine taking a shower like this every morning,' I said.

'Wouldn't that be amazing?'

'You say that now,' he teased, 'but, earlier, weren't you complaining about how cold it was?'

I rolled my eyes. 'It's okay once you're used to it.'

Something wild flashed across his face and suddenly he disappeared under the water. I stared wide-eyed at the place he'd once been.

'Kaelan?'

Without thinking, I took a deep breath and went under, kicking off the bottom to move out from the direct hit of the water. When I emerged, I blinked several times before the new surroundings made sense. Where the water stopped, dark, smooth rock began. The spray from the falls hit it, making it gleam like a jewel.

I hoisted myself onto the ledge and crawled forward, seeing he was there already.

'What are you smiling about?' I asked, plopping myself down next to him.

He smiled wider. 'Nothing.'

I poked his ribs before looking around the cave. It was deep enough that the back half was dry, but it was still barely an indent into the rest of the massive rock wall. I watched the waterfall, noticing how the sun glimmered through from the late afternoon outside.

I turned back to Kaelan. 'Thank you for bringing me here.'

He smiled. 'You're welcome.'

I crawled onto his lap and wrapped my arms around his neck. He had a question in his eyes, but whatever it was, he didn't speak it aloud.

'I love you, Kaelan Costas, forever and always.'

He was grinning now. 'I don't think I'll ever get tired of hearing that.'

I laughed and kissed his forehead, then the tip of his nose and, finally, his lips.

It was almost dark by the time we began to drive back home, and I drifted in and out of sleep again, weary from the stress of the past few weeks. When my phone beeped in my hand, I almost ignored it, but the thought that it might be Karlie or Luna made me check the message.

It was a text from a number I'd never seen before.

*"You'll never guess what's around the corner, little bird. But don't worry your pretty little head over it. I'll see you soon."*

I clutched the phone harder and read it again, wide awake now. It must've been a wrong number, either that or a prank. But then, why did the wording sound familiar?

The realisation hit me like a kick to the gut.

Kalip.

He'd called me "little bird".

My mind flashed back to the stuffy classroom, to his slimy mouth on my ear. It could have been a coincidence, but the feeling of unease in me said it wasn't. I sucked in a breath.

The last thing he'd said to me was "see you soon".

'Are you okay?'

I started, darting a glance at Kaelan. Of course, he'd notice something was wrong; I couldn't hide anything from him. He knew me too well.

His face was unreadable as I explained and, once I was done, he began to speak. His tone was controlled, calm.

'If it's him,' Kaelan said, 'there's no point getting worked up. He just wants a reaction – he just wants to scare you. Don't let him.'

'I can't just ignore this, Kaelan!'

We began to slow down, taking an exit off the motorway.

'I'll talk to Viviana tomorrow,' he said finally. 'She'll know what to do.'

# CHAPTER 34

## KAELAN

'Ah, the lovebirds have returned,' Rheo simpered as we entered the kitchen. 'I'm on facetime. Come, say hi.'

He turned his phone around as we stepped closer. My *mamá* was on the screen, sitting on her old wooden stool.

'Oh! Kaelan, you are too skinny!' she said in Greek, putting her eye up against the camera. She sat back onto her stool. 'Ah, and who is this?

I glanced at Chiara. Her eyes were wide, taking in the woman on the screen. She was only twenty-two, but the sun, sea and stress made her look much older.

Wrapping my arm around Chiara's waist, I made the introductions. *Mamá's* English had improved over the years, and there were only a few words here and there that I had to translate. It was going well until she started interrogating Chiara: "where do you work?"; "how much do you earn?"; "can you cook?".

Chiara was shaking almost imperceptibly, but it was there. I held her closer, realising this might've been a bad idea after the text from Kalip.

'Kaelan, *mátia mou*, were you listening?' *Mamá* was speaking in Greek now, peering into the screen. 'Where is your cross, the one I gave to you? Do you not wear it?'

I cast a look at Rheo. '*Mamá*.'

'It will protect you against the *mati*.'

I bit back a smile as she wagged her finger at me.

'Kaelan, this is the facts! And I tell you, Chiara will get the *mati*.'

Chiara looked up. She was chewing on her lip so hard she almost drew blood. 'What did she say?'

I shook my head and lowered my voice. 'It's stupid. There's this curse called the evil eye – *mati*. It brings bad fortune and, in extreme cases, death. *Mamá* is concerned you might get it, but don't worry, it's just superstition.'

Chiara didn't seem too relieved.

I switched back to Greek. 'Anyway, why would Chiara get it? You think people will send it to her because they're jealous of her?'

Rheo sniggered, but *Mamá* was serious.

'Yes, yes, she is very talented and beautiful, but I am talking about her heart.'

'Her heart?'

*Mamá* shifted in her seat and pursed her lips. 'It is *skoteinós*. Filled with pain and shadows that will attract the *mati* to her. Are you certain she is your mate, *mátia mou*? It is strange that your soul would choose someone like her to be its match.'

*Someone like her*. As if Chiara was a mistake. As if she wasn't the most genuine, astonishing person I'd ever met.

I swallowed hard. 'Yes, I'm sure.'

*Mamá* looked taken aback by my bitter tone, but I didn't understand why she was telling me my mate wasn't good enough for me.

Chiara looked upset. I could tell she didn't want to ask

again what we were talking about, but she knew from my expression that it was bad. And about her. *Mamá* had kept looking at her as she talked, her eyes narrowing as if Chiara couldn't be trusted.

I didn't realise how hard I'd been squeezing her hand until she looked down and back up at me questioningly.

*Why is my heart hurting?*

*Mamá* switched to English to target Chiara herself. 'Are your parents vampires? Were they turned against their will or not?'

Chiara froze. It took her a while to get her words out and her voice was rough when she spoke. 'I-I don't know if they were turned willingly. I don't know my real parents.'

'What do you mean you don't know? You are an—' here, she switched to Greek to ask me how to say the word.

'Orphan,' I blurted.

Chiara looked at me like I just punched her.

Her hand slipped out of mine before I could stop it.

'Wait! Please, I love you,' I whispered.

She said nothing, turning and walking out the back door without another glance. She took my heart with her.

'*Mátia mou*, I am trying to protect you.'

I turned to face *Mamá*. There were years of hardship in her eyes and in the lines on her forehead.

'This girl will hurt you even more than that Tasha, I know it.'

I shook my head. 'You don't know that. Look what you did to her! You were way out of line, what does it matter if she is an orphan?'

'Kaelan.' Rheo put his hand on my shoulder, but I shook him off.

'I can't do this right now.'

I left without saying goodbye and stormed out through the back door. Luna was reading and Nico was in our vegetable garden. Chiara sat on the grass, facing away from me.

I wished I knew what she was thinking. I wanted to apologise, but she probably wanted space.

Nico looked up suddenly, then started to run, hopping over plants. The corner of my lip turned up. Come to think of it, it smelt like something was burning.

'Fuck!' he cried, throwing up the barbecue hood.

I peered over Nico's shoulder at the overcooked lamb. 'You can still eat the parts that aren't burnt.'

'Possibly. Someone get me a plate!'

'I'll get it.'

I turned my head in surprise at Chiara, who was already brushing off her clothes.

'I'll go with her.'

She started walking towards the door. 'I can do it alone.'

*Shit.*

As soon as she'd left, Luna rounded on me. 'Right, now I know something's wrong. What did you do?'

I cleared my throat. 'My *ma*—'

And Chiara was back outside again.

I scratched the back of my head. 'That was fast.'

She ignored me and put the plate on the table a little too hard, then turned to walk away.

I grabbed her arm. 'Chiara, please, talk to me. I'm sorry I... I didn't know she would act like that.'

'It doesn't matter,' she said bitterly. She couldn't meet my eyes. 'Your mother's right. I'm just an orphan.'

Her chest heaved. I knew the words she wasn't saying.

253

'Can we just go to my room to talk?' I swallowed. 'Alone?'

Her voice was dead, thick with tears. 'What is there to talk about?'

I clenched my fists to prevent me from reaching out again.

'Please,' I begged.

A second passed.

Chiara was staring at the ground now, tears pooling in her eyes. I wasn't breathing.

'Okay,' she choked out, finally.

Finally.

'Can I... hold your hand?'

# CHAPTER 35

## CHIARA

It was tearing me up from the inside out. I wanted to scream.

I wanted to hurt him for being so perfect and loving me when I wasn't.

I was empty as I let him guide me through the darkened hallways as the sun went down outside. I didn't see the walls as I passed them or hear the sound of his tortured breath. I could barely even feel his hand in mine.

'Chiara?'

I looked at him, his deep blue eyes made out of love that made no sense. Whatever he saw on my face made him collapse a little. I watched as his eyes started glistening and he squeezed my hand as if to ensure I was still there.

'Tell me how to make it better.'

He tried to control the shaking of his voice, but he was failing miserably.

I stared at him. It was my fault he was in pain.

My gaze dropped to our hands. I hated myself for making him hurt; he should have never even met me in the first place. The question slipped out of my throat more easily than I thought.

'How can you love me?' I asked.

Kaelan drew in a breath. 'Chiara, look at me,' he whispered, bringing his fingers to my chin.

I lifted my eyes and what I saw in his made something in me die a little.

'I love you because you're *you*. You're kind, creative, and you're funny.' He smiled, then cupped my cheek when I dropped my eyes again. 'But you're also so much more than that. I can't even tell you how much more. You're everything to me, Chiara. And I don't care if my *mamá* doesn't see what I see, because all that matters is that you see.' He rested his forehead against mine. 'You deserve everything, *koúkla mou*. I would do anything for you.' He buried his face into my neck and whispered, almost like it hurt, 'I love you so much.'

I didn't know what to say. I wrapped my arms around his back, resting my head against his until we were so close we were almost one.

He loosened my heart and made it more pliable to his touch. My love for him overflowed as we held onto each other tightly, as if one of us would slip away before the other could grasp them.

It wasn't until much later, as we lay beside one another, that Kaelan spoke again.

'Chiara?'

'Mm?'

'Will you mate with me?'

I opened my eyes. 'What do you mean?'

He turned to face me, touching my cheek. 'There is a ritual we do when we decide to commit to our mates. A piece of my soul would move to yours and a piece of yours to mine.'

'So, it binds us together?'

'Yes. You can only mate with one person.'

My lips parted. 'You never mated with Tasha?'

'No.' He shook his head. 'Never.'

'I'd still be me, right? After?'

Kaelan looked into my eyes for a heartbeat, then laughed. 'Why wouldn't you be?'

'I don't know how it works.'

'I told you what happens – there's nothing else to it, I swear.' He tilted his head. 'Although some people claim they share dreams.'

'Dreams?'

'Not every single dream you have, just some.' He shrugged. 'Could be fun, right?'

I wasn't sure if "fun" was the word I'd use to describe it. Did that mean we would share nightmares too? My heart was beating loudly against my ribs and I was probably gripping his hand tighter than was comfortable.

'We don't have to if you don't w—'

'I want to.' I swallowed. 'H-how do we do it?'

He ran his fingers lightly down my arm. 'Do you see this vein here?'

I nodded.

'I have to pierce it, and drink some of your blood, and you have to do the same for me. It's not much.'

'Will it hurt?'

'Not at all.'

I watched as he bent his head over the inside of my arm. His lips felt good against my skin and he grazed his canines over my vein. As the pain of his teeth sinking in was instantly transmuted into pleasure, I gasped. He sucked on the wound and I felt my blood running from me into him. My breathing was shallow and rapid, and it took everything in me to keep still. He licked the wound, then pressed his thumb over it and wiped his mouth.

I stared at him, unable to utter a single word.

'What?' His eyes were shining.

I regained control. 'Nothing. It's my turn now. Close your eyes; I don't want you to watch.'

He bit into his smile and did as he was told.

I mimicked his movements, hesitating before I sunk my teeth into him. But then, there was no turning back. He groaned softly as I began to drink. His blood tasted better than anything I'd ever consumed in my whole life.

When I was done, I licked the wound and pressed my fingers to it. Kaelan's eyes were wide as he breathed heavily.

'Did I—?'

His hands were knotted in my hair before I could finish, his lips on mine. But I needed more. I pulled off his shirt and he grinned at me through his hair. I raised my arms, watching him as he hooked his fingers under my own t-shirt.

He paused. 'Are you sure?'

I nodded.

Soon, it joined his on the floor and I pushed my palms against his chest until he was flat on his back on the bed.

I'd never done this before, but Kaelan always had a way of making me feel safe. He stroked his fingers down my arms as I unbuttoned his trousers. I bit my lip, unsure, but his eyes held mine with that steady calm.

I wanted him more than I'd ever wanted anything.

*I can't believe I did that.*

My eyes cracked open to find the stale grey light of morning entering the room. Kaelan was holding me. Everything was quiet.

It felt like something big had happened last night. Maybe it was his blood that now ran through my veins or something about the energetic exchange that happened with it, but I was feeling... really good.

He was so warm, but if I stayed any longer, I would have difficulty getting up again. I pried his arms off my stomach as gently as I could manage and slid down the side of the bed until I landed on the floor.

I peered over the bed at Kaelan, checking he was still asleep. My heart felt so full with him; my love for him. I smiled. He was absolutely gorgeous.

I pulled my phone from the side table onto my lap. There were no new text messages. Thinking of text messages made me remember the one I'd gotten on the drive back from the waterfall, the one from an unknown number. I clicked on it again.

*"You'll never guess what's around the corner, little bird. But don't worry your pretty little head over it. I'll see you soon."*

Why was it still bothering me? It was probably an empty threat as Kaelan had said, designed to scare me. It just felt so out of the blue, out of place in my perfect happiness. Kaelan made me feel like I was walking on clouds, but this message now brought me crashing back to Earth.

A shiver ran through me and I put down the phone.

I recalled what had happened yesterday, when his mother had made it all too clear what a letdown I was. The ache I'd felt then resurfaced now. I'd wanted his mother to, at the very least, accept me. But she hadn't. I felt a swell of pain hit me in the chest and I pressed my hand over my heart as if that could prevent it from spreading its poison to the rest of my body. How could she, though, when even my own mother abandoned me?

It was amazing that I still harboured the desire to find my mother, even when she so clearly didn't want to be found. If she had, she would have left me with something.

All I had was a huge gaping hole where she should have been.

Downstairs was completely quiet as I made my way into the kitchen. The Costas brothers were all morning people and they were usually up before 8 a.m. I frowned at the empty kitchen, but began to make a big pan of scrambled eggs anyway, in case they woke up. My thoughts circled back to the text and Kalip.

Wasn't Luna usually downstairs too? The girls and I were supposed to go into central Paris today. She should be up, getting ready by now.

I stared at the yellow eggs. Something felt wrong.

'Are you okay?'

I started, pressing my fingers between my brows. I hadn't even heard Kaelan come up behind me.

'Don't scare me like that!'

He opened the fridge, expressionless. 'My bad.'

'Did you wake up on the wrong side of the bed or something?' I teased.

He shut the fridge and started rummaging through the pantry. 'No, I'm fine. Hey, do we have any cereal?'

I opened and closed my mouth. Kaelan hated cereal.

'N-no, I don't think so. Since when do you eat cereal, anyway?'

'I'm bored,' he announced as he slid into the stool behind

the counter. 'Come to think of it, I'm not really hungry.' His eyes glinted. 'For food.'

*What the fuck.*

I frowned at him. 'You're acting so weird today.'

'Am I?'

He tilted his head, viewing me like I was some kind of new animal at the zoo. I only realised I had been backing away from him when I felt the fridge door against me.

*This isn't right.*

Kaelan sat back and yawned noisily. 'You know, Chiara, it's quite funny how long it's taken for this charade to end.'

He smiled widely, but it was nothing like the beautiful smile that belonged to Kaelan.

'What do you mean?'

My heart pounded in my chest as he stood.

'My, my, I thought you would've read the eloquent text I sent you by now.' His eyes slid over my expression of shock with a satisfied gleam. 'Ah. So you did read it. You see, I thought it would prepare your mind nicely. For what's to come.'

All my blood fell into my feet.

'What did you do to him?' I choked.

He laughed, but the beautiful sound that Kaelan usually made was now mechanical. I looked at the man I loved, whose mind and heart had been stolen and I felt disgusted.

'That isn't your concern, now is it, little bird?'

His teeth decorated his face with a garish smile. I grabbed the fridge for support. But my fingers passed through it.

I tried to run, but I couldn't move. Not even to lift my pinky finger.

'I wish it didn't have to be this way,' Kalip said. His gaze was penetrating.

I watched, helpless, as he came to a stop centimetres from me. I stared into Kaelan's face, the one I knew so well. But I didn't see someone I knew in the planes of his cheeks, in the slope of his nose. My insides felt like they were tearing themselves apart, like my mind was breaking because my eyes were not showing me the truth.

'It is a pity,' Kalip whispered, 'that I can never have you.' His voice was Kaelan's too. It was horrible. 'I like getting what I want, Chiara,' he grinned, 'but you probably know that by now.'

Suddenly, his eyes flashed pitch black. That was when I lost myself. Those black holes were growing larger and larger until I was consumed.

I was numb.

Cold.

My bones were cold and my mind had left me.

I knew nothing else.

# CHAPTER 36

## KAELAN

I'd been through the entire house, top to bottom. I couldn't find her anywhere. I racked my brain to think of all the places she could be. What if she went for a walk somewhere? I thought of last night, how our blood and souls mixed. Maybe it had scared her. I pushed back my hair with both hands.

Just as I was trying to rationalise my thoughts, the doorbell rang.

I swung open the door, half expecting it to be her. I didn't bother hiding my disappointment when I saw it wasn't. From her black leather trousers to her large curls, it was Viviana, through and through.

'Where's Chiara?' she said before I got a chance to ask what the hell she was doing on my doorstep on a Sunday morning.

'I don't know. I can't find her anywhere.'

Viviana's face paled. 'May I come inside?'

My heart was beating fast as I led her into the kitchen. If Viviana was here, something must be wrong.

'Ah, Viviana,' Rheo cried as we entered the kitchen. 'What brings you to the Costas household at this fine hour?'

Viviana ignored him completely, turning around to glare directly at the fridge. 'Something happened here.'

I gritted my teeth. 'If you know something, I suggest you say it within the next five seconds.'

'Kaelan.' Her eyes cut into me. 'This won't be easy to hear.'

'Shit, what's going on?' Rheo asked, coming to stand beside us.

I took a deep breath to prevent myself from strangling him.

Viviana glared at him, then looked me straight in the eyes. 'Chiara has been kidnapped.'

I lost my breath.

'How do you—' I swallowed. 'Are you sure?'

She nodded. 'Positive. He was here. The illusionist.'

'Kalip.' It came out like a growl. I pushed my hair back with both hands, forcing myself to breathe. How was it possible?

I groaned. The text. The fucking text.

I should've known. Why hadn't I acted on it last night? It was never an empty threat when it came to him.

'How the hell did he get into our house?' Rheo snarled.

That was the least of my concerns. 'Viviana, can you find out where she is?

She shook her head. 'I'll do what I can, but I can't promise anything.'

Something searing hot pierced my heart. It hurt like hell.

Viviana looked as if she was going to say something else when we heard laughter outside the door. Nico and Luna tumbled into the kitchen, practically on top of one another.

Upon noticing Viviana and the look on my face, they figured out pretty quickly that this was not the time to be cheery.

'What happened?' Nico asked, pulling Luna to his side.

I sat down and put my head in my hands as Rheo explained the contents of the last ten minutes, making up an elaborate story about phoning the cops for Luna's benefit. I glanced at her. She looked like she would probably rain down the questions on Nico later since she wasn't falling for Rheo's bullshit.

Not like any of it mattered anyway.

The air felt dense, as if the room was packed with rain clouds. It felt like something catastrophic just occurred, like World War Three had just been announced on national television. Rheo was now in a state of giddy terror, high from the soul-destroying news he had the privilege to distribute. I couldn't see Nico's face from this angle, but I knew by the set of his shoulders that his entire body was tense. Luna looked even worse, like she was angry, distraught and in disbelief all at the same time.

I couldn't process it.

How could I when she was literally in my arms just last night? It felt like Chiara was going to wander in through the door any time now. She'd laugh, a smirk on her lips, and joke about how she'd got us all pretty good. But it wasn't a joke. I would have laughed at how crazy the situation was, except it wasn't funny. The clouds in the room pressed against my chest, mixing with my thoughts until they were fuzzy and confused.

'That's a good question.' Nico's voice brought me back to the present. 'How did he get in?'

'I was asleep, I have no idea,' I said.

Luna frowned. 'What? No, you weren't. I opened the door for you – you said you'd been on a morning walk to clear your head and forgot your keys.'

I stared at the table. *Fuck.*

'Oh, yeah, I remember now,' I said to Luna, before glancing between Nico and Rheo. 'I must've been half asleep.'

I could tell they had clocked what had really happened by the intensely disturbed expressions plastered to their faces. They looked the same way I felt.

I'd been scared to lose her all this time, but I never would've guessed that she'd be taken from me instead of leaving through her own free will.

God must have a sick sense of humour.

# CHAPTER 37

## CHIARA

When I woke up, I was in pain. It took me a while to register that my ribs were pulsing and I peeled up my shirt to find that they were bruised and swollen. I covered them again. This wasn't even my shirt. Someone had changed my clothes and put me in this and some thin shorts that looked like they were covered in engine oil and a little blood.

My head was pounding, trying to remember what exactly had happened. It was all so black and cold and then... nothing.

For the first time, I looked around me.

The floor was milky white and so were the walls, and ceiling.

I stood up and turned, realising what had happened with every quickening breath.

My heart sank six feet deep. My knees buckled to join it.

*This has to be a nightmare.*

But the pain in my ribs told me it was real.

*There has to be a way out.*

My breathing hitched and I tucked my hair behind my ears. It was hard to tell where the wall and the floor met each other. When I looked closer, I saw that the walls weren't even solid. They were made of mists, roaming in and out, back and forth, dancing upon the retina like a taunt.

I pressed my palm against the mists, discovering a solid wall beneath, and when I knocked on it, the sound that returned was hard, like I was inside of a slab of concrete. I ran my hands over the walls, feeling for cracks, vents, anything. But all was smooth. All, apart from one wall.

I felt the hinges of a door, the space where two materials took a breath. But it wasn't even large enough to stick my pinky finger inside. There was no handle on the door, no lock.

I was in the centre of the room again, staring at the six bleak walls that had me in a box.

Trapped.

I screamed over and over, my chest growing hot. I threw myself against the door and the jolt ran through my bones, but I didn't care. I cried out and did it again, pounding my fist.

'You can't leave me in here!' I screamed, even though I was all alone.

Alone.

I sank against the door.

The next time I awoke, there were two bowls. One was full of what looked like mashed potato and the other was water. I wondered if someone had opened the door to put them inside, but my hope dwindled into smoke when I noticed the bowls were left in front of a slot-shaped crack at the base of the door. It was jammed shut and would not budge no matter how hard I banged on it.

Maybe, if I refused to eat, Kalip might have to intervene, giving me a chance to escape.

*Unless he brought me here to die.*

I sniffed at the mashed potatoes suspiciously, though I was too hungry not to eat them. My ribs ached dully now, but the skin over them was still swollen and the water was cool. I dipped my fingers in it and dabbed my burning skin.

Using water for things other than drinking was a mistake I learned never to make again.

Day and night were indistinguishable here; the same mists rolled in and out through the walls, with the same bleak light emitting from every surface, no matter what time I could possibly conceive it to be. I wanted to keep track of the days, but it was impossible. I slept at seemingly random times, waking abruptly because of the nightmares.

They were all the same; Kaelan's face, the twisted smile and the cold of his eyes making it seem like his soul had left his body and another cruel one had enslaved it. He was dominating and controlling.

And I could do nothing.

That was the worst part of all; when I tried to scream but had no voice, tried to run but my limbs were as heavy as the Earth.

Every time I woke up, I was covered in sweat, panting and glancing around the same six walls over and over again as if Kalip would magically drop down from the ceiling. It took me a while to calm myself down, and even after that, I would stare hard into the mists and sometimes I would see faces.

Like someone was watching me.

Every day I was terrified that Kalip would come in and do something terrible to me. But every day, he proved me wrong, and every day I gained a little more confidence in my fantasy that he wasn't going to torture me, rape or kill me, or all three.

I lay down on my back and closed my eyes. I imagined I was

lying on the ground, the smell of sweet grass around me. The sun was warming my face gently, bathing my bare skin in its glow. When I moved my fingers, I could almost pretend they were feeling the soft blades of grass, not the rough concrete floor I was getting accustomed to.

Eventually, this fantasy wasn't enough and I began to dream about Karlie and Luna and what our travels might be like; smells and tastes of food; rich colours and sounds; people with smiling faces; cities, rivers and mountains.

Whatever was happening to me now had to be temporary, a small blip in the hundreds of years that would make up my life.

I thought of Kaelan, his honey-tan skin, the laugh in his eyes that ran deep like the ocean, like the sky, the way he carried responsibility on his shoulders and made it look like a pair of wings. I wanted to see all the places he'd seen as he grew up, and meet all the people who were threads in the intricate network of his past. I'd already done things I would have never dreamed of doing for him, and I knew a lot more was still to come.

This world wasn't done with me yet.

As if my determination had been sensed, there was a click in the door.

My heart leapt. That was a new sound.

In the time it took me to scuttle against a wall, the empty space where the door was glimmered, and a man stepped inside my room.

My blood froze.

I should have listened to the fear.

'How delightful to see you, little bird.'

Suddenly he was gone, only to reappear crouched in front of me.

I started against the wall, hitting my head. His gaze bore

into me for a few seconds too long, and my heart rate did not slow down.

'W-why am I here?'

'Why?' His grey eyes glistened with life as if seeing me threatened excited him. 'For me to play with you, of course. Oh, don't look at me like that.' He ran a cold finger down my cheek. 'I didn't mean it that way. Though, if you so desire—'

I grabbed his arm and hurled it away from me. 'Don't fucking touch me.'

Ducking away from him, I started crawling towards another wall before standing up and stumbling to the other side of the room.

'You're sick, you know that?' I spat at him. 'What are you planning to do with me?'

He smiled wider. 'While I adore the compliment, I feel it is wholly misplaced. Why, you barely know me.' His eyes glittered darkly. 'But I do know you.'

He disappeared again and my heart went flat. I held my arms in front of my chest as my eyes darted around the room, my ears straining to pick up any noise.

He appeared in front of me. 'You asked what I plan to do with you.' He shoved me against the wall with his arm barred over my throat before leaning his head into the crook of my neck. 'Oh, Chiara,' he muttered.

I whimpered as he breathed me in.

'The things I want to do to you.'

I swallowed hard, my mind whirring through all the ways I could escape. I waited till he looked at me before I spat in his eye. It caught him off-guard enough that I had time to wind my foot around his and pull, taking his leg out from underneath. I pushed on his chest hard, watching his arms flailing.

He collapsed onto the floor and I smiled.

My relief was short-lived.

He yelled. It was primal, animalistic, guttural. It drove him back up to standing and his fingers were around my neck in milliseconds, cutting off my air supply. He slammed me into the wall.

'Do not make the mistake of thinking, for one second, that you stand a chance against me.' His voice shook with fury. 'I will break you until you beg me for mercy.'

He let go of my neck and I gasped. This time, he slammed me onto the ground in one smooth swoop as if I were a rag doll. I cried out in pain, which heightened into a scream when he kicked my ribs.

Then he was gone.

I didn't move.

My ears strained again, listening to the silence as if it would tell me whether he was still in the room or not. I ventured a look around. Had he left for good? I held my breath, waiting for it, anticipating another attack. But then the door clicked closed.

I listened closely for a few moments more to ensure it wasn't a trick. The only thing I could hear was the sound of my strained breaths.

*I'm safe.*

All of the air left my body as I released my muscles. I was shaking badly. I lay on the concrete like a dead thing, curling in on my own bruised, swollen body as silent tears streamed down my cheeks. I lay there until all the fear went away, until all that was left was numbness.

As I stared at the wall, the endless mists rolling in and out, I thought of how everything I'd dreamed of for my future was just that: a dream.

That was the worst pain of all.

# CHAPTER 38

## KAELAN

My feet pounded against the concrete pavement as I ran and the force of each step shot through my body. It was the good kind of painful.

Five days.

Five days without her and the reality of the situation had finally sunk in.

Reality felt like shit.

I growled and ran harder, furious at myself for letting it happen. I should've been more careful. That day on the cliffs, I'd sworn to always protect her, no matter what. When I promised something, I meant it with every fibre in my body.

I'd failed her.

My phone buzzed in my shorts pocket. I slowed down, panting, and checked the message.

I almost dropped the phone.

I'd been sent a photo from an unknown number. She was lying on a white floor, dried tearstains on her cheeks. She looked like she'd been beaten.

I was going to kill Kalip.

It didn't make sense – why was he showing me what was happening to her? It was almost as if he wanted to get under my skin. Like he was torturing both of us at the same time.

I shut off the phone to prevent myself from looking at the photo again, but it was too late; it was already burnt into my memory. I saw it when I closed my eyes.

Why couldn't Kalip have taken me instead?

Why her? Why?

I wanted to hold her, kiss her, tell her she's one of the strongest people I've ever known.

Fuck that.

I wanted her back.

'Viviana?'

It was thirty minutes later when I showed up at her flat, knocked hard on her door and waited, listening. But it wasn't Viviana who opened it.

'Who are you?' I asked the woman with blonde dreads, a nose piercing and a ton of bracelets.

She grinned, sticking her tongue between her teeth. 'And who is you?'

'Look, is Viviana here or not? It's important.'

She cocked her head, analysing me. It made me uncomfortable, to say the least.

'She not here,' the woman finally said. 'She down in the woods.'

I could still feel her watching me as I jogged down the hallway. She was strange, like Viviana.

The further I walked towards the woods, the darker my surroundings became. Deep within the trees, I spotted her candles, tiny pinpricks of light in the distance. As I got closer, I saw she was sitting in the middle of them, her old, ragged cards laid out in front of her.

Viviana didn't open her eyes at the sound of my arrival.

'I knew you'd be back,' she said.

I scoffed; she didn't need to be psychic to know that.

'You said you'd help me.'

'I am.'

'Are you? Because I don't know if you know this, but Chiara is being tortured as we speak.' I was struggling to keep my voice stable. 'We don't have time. Whatever you're doing,' I glanced at the cards, 'you need to do it faster.'

'Kaelan.' She opened her eyes and I watched as her pupils dilated and then constricted. 'I really don't think you are in the position to be making demands right now. These matters take time and can absolutely not be rushed. Not to mention the fact that Kalip is highly skilled at bending reality. Uncovering Chiara's predicament may be a little trickier than I first anticipated.'

'Her "predicament"?' I almost laughed. The look on Viviana's face was the only thing making me hold back the bitter retort I had ready to go. 'Alright,' I sighed. 'Thank you for helping. I appreciate it.'

'I have found out something else.' Viviana twisted her mouth like she was trying to figure out the best way to let me down easily. 'I do not believe that Kalip is the one truly behind this.'

My heart was pounding loudly. Too loudly. 'What do you mean?'

'You told me something felt off, almost personal. It was unclear what ties Kalip himself could have to Chiara, or you for that matter, besides being your former Chemistry teacher.

However, I do believe that he is working for someone else. He is merely a puppet, pulled by the strings of someone with greater motives. I don't know who,' she said quickly, noticing the look on my face, 'but I'll try to find out. And... another thing.'

My palms were sweating, either from the heat of the candle flames or the panic rising inside me. Probably both.

'She wasn't kidnapped to torture her alone. That was... not really the aim here. The aim was to hurt you.'

'What?' I shook my head. 'That's impossible. No one I know would want to torture me.'

Viviana levelled a cool look at me. 'Are you certain?'

'Yeah. I think I would've known if I had pissed someone off that badly. There has to be another reason.'

She looked doubtful but didn't contradict me.

I turned as another set of footsteps sounded behind me. The woman from Viviana's flat.

She lifted her skirt and walked straight between the candles, and I could've sworn she was on fire. She and Viviana sat opposite each other, with a pile of smoking herbs in between them. They held hands and closed their eyes, taking a deep breath at the same time.

Maybe it was best I left the spell stuff to them.

I'd already started to walk away when Viviana announced they would try a location spell.

I scratched the back of my head. 'Do I, uh, should I go?'

Viviana rolled hers eyes. 'This won't take long. I doubt we'll find anything.'

'Excuse me?'

The other woman nodded in agreement. 'Best not to bring up hopes. Sit by the tree and wait.' She pointed a bony finger towards a particularly twisted, moss-covered tree.

I didn't know what else to do, so I sat on the roots and looked at their circle of light before leaning my head back. They began to hum, chanting in a language I'd never heard before.

I closed my eyes and saw Chiara laughing. When Chiara laughed, her entire face lit up and it sounded like a stream bubbling up and spilling all over the place. It was contagious; it made me laugh, even when I didn't know what was so funny. We used to laugh a lot together.

'Kaelan.'

Viviana's voice sounded so much like Chiara's at that moment that I shot awake, searching for her frantically.

But she wasn't there.

'D-did I miss anything?' I asked, failing to keep the hope out of my voice. 'Wait, did you find her? Do you know where she is?'

Viviana gave me a small, sad smile and her friend turned to stare at me.

My shoulders sagged. I should've known it wouldn't be that easy.

I was lying on my bed, staring at her side of the bed. It was summer, my favourite season, and the air was sticky. If she were here, we would have held each other despite the heat, although it was more comfortable to sleep apart. We would have talked until the sun started to rise; she would ruffle my hair with a sleepy smile and I would kiss her heavy eyelids.

But she wasn't here.

I could almost still see the dent her body had made in the mattress. Her smell was all over these sheets.

I rolled onto her side and squeezed my eyes shut.

*I wish this was a nightmare.*

If this were a nightmare, I would have woken her up by now with my whimpering and buried my face into her neck. If this were a nightmare, she would have stroked my hair and hummed to me until I calmed down, until my entire world was entirely her in that moment.

But when I opened my eyes, the bed was empty.

That was the reality.

The photo of her tear-stained cheeks came to mind, her body broken. I remembered it and my heart cracked. Alone in my room, I let myself cry. It made her pillow wet.

God, I missed her so much.

# CHAPTER 39

## CHIARA

It was becoming more and more apparent to me how this game was being played. Kalip hadn't returned since our first encounter, but that didn't stop my anxiety from ripping through me.

In the silence, I would listen. Listen for the sound of the door clicking, for another pulse, another breath being taken. Sometimes I'd convince myself I had heard something and my heart would beat so loudly that I was sure anyone standing on the other side of my door could hear. I couldn't sleep either; I was scared he would come in when I was most vulnerable, and even worse, I wouldn't even know if he had. Every time I woke up, I thought about it, wondering whether the space felt any different. Kalip was long past being just a man now; in my mind, he was an evil god, a magician who could bend nature and people's wills with a single pointed thought. He could disappear into thin air. He could paralyse people. He could possess the man I loved.

I looked around at the prison that had become my entire existence. It was crazy how easy it was to get used to something. Like being trapped in an illusion.

Kaelan's perception of reality was usually a lot more

accurate than mine was, but right now, he wasn't here to pull me out of it. I was getting lost in my own mind.

A bang sounded against the door, so loud it reverberated through my chest. I cowered, shivering against the wall – was it Kalip?

That was when the winds started.

The air was no longer still; it pulled together and rushed toward me. The winds were fast, getting faster and faster, and I seemed to be their sole target. I was shoved back into the wall by fingers of harsh nothingness, confused, startled. Where had they come from? I squinted, trying to make out a vent I'd missed or a fan that could be the source. But it was as if the air had collated in on itself and had decided collectively to hurl at me.

I tried to breathe, but there was so much air that it was difficult. The winds threw me sideways and I fell onto my forearms awkwardly, pain shooting through to my shoulders. My hair was whipped across my face as they picked me up again, slamming me onto the ground as I cried out. I tried to get up quickly, I tried to run, but they snatched my legs out from under me and suddenly I found myself in the air itself.

There was so much air, air in my mouth and my nose, lifting me up and pulling me around and around in a harsh spiral.

*I don't want to die.*

I tried to scream, but the noise drowned out my voice.

*I am not going to die.*

I thrashed and cried out as I tried to disentangle myself from the spinning wind. I couldn't breathe.

I couldn't breathe.

There was so much air that I could not breathe.

'Mumma, there's no food in the fridge. What am I supposed to mak—'

'Stop your complaining, Chiara, you're giving me a headache.' My foster mother pressed her hand to her lined forehead.

She got migraines all the time and took a lot of painkillers, which didn't really help. She usually blamed me as their source.

'But what am I supposed—'

'Shut up.' Her eyes flashed, but I saw what was underneath the anger: disappointment.

She got up stiffly and ruffled her hands through her hair with a sigh.

'Where's Dad?' I whispered.

My mum scoffed and started towards the door. 'Fuck if I know.'

I followed her, handing over her coat and hat. It was late, but they always went out late.

'There's pasta in the pantry. Now, kiss me goodbye.'

I planted one on her sallow cheek, and she gave me a shadow of a smile in return. That was how it always went; I gave her more than she gave me, but the little she did give made it worth it. Then she was gone and I was alone in the house yet again.

I never minded being alone; I was used to it. I liked the peace and quiet because I knew it would be anything but when one or both of my parents came back. I would set up my paints and canvas in the living room, painting scenes from movies I'd paused on our small TV. I was always so proud of my work, but my mum said they could be better and my dad didn't even pretend to care. Sometimes I looked at my painting and got mad, swiping a whole line down the middle. Then I would get mad at myself for ruining it and throw the canvas on the ground.

*Their voices woke me up that night.*

*Mumma was yelling at Dad because he smelt like another woman's perfume. I shoved my head under my pillow. I had school tomorrow but there was no point telling them to be quiet so I could sleep. They wouldn't care – they'd yell at me too.*

*I hated it when people yelled.*

*I started humming the same three notes over and over, the ones I always used to drone out their voices when it was 2 a.m.*


I groaned.

It felt like I'd just fallen from a ten-storey building. My entire body was so stiff, so sore. Never mind Kalip coming in to torture me; it seemed the room had a mind of its own. Kalip didn't even have to dirty his hands. I squinted at the whitewashed ceiling, at the mists roaming across the walls. It all looked so deceitfully innocent, and maybe I'd been ignorant given that from those very walls seemed to drive a force that had a lust for blood.

I could've died.

I stared at my palms and then down at the rest of my body, as if I were seeing it for the first time.

*If Kalip wants to kill me, he will have to try a little harder than that.*

# CHAPTER 40

The ache in my stomach had dulled to a steady hum. I could tell when a meal was due by the wax and wane of hunger in my body. Having found no other way of escaping, I'd decided to try a new strategy.

I positioned myself by the door, right in front of the slot. The few times I'd been awake long enough to hear the person delivering my food, I'd realised it wasn't Kalip. There was always a soft grunt after the bowls were set down; a woman's voice.

Now, I waited for her to come again. Each time I felt myself drifting into my thoughts, I would slap my arm to snap me out of it, watching, waiting in the silence for the slot to creak open. Finally, it did. My breath hitched and I shoved my arm through as fast as I could, grabbing hold of the arm as I begged her to help me. The woman on the other side yelped. She yanked her arm away and pushed the food through, slamming the slot shut.

'Please!' I cried out, slapping the door.

Nothing.

Sighing, I started on the food, moaning as it hit my lips. In another life, I would have absolutely abhorred it, but that was then and this was now. Now, the unidentifiable mushy substances tasted like heaven.

When I was done, I licked my fingers clean, then the bowl, but it still wasn't enough. I had to learn to be satisfied with what I got. I saved the water bowl and pushed it next to me against the wall; this, I'd learned, was even more precious. I could only take a few sips at a time when I was thirsty. Water was my liquid gold.

After mealtimes was nap time. I didn't know a better way to waste away the days here, and they would be wasted no matter what. This was no life. But still, I clung to the hope that I would get my life back one day, whenever that might be, and I hoped it would be sooner rather than later. Kalip and his assistant couldn't keep me in here forever; they had to have some kind of ulterior motive. I was tired of waiting.

What was his aim, keep me locked up in here until I went insane? I could have tossed and turned for hours, my mind running around in endless circles, trying to come to a conclusion when I didn't even have all the pieces of the problem.

It was utterly futile.

Sometimes, I liked to imagine the paintings I would create when I left this place. In my mind, I painted Kaelan and I sitting on the edge of the cliff, watching the sunset. It had been the first time I'd known I loved him. I'd never forget the way he'd looked at me that evening. It made something deep within me pulse with recognition.

I missed everything about him. I missed our late-night conversations, the way I could talk to him for hours about anything at all; he always had an interesting reply that I could bounce off of, our conversation taking paths into territories I didn't know existed. I missed the way he built me up when I tore myself down, the way he was consistent and reliable. Loyal. He was a good person. I missed the way he threw socks at me when I wouldn't get out of bed and the way he kissed the fingers of my free hand when I was painting. I missed his smell of smoky wood and lemongrass. It smelt like home.

I imagined lying next to him, bare skin on bare skin, holding and being held. His heart was beating in my ears. I'd always loved the sound of it, especially when I could feel both of our hearts beating at the same time. He used to pull me as close as possible and we would laugh because it wasn't enough. He would dip his head and kiss my shoulder and the slope of my neck.

But it wasn't Kaelan I was holding onto now, warm, alive, real, but the floor. Cold. My heart squeezed so hard it managed to wring out a tear from my eye. I gasped softly at the pain as the tear rolled all the way down my cheek, falling off my jaw. It was like the aching ran through my bones and my nerves, like he was wired into my very DNA, and not being with him was detrimental to my health.

When everything was taken away from me, I realised the most important things in my life. It was people and my relationships with them that mattered above all else. Karlie and Luna, my soul sisters, whose friendship was incomparable to anything I had ever experienced before. They filled my heart with warmth when all it knew was darkness. They loved me and laughed with me and loved me again. I cherished them with everything I had. Then there were the twins, who made me laugh even more with their stupid jokes and endless banter.

And there was him.

He had my heart, forever and always.

# CHAPTER 41

## KAELAN

The sun touched the waves as I watched her standing on the cliff's edge, looking out at the darkening water with a soft smile on her lips, the golden light bathing her face. I ran my fingers down her arms and interlaced them with hers, my chest against her back.

'I could spend forever with you,' I whispered.

It was perfect.

But then she turned to face me and her expression was anything but.

'What's wrong?' I asked.

Chiara looked so sad then. Her eyes drew me into her world, making me want to do anything in my power to give her happiness instead.

'I'm sorry,' she choked out.

Before I could ask what for, she disentangled her hands from mine.

And stepped off the cliff.

'No!' I screamed, lunging for the edge. But it was too late. Her body hit the water, the water so far down, and went limp.

I bolted awake in a cold sweat. Panting, I instinctively looked over at her side of the bed as if she would still be there.

I should've known better.

Every day without her was torture. Every day was worse than the one before. I couldn't sleep; I must've had that dream dozens of times. And she jumped every single time. I could never save her.

The sun was shining today. It made me angry; it was so completely opposite to everything happening right now that it was almost an oxymoron. It should've been raining, cold and miserable because that was exactly how I felt.

She loved the sun.

I scowled at it and shut the curtains, pulling on some joggers, and slumped downstairs. My brothers were playing some kind of oldies music, probably in another attempt to cheer me up. Like that would work.

'Who even bought this music?' Rheo asked as I walked into the kitchen.

I glanced at our record player, which was playing Dolly Parton.

'Probably Nico,' I said, pinching the bag of crisps out of his hands. 'Didn't you have a thing for her?'

He coughed up a chunk and it landed on Rheo's hand, who screamed.

'Sweet Jesus, gotta say I didn't miss that,' came Karlie's voice from the door, Luna hot on her heels

'Wha-Luna!' Rheo cried. 'Stop letting random people into my house!'

'"Random people"? Did he really just say "random people"?' Karlie waltzed straight in, her eyes alight. 'You know what, Rheo, you are a grade-A pain in my ass.'

'Whatever, I'm sick of your shit.' Rheo grumbled. 'Clearly, we have more important things to be discussing other than our relationship, or lack thereof.'

'Yeah, we do,' she said quietly.

I swallowed hard, suddenly very aware of myself. To avoid eye contact with anyone, I stared at the counter and traced the marble pattern with my eyes. I'd never noticed how detailed it was before, though I would bet Chiara had. Paying attention to little things was something I admired about her. I never realised how much I was missing until I saw life through her eyes.

Karlie pulled out a stool and sat beside me, resting her forearms on the counter. 'It doesn't feel real,' she mumbled. 'I just want my best friend back.'

*Me too.*

No one spoke for a while, and the silence was so heavy that it seemed miraculous the sun was still shining at all.

I couldn't stand being in there any longer. I got up and went out to the garden, sitting on one of the folding chairs. I screwed my eyes shut, wishing all of this would just go away.

*Mamá* called me sometime after lunch, during the mid-day heat. I almost didn't pick up; I really couldn't take an "I told you so". When I did answer the call, I took one look at her and knew that she knew what had happened, but *Mamá* always had subtle tactics, usually to avoid the elephant in the room.

'Come back to Greece, *mátia mou.*'

I inhaled sharply. 'You know I can't. I want to, but not without her.'

'Did I not tell you what trouble this girl would bring?' *Mamá* clicked her tongue. 'And you did not listen, as usual.'

*And there's the "I told you so".*

'You were wrong about her,' I said, and looked my *mamá* in the eyes so she got the message. 'She *is* my mate and I love her, so don't tell me I should move on, that this is my chance to find a nice Greek girl to fill her place.' I frowned. 'Don't you understand? No one can replace her. I don't want them to.'

*All I want is her back.*

*Mamá* regarded me, then nodded. 'Then I will say the *vaskania* prayer. And, Kaelan, where is the charm I made you, seriously? I cannot believe you are still not wearing it.'

I laughed, rubbing the back of my neck. *Whoops, I might've lost that one.*

*Mamá* closed her eyes and started rocking back and forth slowly on her chair. I closed my eyes to listen as she spoke the prayer against the *mati*.

'There. I hope it helps,' she smiled. 'Remember, *mátia mou,* there is something to be learned from every hard thing in life, and that is good because there are many hard things!'

'*Mamá*,' I groaned, rubbing at my eyes. 'You're like Chiara – you think there's some kind of deep reason behind everything, but sometimes bad things just happen for no reason and that's life.'

'No, my son. There is always something to be gained in a situation where it looks as though you have lost. If she is your mate, something you seem to be certain of, then all the evil forces in the world cannot keep you apart.' *Mamá* leaned back and gave me her knowing smile. 'She will find her way back to you. Do not give up hope.'

# CHAPTER 42

## CHIARA

The sky was bloody and golden. We were on a cliff.

I died.

Another dream about him, where we were lost to one another, pulled into two separate worlds.

I hated these six walls.

I didn't notice at first when the floor became wet.

It roused me slowly from my lamentations, and when I saw the fine layer of water covering the ground, it didn't occur to me to become alarmed. I went back to my thoughts. But then I felt myself becoming more uncomfortable as the water rose.

I sat upright. This was unnatural, but, then again, so was everything else I was experiencing. The water was clear, lukewarm and past my hips where I sat. I stood and waded through it, peering at the corners of the room to make out where it was coming from. But then I remembered the winds and how they had arisen suddenly out of nowhere.

A sob ran through me.

*They're trying to kill me again.*

The volume of water was getting larger by the second until I was floating in it. It looked as though the room itself was weeping.

I screamed for help, trying to keep myself afloat. No one would care, I knew, but I screamed again anyway. I had always loved the water, but like with everything else, Kalip had managed to turn it into a weapon.

I took breaths as large as I could manage, over and over again, as my body rose closer towards the ceiling. All my life, I'd been fighting against something. And when I had nothing externally to fight against, I had to fight against myself. Well, now I was sick of fighting, but I would when I had to. My will to live was stronger. If I'd wanted to give up, I would've done it long ago, before I even got trapped in this room.

*I will not die.*

I floated on my back and began to slap my palms against the ceiling, trying to find a weak point. There were no panels, only concrete.

It was solid.

A cry escaped my mouth. I trod water as my heart beat faster, looking around and around, but there was absolutely nothing I could do.

I forced myself to take deep breaths until my face was pressed up against the ceiling and I was breathing in the plaster because there was no more air.

I took my final breath and my head went under.

It was quiet.

Dark.

I kept still, even though the panic was rising inside of me. My chest contracted horribly and my lungs protested.

In the black behind my lids, I saw Kaelan.

I had to take a breath.

I woke up coughing. I was choking on water and air, my lungs on fire. My clothes were soaked, my hair was soaked and the floor was soaked. I was heaving and heaving, and I vomited once, then twice.

*I'm alive.*

I took another breath gently, easing my lungs into it. How had I cheated death again?

Then it clicked.

They must've known, Kalip and the woman, what my breaking point was. They must've known to stop at the right time so they didn't push me over the fine line between life and death.

I closed my eyes. My mind was blank now, blanker than the ceiling and the walls. For the first time since being here, I just noticed. Noticed what it was like to be alive. I was wet, cold, my entire body was aching and my lungs were burning. But I was alive. And that was everything.

Water and air. It was like this room was alive, too, with a more sinister intention than just being.

Dragging myself to the doorway, I waited, knowing it was only a matter of time until the slot was wrenched open.

The click sounded. Before the bowl could be pushed through, I stuck my hand through the gap and grabbed onto a plush arm. It was the only contact with a person I'd had for a while.

'I'll do whatever you want. Just help me. Please.'

The woman growled and yanked her arm away, but when I

didn't let go, she started to close the slot more and more until the metal cut into my arm. I snaked my arm back through just as the slot clanked shut. I stared at it. It took me a few moments to realise that this was a double loss; she hadn't given me the food or the water.

I slumped back onto the wet floor again. When I next looked up, the mists had started to shift, morphing into something darker. I watched as shadows merged to form smoky-looking trees.

I placed my hand on the wall. It looked so real. But it was just another illusion. The ceiling grew dark until it was pitch black with a tiny pinprick of white light in the centre. I watched, transfixed as the light grew larger and larger until it resembled the moon.

Even as an illusion, it was stunning. Whatever Kalip had been intending, I was sure it was having the opposite effect. He had graced me with another thing that I longed for: nature.

The darker light made sleeping easier, but it was harder to wake up.

When I finally did wake, I noticed another change in the room. A pile of thick sticks, stacked halfway to the ceiling, directly under the moon. I pulled on one of them, expecting the rest to tumble. But they seemed to be stuck to one another.

They seemed to be real.

I began to climb them, but they were too smooth and there were not enough footholds.

I wondered what would be next.

# Chapter 43

## Kaelan

'Here,' I said to Viviana as I placed Chiara's yellow dress on her table. 'She wore that a lot.'

I tried not to cringe when she picked it up and examined it, running her long fingers over the fabric. She needed it for another attempt at a locator spell, but she probably didn't realise how difficult it was for me to even touch something Chiara had owned.

I sat down on her sofa and put my head in my hands. I'd been coming here almost every day, just in case Viviana found something.

Always just in case.

A couple of days ago, Viviana and her friend had found a lead that took us to an abandoned building on the outskirts of Paris. Like idiots, my brothers and I were hot on the trail before the thought it could be a hoax ever crossed our minds. Kalip left nothing but a note saying something snide akin to a big "fuck you". I was so angry I punched a hole through the wall.

Then I got sent the video of Chiara drowning. The pain I felt was so severe, I swear a part of me got disconnected and now I was barely feeling anything at all.

I stretched out on the sofa and tried to sleep. Viviana and her friend were back at the locator spell, my brothers playing cards on the floor. There were probably a dozen better ways to spend this summer, at least for them. Maybe they thought they were doing me a favour by not letting me be alone. I guess it helped.

I woke to a tap on my shoulder.

I sat up wearily. 'Did you find anything?'

When I saw their faces, the last strand of hope dropped like a bomb in my stomach. How long had it been now? The seasons were already beginning to change and what had they found? Nothing, then a fake lead and then nothing again.

'You're both useless,' I spat. 'You're not even trying!'

'Kaelan, do you really think that we'd sit here and not try every day?' Viviana responded, like she was talking to a child. 'We have sacrificed our time for this—'

'I don't care!' I stood up. 'You don't get it. She's dying in there.' I pushed back my hair. 'We should be... I should be doing more than this.'

Viviana fixed me with her cool gaze. 'There's nothing you can do but wait and trust. We're doing the best we can.'

I clenched my jaw. 'Well, it's not enough.'

I moved past her and shoved through her bead curtain into the kitchen. I wanted to get away from it all, but didn't know where else to go. Everywhere reminded me of her. Nowhere was safe.

'Well, that went nicely.'

Rheo's voice sounded like a fly buzzing in my ear. I slammed my fist against the cabinet, then collapsed over my arms onto the counter. I could hear them whispering out there. Every word was like a brick to my head.

Unstable.

Depressed.

I was good at controlling myself; I'd had a century to learn. But, right now, controlling my anger seemed a little counterintuitive. I lifted my head and came face to face with a bottle of whiskey. I glanced behind me and then grabbed it. The last time I'd got drunk was at my father's funeral. I hated alcohol; it reminded me of him.

I took a swig and winced. It tasted like poison.

Good.

I was about to take another when someone grabbed me and slammed me into the fridge.

The bottle fell from my hands, clanging to the floor.

'What the fuck do you think you're doing?' Rheo demanded, digging his arm into my throat. 'If you think,' he grunted as I struggled, 'that I will sit and watch you destroy yourself like Father, you're seriously wrong.'

Rheo let go. Then he picked up the whiskey bottle and threw it out of the open window so fast I didn't have time to stop him. I started to growl, but he shoved me into the fridge again.

'That's enough, Kaelan.'

I caught his shoulders too, pushing into him as hard as he pushed me.

Then, as soon as it had come, the fight left me.

I let my arms fall and forced in a breath to steady myself.

'I'm sorry,' I murmured.

Rheo's fists were still clenched, but he was already a lot calmer than I was.

'I get it,' he sighed. 'I do. But you're not going to find her faster this way. What would Chiara think if she saw you now?'

I stared at my feet. 'She'd think I was a monster.'

Rheo didn't say anything. Rheo always said something.

I knew it was because I was right this time.

My hands pressed into the leather of the steering wheel. It was starting to cool down again outside now that the hottest part of the year was over. The days were getting noticeably shorter. It all just reminded me of how long she'd been gone.

I pressed harder on the accelerator. There was no way I was giving up on Chiara. I didn't care if it took until the leaves turned brown, until they started to fall off or if the whole cycle started all over again. As long as she was alive, there was a chance. We would have to find her one day, someday, and soon.

*Please be soon. Please.*

I didn't know where I was going until I was virtually at my destination. It was the hill we'd climbed the day I went running and she'd fallen out of a bush onto the pavement, covered in blood.

I lay down on the bench where we'd had our first kiss and watched the colours of the sky. I thought of how Chiara closed her eyes when she was feeling the wind like she was making a wish.

She was teaching me to have hope.

I looked at the sky again and saw what she would see. She would also think the sky was beautiful, and it would make her happy because anything beautiful did. She might paint it later. She saw the world through the eyes of an artist who appreciated both the details and the bigger picture. She could put things into perspective in a way that took me years to learn.

298

If I were learning hope, then I would become an A student. If I were learning to hold myself together, I'd still be doing pretty well. If I had to learn how to live without her... I didn't want to think about that. It wouldn't happen. Besides, that contradicted the whole hope thing.

When we found her, I would give her all the time she needed to recover and then I'd ask her if she would come with me to Greece. I had so much I wanted to show her: the home I grew up in – where my *mamá* lived now – our favourite beach with the rocks you could climb and see the entire ocean from the top of. I smiled at the thought, but my smile faded when I realised it might never happen. Nothing was certain. I could have hope, but it seemed pretty fragile. Maybe hope worked for Chiara and *Mamá*, but I needed something more tangible than that. Something more reliable.

Like a reason.

*You have to make it out alive,* I thought, *and we have to find you because the alternative is not even possible.* No, that wasn't good enough. *We are definitely going to find you because Viviana is one of the most powerful witches and I'm pretty sure I can't live without you, so, you know, that might count for something.*

The stars were starting to show by the time I got off the bench and wandered back down the hill through the trees that threw shadows everywhere. A bird was chirping. I wished it would shut up. When I glanced up from the ground, I swore I saw her long hair flash between the trees.

My heart stopped.

I rubbed my eyes and I heard her laugh catching on the wind.

'Chiara?'

I started to run to catch up with her; maybe we were just playing a game. But she wasn't behind those trees. She wasn't here at all. I cried out, looking around the empty forest.

*I'm going insane.*

I leaned my forehead on a tree and squeezed my eyes shut.

*She's not here.*

I sunk to my knees and it hurt. Everything was hurting.

*I don't want to live without you, please. I can't take it much longer.*

'Kaelan,' she whispered.

Her lips were against my ear. There was gold in the sky and it poured onto the ground. Chiara looked back at me, her green eyes sparkling with mischief, her hair loose.

We were free.

Her laugh echoed in my ear as we ran together to the golden stream and stepped in. I watched for a second as she danced to the rhythm of the wind before I took her hand and showed her how to slow dance. She was against my chest and I could hear her breathing and feel her heart beating.

'I could stay here forever,' I whispered.

Suddenly, she pulled away and the expression on her face was the one I hated to see the most.

'But you don't love me,' she accused.

I gaped at her. 'How can you say that?'

She looked back defiantly and held her head high. 'You haven't found me.'

My feet were sinking into the mud. I tried to reach out for her, but she shrugged me off.

'Chiara, I have been trying this whole time. I can't... please, I need you.'

She studied me with those eyes, but she herself was impossible to read. 'I need more time.'

It felt like a punch. I swallowed the hurt, but only because it was her.

'I'll be waiting.'

I could feel her gratitude as she leaned in and kissed my cheek. I wanted to pull her close to me and hold her one last time before she left again.

But she had already slipped through my fingers.

# CHAPTER 44

## CHIARA

We were dancing in a river and the sky was gold.

I let him go.

I blinked at the moon above the pile of sticks, confused when I first woke. It was so bright it almost made up for the rest of the walls, covered in dark stormy woodland. I remember my dream still and how Kaelan had told me he was looking for me. Was he really? How hard to find must I be?

I rested my hand on my stomach. Tap, tap, tap went my finger against it, my skin so taut I might have been beating a drum.

Maybe it was a good thing I was gone. Maybe Kaelan would find another girl and she would actually be his mate. I couldn't be his; this wasn't how our story was supposed to end.

I wasn't supposed to die.

The woman with the plump hands hadn't returned with food or water since I'd grabbed her. I didn't know how long it had been since then. My body had started to shut down a while ago.

I could feel it letting go.

The air was abrasive as I dragged it in through my nose and as it hit the sides of my tired lungs. My bones nestled deeper

302

into the concrete floor.

I dared to close my eyes.

I remembered Luna and Karlie and how they'd decided in that alleyway to be my friends when I was a complete stranger. My life had taken a completely unexpected turn because of them. I remembered Luna; how strong-willed she was, yet soft at the same time, speaking her opinion in a way that would not offend. How she cared for every living soul as if she were their own mother.

And Karlie, her sassiness and how she could make anyone feel comfortable in her presence. She was sweet all the way down to her core. I remembered the way she danced and the way she made me laugh until it felt like I'd gained six-pack abs.

They both loved fearlessly though. I'd always admired that. It didn't matter to them if it was reciprocated or not; they gave it anyway. I'd learned from them that, more often than not, if you gave love, it would be reciprocated, and that the act of giving love filled you up with enough of it that it didn't matter anyhow. I remembered how held I felt in their arms and how seen I was. They loved me even though I was messy, all good and bad things combined.

A pang welled in my heart and I sighed. I wish I could've said goodbye. I never got the chance to tell them I loved them one last time.

I opened my eyes to see the moon. Every time I opened my eyes and saw it, it was a miracle. Another moment of life. Though it was silly for Kalip to forget to put stars on the ceiling. If it was a clear night and you could see the moon, you could see the stars. It was completely unrealistic. He should've thought about that.

My mind blanked again.

I shut my eyes and let my hand fall back onto the floor from my stomach. It felt hollow, like a shell. I suppose that's exactly what I was now. I could feel the life slipping out of me by the minute.

Kaelan's beautiful, deep blue eyes came to mind. He was there, in Chemistry class, then kissing me in the cleaning cupboard and running next to me up the hill. He held me on the clifftop, singing his mother's lullaby to me until I fell asleep on his chest. He was telling me stories on the grass. He was laughing at me trying to pronounce Greek words. He was whispering that he loved me in my ear.

If Kaelan were here now, I mightn't have been as scared to go.

The rest of my life was being taken away from me, but the whole life I had lived already couldn't be taken away. I was so glad that I had been given it in the first place. I was so lucky to have met my best friends, so lucky to have met my mate.

My chest contracted, my thin muscles barely able to move. I could do nothing but lie there and remember.

I tried to think of Kaelan laughing again, but I knew he wouldn't be laughing if he saw me like this.

*I will protect you now, my love,* I thought. *Until we meet again.*

His face was the last thing I saw before my mind slipped away.

And

I

let

go.

# CHAPTER 45

## KAELAN

I choked awake. My heart was pounding in my ears like I'd just run a marathon. I swallowed, shutting my eyes again.

Something was wrong.

The day started off normal: empty, colourless. I ran my fingers over her side of the bed like I did every morning and night, in case I could still feel the dent of her body and the remnants of her memory. But normal went to hell the second I checked my phone.

The text was from the same unknown number.

*"She's dead. Whoops."*

I clicked on the photo underneath it with shaking fingers. Everything stopped.

She was so thin she looked more like bone than skin.

I let out a strangled noise, my eyes tearing across the photo. *She's dead.*

I threw the phone across the room. The pain was blinding. *She's gone.*

I punched the bed over and over again and cried out with every hit. The tears made my shirt stick to my hot skin.

Rheo and Nico came running and Rheo was on my back in seconds, holding my hands behind me as I thrashed.

'What is it? What happened?'

I couldn't say it. My heart was breaking. No, it was already broken. It was exploding.

Nico showed him my phone. Rheo made the sound of a wild animal before getting off me.

I was crying so hard it hurt. Everything hurt. Rheo and Nico tried to fix it, but how could they stop me from shaking when they were shaking too? I heard Luna's voice somewhere in the room and then she let out a sound that made me cry harder. The next thing I knew, she was at my side, telling me to breathe even though she struggled. But it was too hard.

'I can't, I can't.'

'Kaelan, please.'

*Please what? Please calm down? I can't.*

'She's dead,' I moaned, rocking now. 'We were too late.'

Luna somehow managed to wrap her arms around me to try to hold me. But all that did was remind me of Chiara. I cried out and pushed her off me, collapsing into Chiara's side of the bed. I shoved my face into her pillow, trying to smell her and trying to suffocate.

'Kaelan!'

*Let me be with her.*

'Kaelan!'

It was Rheo, shaking me violently.

'Kaelan, listen to me. Viv said it's only temporary. Chiara isn't supposed to die. She will come back.'

I started to shake my head and I couldn't stop. 'The dead don't come back. It's impossible.'

'Well, I'm no psychic, but two highly skilled psychics say otherwise. There is a way. There has to be.'

My head was pounding.

I wanted to die.

I wanted to be with her.

'Kaelan, did you hear me?' Rheo yelled. 'It's only temporary. Listen, for the love of God!'

I looked at the three of them, blurry, standing over our bed.

Luna's face said it all.

'Get out,' I said quietly.

No one listened.

'Get out!' I screamed. 'Get out, get out!'

They did. And then I was alone.

I tried not to think about her. But it was impossible. She was everywhere. I closed my eyes and she was laughing. She was kissing my forehead, then my nose and then my lips.

'I love you,' I whispered.

I would have given anything to hold her hand again or hear her say my name.

To see her smile.

*Temporary.*

I couldn't believe that. How could I believe that?

# CHAPTER 46

## CHIARA

Hand after hand reached out to shake mine, ashy and somehow there, yet somehow not. They were congratulating me, though what for I didn't really know. It was dark and I lost track of where I was going, but the hands of my ancestors seemed to push me closer towards the light.

Except one.

I looked into his face and I knew. He had the most pride for me of them all, and if his body was more than a shadow, I would have seen his chest was swollen with it too. This was my real father. I held onto his hand.

'I wish I had known you,' my voice echoed.

He didn't say anything, but somehow I felt comforted knowing he felt the same way. Then came a great mist, and he and the rest of my ancestors were swept away and I turned and walked into a room. I recognised this room. It was my foster parents' bedroom, back in the old house I grew up in. My foster father was there, sleeping on the bed. But he was alive and I was dead. In a cloud above his head, I watched his dreams play out like a movie.

I knew something I'd never known.

I knew he was tired of his life and I knew he had a hunger

for something more, but he didn't see a way out of his world. He was trapped, wanting to fill a void in him, using women and alcohol to do it. I also knew he regretted how he'd treated me. Though it hadn't felt like it, I had always been the glue holding the tendrils of our family together.

'You did the best you could,' I said, and my voice sounded like the shadows. There were so many reasons he'd acted the way he had. 'I forgive you,' I whispered, hoping my words would permeate into his conscious mind so that when he awoke, he would remember.

I walked out of the room. I was in another building, another bedroom. My foster mother was sleeping in that bed, and she was with another man. She was pregnant. I put my ear against her stomach, listened and smiled. My foster mother looked better than I remembered having ever seen her. She was content. I had more than enough love to give to both of my foster parents. It was they that I had to put to rest, them and my past. My foster mother was abused as a child and married my foster father when she was too young. She was never able to have children of her own. Until now.

I bent to kiss her forehead and whispered, 'I forgive you.'

Looking at them now, they seemed like pieces of a story that had already been lived out. My story. But though my past was a part of me, it wasn't me at all. I was something more. I turned to look at her one last time, and then I walked out.

It was dark again. I didn't feel pain. I didn't have a body at all. It was easy to navigate the darkness, though, to move through it with a vague purpose in mind.

Death is seen as bad because we do not understand what happens in darkness, on the other side of the light. But maybe life and death are lovers; equals and yet opposites. Maybe one should fear neither and embrace them both.

I found who I was looking for. She was sitting like she was waiting for me, her hair the same as mine. She was a few years older than me and her eyes were a warm brown.

*Mother.*

She was alive.

I could tell by the way she glowed that she was not dead like my ancestors. Yet she was here, in this realm with me. I started towards her because I had no fear. The closer I got, the more I could tell that she was, in fact, made of light, shimmering like nothing I'd seen before.

But her shimmers were made of tears.

'I am glad you forgave them, your foster parents. It was the only way to let the hurt go.' Her voice echoed in the emptiness. 'But I don't think you will be able to forgive me.'

'Why?' I asked.

'I'm sorry.' A silver tear pooled in her eye and dropped, silently. 'You were not supposed to die.'

'I don't understand.'

'You need to go back,' she said, with a voice that was crystal clear. Her eyes started to blaze.

Suddenly I heard something scrape next to my ear, like a match lighting. The darkness dissolved and I blacked out.

When I next came to consciousness, I could feel my body.

I was in it.

I shuddered.

And I took a breath.

And I opened my eyes.

# CHAPTER 47

I inhaled again and again, faster and faster.

*What's happening?*

I glanced around the room wildly, squinting through my foggy vision, but I was pretty sure I was alone. The room was the same, with the same pile of sticks and the same moon.

My heart was beating. It was beating!

I could wiggle my fingers and my toes. My lips cracked into a smile.

I was alive.

I had perfect clarity about what had happened, yet I didn't feel like it was anything bad. I felt something else entirely: light.

My mind was completely light.

It was remarkable.

I breathed in the air and it was invigorating. It felt like something completely profound had occurred, and maybe that had everything to do with meeting my real father and then... my mother. She was alive too. I couldn't believe it. I had met her! I knew what she looked like and sounded like. But where was she in this world? How did she know I had died? How did she even get into the realm of the dead to meet me in the first place? Now I had another motive altogether to get out, and somehow staring at these walls, I didn't feel the same sense of hopelessness as I had previously. There was something different about the air in here. A kind of finality.

I couldn't believe my body was working again. It was a miracle. I was a miracle. I hugged myself tightly.

*As long as I am alive, I have hope.*

As if on cue, the slot in the door grated open and I looked over to see what was being pushed through. But it wasn't food or water.

It was blood.

I tried to move. I rolled onto my side and managed to slide my leg up, but I didn't have the strength to push myself off the floor. I dragged myself to the door. It was half a blood bag, but it was more than what I'd seen in God knows how long.

The moment that liquid hit my lips was bliss. It was thick and cool and soothed my cracked tongue and my swollen throat. I could almost feel it as it ran through me. Like it was reawakening every cell.

Like it was medicine.

I slept afterwards, and when I woke I had the strength to sit up. Another half a blood bag was waiting for me by the door. Something about the blood was like magic, better than food or water. I thought of how my mother said I wasn't supposed to die. Was that really true? Was that why they were giving me blood?

Several days or several long periods of sleep passed and I would sip a little more blood after each one. I started to get half bowls of water too. I'd forgotten what water tasted like: it was another kind of liquid gold, of liquid life. All of the things I was consuming were giving me life.

He was in my dreams the next time I slept. We were in a

meadow of dark green, luscious grasses. The sky was pale pink.

'Come back, please,' Kaelan said, his eyes filling with tears.

I caught one as it rolled off his bottom lashes. 'Just a little longer, I promise.'

I gazed past him at the meadow. The air, too, was sweet, like the view.

'Why?'

I looked back into his eyes, deep like the ocean. I cupped his wet cheek and gave him a small smile. 'You know why. All I ask is for patience.'

He closed his eyes and breathed. I kissed him then. It was salty and full of pain and longing.

When we broke apart, we were both crying and I pressed my forehead against his. The air was warm because our breaths were shared.

'Chiara. I have something to tell you.' He took his forehead away from mine to look at me. 'The woman who feeds you? She's your real mother.'

I stared at him.

And the world spiralled into darkness once again.

I shot up, panting.

"I don't think you will be able to forgive me," she had said.

Because *she* was the one working for Kalip.

*She* was the one who had killed me.

Out of the corner of my eye, I saw a spark of orange burst into flame in the middle of the pile of sticks.

I couldn't begin to fathom how the one woman I'd been searching for my entire life had been right behind this door.

She was probably in this building right now. I wanted to cry and scream. It was so unfair.

She was my mother, whom I'd spent years dreaming about, yearning with everything in my body and soul that I could meet her even once, even just for a minute. It was what I wanted most. It was all I'd *ever* wanted.

It made me pissed as hell.

I grabbed the floor to prevent myself from tearing out my hair. The flame in the heart of the pile grew larger and higher until the tip of it kissed the air above.

She'd spent my entire life avoiding me. Not once had I ever received a letter, an email or a phone call. I didn't even know her name.

The burning in me grew hour by hour. I was growing stronger, my body starting to look healthier and I found I could even stand up when I put my mind to it.

I knew my mother wasn't sorry like she had looked in the afterlife. If she was sorry, I wouldn't still be in this room. But I could feel the shift in the air.

I knew change was coming.

The fire roared all day and all night, accompanying the silence perfectly. The pile of sticks did not diminish even though the fire was so large it lit the entire room brighter than the fake moon above. Although I supposed the fire must've been a kind of illusion as well, it was so hot I knew I would be a fool to touch it.

I was wondering when something would happen. I wondered when she would finally show her face and stop cowering behind the door. She owed me an explanation. A really long and detailed one. I deserved that. Then she would let me walk out a free woman because I deserved that as well.

And if I never wanted to see her again, that would also be my decision.

I tapped my bare foot on the concrete and waited. I'd been doing an awful lot of waiting and I was sick of it. I wanted to confront her and make her feel sorry for what she'd done to me. She was supposed to love me, to take care of me. I grew up and barely knew what love was because of her.

I was sick of making excuses for people who didn't show up for me. That wasn't my responsibility. She should have been there. Why wasn't she there?

My head hurt.

I stood up and paced the room, back and forth, wall to wall. I hadn't thought about Kaelan in days. But I was thinking about him now. Something was different. I was sure of it. We were going to see each other soon. It had to be soon. My anger towards my mother changed when I thought about him.

I wanted him almost as badly as I wanted the truth.

I took a breath to steady myself. If I was going to find out anything, I had to keep my head. And I'd have to be tactful, most definitely. I started to pace the room again to think of a strategy.

That was when I saw his face.

In the shadowy forest illusion of the wall, the blue of his eyes stood out against the copper of his skin. I rubbed my eyes to make it go away, but all that did was make the vision stronger. I watched as Kaelan, the whole of him, walked towards me, looking at me like he usually did, as though he could see all the way into my soul. I frowned and went to meet him, feeling a pull beyond words. He wasn't real. I knew he wasn't.

And yet...

He held up his hand as though he was on the other side of

a glass pane. I did the same, pushing my palm into his. Except I didn't meet flesh as I half expected to, but the wall.

I gave him a small smile. 'I miss you.'

Then, he smiled.

I'd always thought his smile was the most beautiful thing I'd ever seen. But now, it was heartbreaking. My breath caught at the voracity with which I longed for him.

When I met his eyes again, they were not blue but steely grey.

This was not Kaelan.

I jumped back from the wall.

It was a disgusting transformation; his golden skin into sickly pale, his soft hair into greasy slicked back strands. Kalip grinned at me. And then, just when I thought the scene couldn't get any worse, he stepped *through* the wall.

'My, it feels good to be back,' he exclaimed, shaking out his stocky limbs.

I became acutely aware of my posture: caved in on myself, trembling.

*Chiara Beaufort, you did not just die and come back to life to be usurped by a misogynistic dickhead who uses an entire tube of hair gel in one application.*

I brought my eyes to Kalip's, which were already on me, and I gave him a look I hoped conveyed the extent of my detestation for him.

'My, my,' he said, his eyes gleaming, 'death seems to have done you a favour, little bird.'

I clenched my fists and bit my tongue to prevent myself from screaming at him.

The corner of his mouth flicked up. 'The truth is, Chiara, I've had enough of these games.' He began to walk closer as

I backed away. He did it slowly, like he was savouring every moment. 'I think the time has come, wouldn't you agree?'

I swallowed down the fear and forced my chin up. 'For what, Kalip?'

As he stepped closer, the shadows from the forest began to draw in around him, swelling over his feet and behind his back. They weaved around him as if they were part of him.

'You are nothing,' he said, his voice echoing off the walls. 'Nothing but an insignificant little girl. Unlovable.'

The last word wiped the false confidence from me. 'That's not true. People do lov—'

My voice trailed off as he grew taller and broader, as his clothes began to rip. His face darkened and his eyes turned pitch black. There was no time to scream or panic as he grabbed me and forced me up against the fire. It was sweltering, so close to my back that I was sure my clothes would disintegrate. Panic sliced through me.

'You are nothing,' he repeated, and his voice echoed a thousand times off the walls.

His fist was clamped around my neck. I knew what it felt like to be unable to breathe, but the shock of it alone always took my breath away. Kalip forced my head further back towards the flames.

I'd once heard that burning alive is one of the most painful ways to die. And in all the time I'd been here, all the times I'd looked death in the face and had chosen to live instead, I'd realised it wasn't death that I feared.

It was the pain that came before.

I looked into his lifeless eyes, two pools of nothingness and wondered, *how did you become like this?*

My voice rose, hoarse and broken. 'You want to kill me?'

Kalip laughed. It was a metallic, bitter thing. It revealed what lay under the façade of nothingness: a hunger that needed murder to feed it.

He was insatiable... and much stronger than me.

Fear spread through my body like wildfire as he gritted his teeth, digging his fingers in harder and pushing my head closer so the tip of the flame began to lick my hair.

'Kalip!' bellowed a woman's voice. 'Release her!'

The fire went out. Kalip dropped me and I collapsed into a heap at the base of the sticks. My hair had not caught fire, but I was sweating and burning anyway.

'Get out of my sight,' she snarled. 'I will deal with you later.'

Her voice was power.

I clutched at my burning throat and blinked through the now darker room to see that Kalip had reverted to his original size and was standing in the middle of the doorway, the door left wide open. He glanced at me, licked his lips and slinked away.

I was trembling on the floor and the woman threw herself down to meet me.

'I'm sorry, Chiara, I—'

She swallowed, shaking her head. Her hand was on my arm. I recognised those hands.

My mother.

She looked slightly different than when I'd seen her in the land of the dead.

'Are you my mother?' I asked.

I wanted to be certain.

She collapsed.

'Oh, *ma chérie*,' she cried out, scooping me into her arms.

'Get off me!' I yelled, writhing free and crawling a few feet away. 'You have no right to come in here and act like you care about me when I haven't seen you *once* my entire life, not to mention after what you've just done!'

Tears pricked my eyes, but there was no way I would cry in front of her.

The corners of her mouth dropped. 'I told you that you would never forgive me. I did not know you were my daughter until it was done.'

Her voice was melodious, and I'd have thought it was charming if I didn't know better.

'Until what was done? Kalip was obviously working for you!' I shook my head, exasperated. 'Why would you kidnap your own daughter?'

'Revenge,' she said, her eyes glinting with insanity. Then she noticed my face. 'I'm sorry. I did not mean to scare you. I'm not very good at this.' She smiled and looked normal again. 'I should explain. Yes, that is what I will do. I will start at the beginning and leave nothing out.'

A part of me didn't want to listen. I didn't think there was anything she could possibly say to redeem herself. But I had to know the truth.

'I gave you up for adoption, Chiara, because I could not look after myself, let alone a baby.' She closed her eyes and her face looked much older than it was, filled with pain. 'Your father was murdered.'

She and I drew in a breath at once.

'He was the love of my life,' she said. When she opened her eyes, I saw the years of nightmares in them. 'I was pregnant with you when it happened. I don't want to tell you how; I don't want to relive it again. But a vampire killed him and I killed the vampire in return.' She rubbed her thumb into her palm. 'I had no money and didn't want to return to the flat we rented. Everything reminded me of him as it was.'

'Why did you never write to me? I don't even know your name.'

She smiled warmly at me and I thought my heart might implode. 'I didn't want to make things complicated. You had a life of your own by the time I could financially support you. I didn't want to take it away from you, to whisk you away to some foreign land; me being a stranger myself.' She laughed a little to herself. 'I thought it was easier this way.'

I dug my fingernails into my palm. 'Did it never occur to you, even once, that your daughter might be living a miserable life and that the only thing she ever wanted was to see her damn mother?' I looked at her, wiping away the tears that had escaped. 'I dreamed of you. I thought there must have been a reason you couldn't take care of me, but that one day you'd show up and apologise.' She, too, was starting to tear up, though I didn't know why. 'But you never showed up. *Ever.*'

Her mouth twitched, but she didn't say anything. I guess there wasn't much to say to that.

She coughed. 'If you do care to know, my name is Catherine. And I know I have been an awful, awful mother—'

'You haven't been a mother at all.'

Catherine blinked. 'Yes. I suppose that's true. But I wanted to say that I do love you, Chiara.' She looked around the room. 'I feel... terrible that I put you through all of this. I would have never done it if I'd known you were my daughter from the start.'

'So, why did you do it then? If it wasn't me, it would have been someone else, is that what you're saying?'

'I— yes,' she admitted. She looked guilty for all of two

seconds before she decided to switch tactics once she saw I wasn't buying it. 'You see,' she started, wringing out her hands, 'I always felt that death was too easy an escape for the vampire that killed Pierre, *mon chéri*, your father. Did you meet him in the underworld?'

'I did.'

Catherine closed her eyes, her face contorted in pain and longing once more. I knew exactly what that felt like.

Thanks to her.

When she opened her eyes next, they were hard. 'The murderer, he had a son. Three of them, in fact.'

Lead shot through my heart.

She gave me a knowing look. 'I watched them from a distance. The younger two I could only bear to look at because they did not look like him. But the eldest... not so.'

I felt emotion rise within me.

'I initially thought it was Dinos himself, returned from the dead. They look almost identical.' Her eyes were darting back and forth manically. 'I started to dream that the son killed my Pierre. Just knowing that this boy was roaming the same Earth that I walked upon, with the same face as his father, the murderer, I wanted to...' She closed her eyes again, balling her fists.

The tears were streaming down my face now, and I stuffed my fist into my mouth and bit down on it.

'I thought about it, taking his life. But I also knew it would not do. His father had made me suffer. I was too quick to kill him; I did not allow him to do the same. But now his son was making me hurt again, rubbing salt into my wounds that were not healed. He deserved to suffer for the sins of his father.'

'You're insane,' I breathed. 'He didn't deserve any of that.'

I felt myself being torn apart. 'How could you?'

'In my head, he and his father were one and the same. The son—'

'Kaelan.' I swallowed. 'Say his name, for God's sake. Or can you not?'

Catherine stiffened. She looked around the room then and smiled slightly, almost like she was admiring it. 'Our minds can play cruel tricks on us sometimes, do you not agree?' When she next spoke, her voice was quieter than death. 'I wanted to make him suffer. There was no way out for me other than his suffering. I thought about it every day and every night as I went to sleep. I had dreams about how I would go about it. It was eating me up from the inside out. You have to understand this, *ma chérie*.'

The term of endearment sounded like poison from her lips. 'Don't call me that.'

'And then, he met you.'

Her smile made me feel sick.

'And oh *my*, has he suffered because of it. It made me so glad.'

I stared at her expression in horror. I didn't want to be in this room with her anymore. 'When did you figure out I was your daughter? Before or after you'd kidnapped me?'

Her joy transformed into something tortured. She must've known for a while.

'After. But I'm not going to say anything else because I know that if I do, it will only make it worse.' She wouldn't meet my eyes. 'If you do not wish to see or speak to me again, I will completely understand. But you must forgive me, *ma chérie*. You must.'

I rolled up my emotions as best as I possibly could and took a deep breath. 'If I ever decide to forgive you, it won't be for you, only for myself. I don't want to be haunted like you are.'

She swallowed down the insult and watched me for a moment. Then she smiled, and this time, it seemed genuine.

'Look at you,' she said. 'So strong and beautiful.'

In the silence that followed, I took a breath.

Catherine looked past me and did a double take. Fury flickered across her face.

I turned.

My heart stopped.

# CHAPTER 48

When his eyes met mine, it was just the two of us. His lips parted and his eyes shone wet. Then, his face broke into the widest grin.

He started to run and I felt my legs move towards him. Until I caught the look on Catherine's face.

'No!' I yelled, rounding off in front of him.

Kaelan looked confused, but he knew nothing of our situation. My mother was on her feet, snarling like a wild thing, curling into herself.

'How dare you!' she screamed. 'You devil! You devil!'

Kaelan pressed his chest into my back and made a sound of pure agony. His fingers found mine and stroked them over and over.

He was real.

He was *here*.

I focused on my mother.

'If you care about me at all, like you claim you do,' I said slowly, firmly, 'then you will not hurt him. Do you understand?'

She was shaking with fury, her eyes blazing.

'Do. You. Understand?'

'Chiara,' Kaelan whispered.

His voice tugged on my heart.

Every muscle in Catherine's body was clenched with the effort it took to restrain herself. 'I want to be better for you, *ma chérie*. I want to be better, so I will go, someplace I can't hurt you anymore. Or—' her eyes flicked darkly to Kaelan behind me, 'or him.'

'And Kalip?'

She swallowed hard like she was swallowing down all the things she wanted to do to Kaelan. When she next spoke, her voice was low and strained. 'I'll deal with him.'

I watched as she slunk around the edges of the room, back hunched, face sallow. Her eyes never left him.

Kaelan slid his arms over my waist, burying his face into my neck. He was shaking. I wanted so badly for her to leave, to just leave the two of us alone already. The agony of it was burning in the centre of my chest.

Catherine paused as she reached the door. It was only now that I realised how badly she was shaking herself.

'I do not know what to do,' she whispered.

I felt the weight of the world in those words.

'Tell me what to do.'

'Get help. Please. Before you hurt anyone else or yourself.'

She turned back to look at me and I saw the ghosts that tortured her reflected in her eyes. There was no emotion in her now.

'Maybe.'

Maybe wasn't good enough, but it was better than no. Kaelan whined a little and it brought tears to my eyes. I leaned my head against his, still buried into my neck.

Catherine held up a business card and placed it on the floor. Then, she left.

I blew out the air I'd been holding right as Kaelan spun me around.

'It's really you?' I asked, running my hands over his cheeks, his jaw, the back of his head. After so many mind games, I had to be sure.

He nodded, his eyes wet. 'Chiara, I—'

'Wait. Tell me something only Kaelan would know. Please.'

His confusion turned to understanding quickly.

'Your favourite colour is green; you love the ocean more than rivers or lakes. If reincarnation exists, you want to come back as a bird.' He bit his lip, still looking at me in the eyes. 'You love the stars. Remember that night when we were on the cliff? I sang you to sleep.'

His gaze held me captive as he started to sing the old Greek words gently and his sweet voice brought tears to my eyes. He clutched onto me with tears in his own. We were already so entangled that when I collapsed onto the floor, he did too.

Kaelan took my face carefully in his hands, his eyes shining ferociously. He brought his lips to mine. Our mouths caressed one another, drawing up the pain and longing that wrapped around our hearts. We pressed closer to each other, until his warmth was my warmth, until our souls fused together and the life was drawn up through us so fully it made our bodies tremble.

We spoke in a language words could not convey.

After some time, I broke away, pressing my forehead against his as we breathed in the quiet, sharing the same air.

'I thought I'd lost you,' he said, running his hands through my hair, down my cheeks, 'I thought... I thought—'

Tears pooled once more in his eyes and it made my heart break all over again.

Finally, he whispered, 'I thought I'd never see you again.'

I wiped his tears as they fell, more and more of them.

I moved his warm hand onto my heart. 'I did die, Kaelan. But I'm alive now. Do you feel it?'

He nodded. I wrapped my arms around him and we held each other again. I needed to feel him, to breathe in his skin.

'I missed you,' I whispered.

He squeezed me harder and nestled his head into my shoulder. 'I missed you too,' he whispered back, words muffled. 'God, I missed you so much.'

'I can't believe you're really here.'

I would have thought it was just another fantasy, apart from how real it felt. When I could feel his skin and breath on mine, when I could feel my heart come alive and tingle with joy this pure, this familiar, I knew it was real.

Words could barely convey how I felt. They weren't even close to being enough. Kaelan must've thought the same thing because he eased off me, and in that moment, I saw something flash in his eyes. Then we were kissing hungrily and he was laying me down on the concrete. Our hands explored each other like it was the first time. And in many ways, it was the first time. And it certainly would not be the last first time.

'I love you, *koúkla mou*,' he whispered with a smile, kissing my jaw, then looking at me, kissing my lips, then looking at me.

I pulled his head into my chest and kissed his forehead, nose and lastly, his lips.

He always closed his eyes when I did that.

'I love you too, forever and always.'

I picked up the business card my mother had left and we walked out of that building together, me and him, hand in hand, bumping into each other and laughing, stealing glances at one another all the way.

And then we met the morning air.

And I felt completely, finally, free.